Revenge Is the Game

Gary,
Thanks for starting the HL# and for making it all happen!
Your friend,

by

J. Alain Smith

J. Alain Smith

ISBN: 978-0-9846196-7-2 (hard cover)
ISBN: 978-0-9846196-8-9 (epub)
ISBN: 978-0-9846196-9-6 (epdf)

Library of Congress Control Number: 2013918993

Printed in the United States of America.

DEDICATION

This book is dedicated to all the people who make things happen in this world, to the ones who wake up in the morning and make a difference every day. The ones who leave a lasting impression on all of us—you know who you are. Keep up the good work.

PROLOGUE

Matt felt the heat of the blast before his mind could register what had happened to the helicopter zeroing in on him. The bullets had come ever closer as they danced across the dusty scorching-hot desert floor of southern Sudan, trying to find the exact range to kill him where he was hiding. Zumbula, standing out in the open, tried to draw the pilot's attention and fired one clip after another from his AK-47 at the open doorway of the helicopter hovering above them. The chopper's door gunner hunkered inside, avoiding the onslaught, and was not able to return fire until Zumbula spent the last clip he had scavenged from his dead friends lying just to his left. He vented his rage as he yelled insane epithets at the chopper in three different languages when the last empty clip dropped to the sandy earth beside him.

Detecting the sudden silence from the AK, the door gunner tentatively peeked out from the shelter of the chopper's bulletproof cabin and firmed up his grip on the .30-caliber Djuriber machine gun when he saw he was safe. The gunner swung the heavy weapon on its pivoting steel arm toward Zumbula, jacking the action back to make sure it was loaded and ready to kill the black bastard waving his arms in defiance at the heavily armed chopper. Zumbula shucked and jived, preventing the gunner from having an easy shot. The gunner hesitated for a split second while admiring the bravery of the bare-chested man, a striking form dressed only in a tribal loincloth in front of him. Then, out of the corner of his eye, the gunner saw for the first time a woman a few meters away from the tribesman. The tall, thin African beauty was attempting to hide from the chopper in the sparse brush below. A fleeting thought of saving her—taking her as a concubine or, worst case, selling her after he had his way with the black vixen—swept over him before he returned his sadistic mind to the task at hand: applying pressure to the heavy trigger setting.

The shock wave from the blast of the camouflaged chopper exploding just above them knocked Matt and Bianca off their feet. Chunks of steel and engine parts rained down on them as the "the Flying Tank" converted itself into a flaming mass of molten steel and aluminum, forged by the jet fuel ignited in the rear of the falling chopper by the air-to-air missile that made a direct hit on it. Matt flung his body over Bianca's, covering her from falling debris, cooing to her through the hellish racket, "Don't worry baby, it'll be OK now, don't worry."

Bianca lay still, her mind whirling, the haze and trance-like stupor she had been living in for the last year as Rashid's captive lifting at the shock of the explosion and making her feel strangely alive once again, yet scared to death at the hell that was going on around her.

"Why are people shooting at us? Where in the hell am I? Where has Matt been? I've been alone for a long time . . . I think?"

The crazy thoughts running rampant through her cluttered brain confused the situation even more as fragments of the shattered chopper that had been shooting at her moments before fell heavily to the ground all around their prone bodies. Matt jerked back and let out a yell of pain, bringing her back to the reality and deadliness of their situation once more. She heard a thunderous crash from behind that shook the ground beneath her when the flaming corpse of the crippled helicopter hit terra firma, an all-engulfing cloud of dust and black smoke blasting skyward on impact.

Matt stood up into a half crouch, pulling Bianca to her feet, yelling, "Come on let's get out of here."

She grabbed for his left hand, recoiling when she felt sticky warm blood smear across her palm.

"Matt you're hurt!"

"I'll be OK, it's just a scratch. Come on, come on," he yelled over the roar of the wreckage, switching his hands so that he led her now with his uninjured right hand.

Caitlin O'Shea appeared alongside of them from where she had been hunkered down and, with her backpack strung over her shoulders, jogged across the rubble and sand at the same pace Matt set. After putting 60 meters between them and the pile of burning wreckage,

Matt turned back to check on the others, seeing to his relief that at least Zumbula and Djuri were running hand in hand behind them. Matt slowed a little so they could catch up. When they arrived, he asked Zumbula about Joseph and Bulu's whereabouts, the two trackers who had been with them in the plane Matt had stolen. The trackers had survived like the rest of them when Matt crashed the King Air only moments before the deadly Sudanese Army chopper had shown up.

"They are dead Bwana. The helicopter gunmen got them. They have joined their brothers and sisters in that heaven you speak of."

Zumbula heard it first, the distinct whine of another chopper approaching them from the opposite direction. He hesitated, looking skyward for the source of the whine while Matt followed his gaze. Horror filled his soul when he realized it was not just one chopper coming after them, it was two.

"Let's go! See if we can make that river washout ahead and hope we find some kind of cover there." They all ran with a new sense of urgency, wondering when the bad breaks would possibly end.

The unmarked black jet helicopters were on them in a matter of minutes, faster than any of them thought was possible. The lead bird swept in low, its nose pointing straight at them, with armed wing pods aimed menacingly at their scrambling group. The pilot expertly maneuvered the chopper into a high-speed sideways slip until he was in position, hovering a mere 20 meters above and 50 meters in front of the terrified civilians. Matt held Bianca in his arms, vainly sheltering her from the dust kicked up by the rotor blades, knowing they were done for and that his luck had apparently finally run out. He stood squinting at the chopper through the sand and dust swirling around them, thinking, *"I've been a lucky guy, made it the hard way, never gave any quarter, never asked for any, but God if you're listening, let them take me but don't harm the others. This is all my fault, Lord, so please spare them."*

A booming voice shook them all as it echoed above the roar of the chopper, "Mister Caruthers, halt where you are. We are here to rescue you, not harm you. Quickly run to the clearing to your right and climb aboard sir."

The group stood transfixed for several seconds, amazed at the American command they had just heard come from a loudspeaker mounted under the chopper's belly. The voice had used Matt's undercover name so he knew they must be on orders from U.S. Intelligence, and he obeyed the order immediately. They all ran as a tight group to the place where the chopper was touching down. Four men dressed in sleeveless desert fatigues, full Kevlar body armor covering their torsos, jumped to the sandy desert surface from the open bay of the helicopter. One waited to assist them at the welcoming open door, while the others swept the area for any sign of enemy combatants. Seeing they were alone, two of the men ran with black zippered body bags and retrieved what remained of Joseph and Bulu. The other warship meanwhile hovered 100 meters above them, turning in a slow circle, menacingly angled forward toward any possible intruders at the smoke-filled rescue scene.

Matt and Zumbula helped the women into the folding canvas seats in the chopper bay, securing their seatbelts. The captain twisted the cyclic control, snatching the black chopper off the ground the instant the last Delta Forces soldier jumped back on board. Slamming the sliding bay door shut, the roar of the chopper dissipated as they rose skyward with stomach-churning speed.

MATT WOKE FROM the nightmare in a cold sweat, realizing when he opened his eyes that he was in his own bed in his Portland mansion, his wife Bianca snuggled by his side, sound asleep. He had relived the nightmare event many times in the past year since it had occurred, but he never got used to it and so far had been unable to shake the actual events from his dreams. He glanced over at the electric alarm clock's glowing red dial that read 2:30 a.m.

"How long will I have to keep reliving that day? How much longer?" He thought as he walked to the bathroom sink and washed the sweat off his face, feeling the coolness of the cotton washcloth offer some relief. When he was finished, he turned and walked back to bed, thankful that Bianca had slept through the night for once and that her nightmares had given her a break . . . at least for this night.

CHAPTER 1

IVAN TATRA GAZED OUT OVER THE DANUBE RIVER WINDING its way through downtown Bratislava, the ancient capital of Slovakia, a crossroads for a multitude of civilizations and the starting point of the historic Silk Road that for centuries had led travelers and merchants from Europe to China. One of the hubs of the Austro-Hungarian Empire before its demise after WW1, the city was now making a comeback to its cosmopolitan roots following decades of decline due to the occupation and pilferage by the Soviet Union after the country had been combined with the Czech people's land to create Czechoslovakia.

The grey mist of rainy drizzle mixed with smoke from the thriving factories gave the river valley a dismal demeanor not lost on its favorite son. As he listened to the lawyer on the other end of the cell phone connection drone on and on, he let himself drift off to his 50-meter yacht moored in Nice, hearing the Mediterranean Sea softly calling him back to the warm embrace of its salty comfort, even at this time of September. Closing his eyes, he could see the young beauties, sunbathing topless on the front deck of his massive craft as he watched them from the bridge. Any one of them was his for the calling, whether for 10 minutes or all night, his fanatical sexual desires were for them to satisfy.

The lawyer's mention of the latest business problems in Bosnia snapped him out of his daydream and back to reality. He was now listening with renewed interest to the developments unfolding there, seemingly out of his control and very dangerous.

"Why didn't I stay out of there to start with?" he wondered. *"The fucking Bosniak and their so-called country have been a mess for 500 years. I should have known better than to get mixed up in that hellhole."*

The partners he had taken on there, a group of Bosnian Muslims he thought were small entrepreneurs who fit his business franchise model perfectly, had turned out to be the local Mafia with their fingers in every part of daily life in the still war-torn republic. It was not just the restaurant business anymore; being partners with these characters could end up getting him killed if he was not careful.

IVAN'S STORY WAS a classic Horatio Alger tale of a poor youth taking an idea and making the most of it. With the breakup of the Russian Soviet Empire, the satellite states such as Poland, Yugoslavia, Romania, Macedonia, Bulgaria, and Czechoslovakia became free nations once again. The Baltic nations of the former Yugoslavia, with its variety of religions and ethnic cultures, fell into immediate civil war, unlike the other nations who had much smoother transitions to freedom. Such was the case with Czechoslovakia. One day it was one country, the next it was two, becoming the Czech Republic and Slovakia. In the land and asset grab that ensued after the two new nations were created, the reality was that the Czechs got the better deal, but it was not a big enough issue to go to war over. The former Communist bosses of the republics who had any gumption whatsoever started handing out national assets and rights to services such as mining, radio, newspapers, television, government services, port authorities, you name it, to their friends and business associates even before the transition from communist government to "democracy" had begun.

What really had a magical effect on the Slovakian nation was that even with all the major industries and businesses being kept under control by a new Mafioso of sorts; the average person was now able to engage in free enterprise at its most basic levels. It meant that the farmer or herdsman who in the past was involved in the unworkable collective plan of the Marxists was now free to expand his herds, to sell his wool and meat and grain on the open market and be paid appropriately for his individual endeavors. Small business sprang up in the cities and villages, where shopkeepers were free to sell their wares, carry the products that their customers wanted to purchase, expand the lines they carried, and set their own prices based on supply and demand, rather than following what some bureaucrat told them was the price. Open-air markets carrying all kinds of goods from electronics to the latest fashions, women's makeup to hand tools, everything the citizenship craved suddenly became available. Of course, a big percentage of the workers soon longed for the good old days under communist rule when everyone got the same paycheck, everyone had a job that you rarely worked more than five hours a day at, and the few basics of life such as food, rent, and electricity were subsidized and cheap. A culture of mediocrity had been created by Communism, and it would take at least a generation to rid the country of its curse.

At 22 years of age, the new opportunities in Slovakia were not lost on Ivan Tatra.

As a student at Bratislava University, he had taken engineering classes, hoping to follow in his father's footsteps, with his impressive math and interpretive structural skills, and land a secure job inside the Communist government. In the summer between his junior and senior year of school he was able to secure a grant that allowed him to take a three-month job in America, working at a resort as a waiter and busboy catering to wealthy Jewish patrons in the Catskill Mountains and refining the English his mother had insisted he take throughout his schooling. He didn't fit in with the other imported workers at the resort. They were brought in on a U.S. visa system designed specifically to fill hard-to-hire positions with willing bodies from Eastern Europe. After 30 days of working at the resort, he and his best friend from home, Jakob, decided they had had enough of the demanding, relentlessly unsatisfied elderly Jews they were waiting on every day. So they hitchhiked to Newark with two paychecks in their pockets and a suitcase each of their worldly possessions.

The first place they saw to grab something to eat after getting dropped off in the heart of the city was a small sandwich shop called Subway. Neither of them had ever eaten at such a place but soon figured out how to place an order. The sandwich they ordered was unbelievably good, like nothing they had ever tasted. The idea that you could have whatever topping and combination of meats, cheese, and sauces you wanted was mindboggling to people from Eastern Europe. Where they came from most meals were eaten at home, and if you went out for food it was to a traditional sit-down restaurant where you ordered off the menu and the food came prepared on a plate to your table. The price, even by what they were used to in Slovakia, was reasonable if not cheap compared to what else they had seen in the United States. They each loved their newfound dining experience so much that they ordered another sandwich, only this time two completely different ones and shared them with each other.

As they were leaving the place, Jakob noticed a "help wanted" sign hanging on the door. Shrugging their shoulders with a "why not" gesture they turned around and applied for the jobs. After a half-hour interview with the pretty, slim-figured middle-aged woman who owned the place, they were both hired on the spot and told to report in at 10:00 the next morning to start their new careers in the restaurant biz. That afternoon they found a flophouse that rented by the week, paid in advance, located three blocks from the Subway and got settled, unpacking their meager possessions in the dingy room.

BECAUSE THEY REALLY had nothing else to do other than work and the fact that they were there to make money to take home with them, they soon began working both the lunch and dinner shifts, opening and closing the store for Mrs. Jansen, the pretty owner. She was thrilled to have the two young good-looking Slovaks working hard for her. The customers loved them and their accents, and it was so tough to get good help at the low wages she paid. She told them they could each help themselves to one sandwich per day, on the house, as a bonus for their hard work.

It wasn't until the boys had been working six weeks straight, not taking a single day off, that Ivan mentioned to Jakob as they sat around after work in their grubby room, sharing a six-pack of beer,

"You know, we should tell Mrs. Jansen we are leaving for home in two weeks."

Jakob hesitated for a second then replied, "I don't know if I am going back to Slovakia, Ivan."

"What are you talking about? We don't have any choice. Our visas are expiring and school starts when we return. We are seniors this year, we are going to be tops in our class, and we have some money saved."

"I like it here in America; I have nothing to look forward to in Slovakia. What, some job that doesn't pay shit and then marrying and living in my village with some local wench who will give me three kids and headaches for the rest of my life? That is not what I want to do."

Ivan was shocked. He realized he had a problem; he had never considered anything except the original plan that included the return airline tickets for home stashed in their suitcases. Ivan was dead tired after another 12-hour shift, and it wasn't worth continuing the argument, so he silently swilled the last of the beer before laying his head down, instantly falling dead asleep.

The next day neither boy said much to the other as they walked to work and started their first shift. They arrived at the restaurant at 9:45, 15 minutes early as usual, Jakob using the key Mrs. Jansen had entrusted to him to open the place. The two of them set to the tasks at hand, preparing everything for the usual opening at 11:00. Jose, the experienced Puerto Rican who cleaned the counters and cooking utensils and performed other odd jobs around the place, arrived at 10:00 going about his chores with his usual cheery attitude. Mrs. Jansen, always a sharp dresser, arrived 10 minutes later wearing a very short skirt, black stockings, high heels, and white silk blouse. Ivan only remembered her dressing this nicely on a couple other occasions.

These are not clothes to serve Subway sandwiches in, Ivan thought as he couldn't help but watch her shapely figure walk down the narrow hallway to her small office located next to the room that served as the storage room/employee lavatory. After five minutes Mrs. Jansen opened her office door, saying loud enough to get Jakob's attention,

"Jakob, will you please come see me in my office about these orders for the rest of the week?"

Ivan and Jose looked at Jakob as he took off his apron, shrugged his shoulders as if to say "What now?" and walked down the hallway without looking back at either one of his coworkers. They had only seen Mrs. Jansen get mad one time and that was over a lazy employee she had canned a couple of weeks ago. She didn't seem that mad today but Jakob had only been called privately to her office on three previous occasions, so today seemed a little unusual.

It was already muggy, the New Jersey summer making the small store stifling by midday. Jakob was still in Mrs. Jansen's office five minutes after he had entered, yet there were still lots of chores to do before they could open for business. Ivan unlocked the main entry door, leaving the chain lock on the front door to prevent it from swinging open all the way, before hustling to the back service door to open it all the way and let the cool alleyway air move through the restaurant. As Ivan turned to walk back down the hallway to the restaurant, the moving air cracked Mrs. Jansen's office door open, just enough for Ivan to get a full understanding of why his best friend truly did not want to return to Slovakia.

In the reflection of the mirror on her office wall, Ivan could see Mrs. Jansen bent forward over her desk, her elbows supporting her weight, her mini skirt hiked up over her exposed bum, while Jakob's pants were bunched at his ankles on the floor and he was pounding her from behind for all he was worth. Ivan couldn't help but stare at the two of them. They had no idea he could see them since they were so caught up in the moment. For one instant he was proud of his friend who was having his way with this older American woman, but the next he felt a twinge of anger that his buddy had never confided in him, never told him what was really going on. As Ivan turned to walk up the hall, leaving the lovers to their privacy, the past weeks' events became clear. Now he knew why Jakob had gone out on his own for two hours last Thursday night, why he had taken so long to go to the grocery store for beer and pizza the week before. With a twinge of envy pecking at his ego, Ivan got back to the task of getting the store ready for its opening at 11:00, not saying a word to Jakob when he joined Jose and Ivan at the counter 10 minutes later.

TWO WEEKS LATER Ivan returned home alone.

Back in Slovakia, Ivan worked at odd jobs after graduation, nothing that paid well or had anything to do with his university education. Good jobs were scarce in his field so he was simply scratching out a living wondering if maybe Jakob had been right after all. He met another college graduate, a raven-haired beauty named Katrina who was able to keep him sexually satisfied, but was somewhat annoying to be around, due to her need for constant ego-boosting compliments. Needing to move out of his parents' apartment, the two of them had enough money scratched together and relocated to a small studio flat in the main town square of Bratislava.

The breakup of the country was in full swing now—the old systems were gone, new businesses and ways of governing were just getting started—it was exciting times for those who could take advantage of the new capitalism and devastating for those who sat by and watched their former free lunch, pensions, and subsidies disappear overnight.

Ivan had finished his shift as a gofer at the office in the printing company where he was working and met Katrina for a beer at the small corner bar in the main square. The usual group of friends their age was hanging out, letting the booze wash away the days boredom. They all drank their beer slowly, since they could only afford a couple on their meager wages and had nothing else to do that evening, like most evenings.

After one large draft, Ivan slipped his hand into the crook of Katrina's arm, and whispered in her ear, "You look more beautiful than ever today, let's go home."

He knew the compliment would work. It always did on her fragile ego, and it wasn't so much that he wanted to get laid tonight, he just didn't want to hang out in the bar any longer. They bundled up against the cold before strolling down the cobblestone avenue toward their apartment. As they crossed the main square, Ivan noticed a shop on the east side of the square that had been a bakery for as long as he could remember. Now its windows were covered on the inside with white butcher paper, and a handwritten sign on the door said "For Rent." Ivan wondered about the store as he stood staring at the covered windows, remembering that it was never a very good bakery, but a decent-sized store, long and narrow like so many other shops in the several-hundred-year-old town squares all over Slovakia. It was about the same size as the Subway shop he had worked in when he was in America.

"The Subway shop, it was this size," he said out loud.

"What did you say?" Katrina asked.

"Ah, sorry, I was just looking at the old bakery, and it reminded me of the place I told you about that I worked at in New Jersey, in America. It is about the same size."

"Do you think your old friend Jakob still works there?"

Ivan laughed, "I would imagine he still does and is very happy there, very happy." Only Jakob's parents had received any word from him; he had not stayed in contact with any of his former friends back home.

Ivan led Katrina over to the vacant shop and peered through the openings in the paper covering the windows. The glass cases were still in place, several small tables and chairs and some utensils still sat right where they had been left when the shop owner locked the door one last time and walked away. Ivan's mind raced—it was all dawning on him. A plan was suddenly percolating in his brain. A dream was becoming a reality, a dream he had never mentioned to anyone because it had seemed too farfetched.

"What are you staring at, my darling?" Katrina quizzed him.

"I was wondering how a sandwich shop like the Subway would work here, in this spot. We have nothing like them in Bratislava; I think people would like to eat them very much, just like in America."

"Maybe so, but maybe not. Besides you can't open a shop to sell anything, we have no money. Come on let's go home, I'm getting cold."

"Wait a minute, think of it, people would have a quick place to pop in, order the sandwich any way they want it, and take it to go eat at their office or home or even here. We know the bread-making machines are in this store already, and Mrs. Jansen, the lady who owned the one in Newark always said great bread is the key to a good sandwich. This place is perfect, don't you see?"

"What I see is that it's going to snow any minute now and all this talk of food is making me hungry. Come on and I will make you a nice Slovakian meal and not some silly sandwich. Come on," she begged, tugging him reluctantly away from the abandoned storefront.

A SLEEPLESS NIGHT ensued, with Ivan tossing and turning, no way to sleep as his mind raced. Ivan got out of bed finally and wrote down all his plans and dreams on a note pad, and in the morning he arranged a meeting with the owner of the shop that was for rent. During Ivan's lunch break, they met for an inspection of the premises. All the baking and cooking equipment, counters, furnishings, everything left behind in the shop would work fine with a little modification. It may not be exactly like a Subway, but close enough. It would have to make do.

The owner was suspicious of the young man and wanted a minimum two-year lease but agreed to throw in all the restaurant supplies, machines, ovens, and utilities at no charge after Ivan bargained hard with him. Ivan shook the man's hand and told him to have the lease papers ready by Friday, three days from now and he would sign them. The rent would start three weeks from today at the beginning of the month but the landlord agreed to let Ivan get in as soon as he paid the deposit and first month's rent to get the place ready for a first-of-the-month opening. Now all Ivan needed was the money for the deposit, the food, and the start-up costs and to pay an employee.

"Where the hell am I going to find that in three days?" he wondered out loud for the world to hear as he ran back to his job, having taken one hour too much for his lunch break.

Visiting his parents on the guise of eating a home-cooked meal with them, Ivan laid his plan out for his father after dinner while his mother took away the dirty dishes and puttered about the kitchen. Ivan knew she was listening to their every word, even though she gave no input to the conversation. She was a strong woman who was an equal in his parents' marriage, perhaps silent in public, but a full partner in the family's affairs.

"Well, son, you are asking your mother and me to gamble away our life savings on this crazy scheme of yours, and if it fails I will be working until the day I die and your mother will have to find a job somewhere to help us get by in our old age."

"Father, I know it may sound wild, and the idea that a shop selling sandwiches can make a lot of money seems farfetched, but I have seen it happen when I worked in America for a place just like what I want to open. I wish you could see one. I know I may not be describing it correctly, but trust me they are very profitable."

"Oh no, I understand that it works in America, but maybe the people in Bratislava will not like quick take-out food. Here we take our time, we sit down for lunch, we have a beer, maybe a wine; we are in no big hurry like they are in America."

"What is happening to our country now is changing all that, I believe. People who are going to be entrepreneurs, who are capitalists, and the people who work for them, will need to be hustling all the time if they want to make it. Big lunch days and dinners will not be an everyday occurrence for all the people, especially the ones in the city."

"If your mother and I loan you all our money you will still be short of the amount you say you need."

"I have a little saved up and I get paid next week. I am going to work at my job until I open the store and I am trying to find some nighttime work to tide me over. I am hoping that Katrina's wages will help get us by."

Ivan's father sat back in his chair, his arms folded across his chest, a stern look etched into the aged wrinkles around his eyes. Ivan let the silence be, he had said all there was to say. It was time for him to listen when his father finally spoke. His mother came in the room, silently walking to the back of her husband's chair and gently placing her hands on his broad shoulders, she gave him a subtle squeeze of support. Ivan didn't know what to say or do. He had never seen the two of them team up like this before in a conversation; he figured his plan was doomed.

His father rubbed his day-old chin whiskers in contemplation before continuing, "First of all, this is my first piece of advice: I would not depend on Katrina for anything in your life. She is not the type of woman to spend your future with. I doubt she will support your efforts and sacrifices at the level that will be required of you. Your mother and I have spoken of your future before and we both believe you are capable of great things. We know you can work hard, your grades in school and your desire to achieve in sports proved that to us. We never knew where to direct you so you could accomplish your dreams, the same ones that we wish we could have had the chance to pursue when we were younger."

Ivan's mother squeezed the back of her husband's neck in support of this last statement; their generation never had a chance for any sort of success under the old communist rule, try as they might.

He went on, "I would have to assume that in the worst-case scenario, if your plan does not succeed, you will take care of your newly financially broke mother and father when they are old."

He said it with a smile, and Ivan's mother smiled at him as well and spoke for the first time, "We know you will do just great and I want you to remember that you always have some free help whenever you need it at the shop. I can cook and clean just fine I suppose. I've been doing it for your father here for quite a few years and he doesn't seem to complain too much."

His father laughed loudly as he gave his son one last jab, "They better be good sandwiches, because I will be by for my free one at least once a week!"

Ivan jumped up from his seat, giving them both a big hug, all three of them crying in joy as he said, "Once a week? You mean once a day for free. It will be my interest payment!"

THE STORE OPENED on schedule after Ivan worked nights and weekends getting everything ready. He was able to find a different position working four hours per night instead of during the day at the same office he had been working for. It took time for the first week's customers to figure out how the system worked, how they could order the basic sandwich and then get whatever custom toppings and sauces they desired added to the meat and cheese. He trained four pretty girls from the university how to work the counter while he ran the cash register and assisted new customers with ordering. Two of the girls worked the lunch shift, and two worked the dinner shift. The old main square area of Bratislava also held several of the most popular bars where the young people went on Friday and Saturday nights, so Ivan quit his other job and stayed open to serve the hip drunks who staggered by on their way home. All the other restaurants and shops in the square were closed by 8:00, so he had the bar crowd to himself and had some of his best sales after normal hours. Businesses soon found out they could call his shop an hour before they wanted their orders, and Ivan would have a pretty young co-ed deliver the order right to their office. The vivacious girls always got good tips, so he had no problem getting cheap part-time help to handle the workload.

His father had been right about Katrina. She moved out a month after the shop opened. She didn't want to work there, to help with the cleaning after he closed up, to assist him on weekends, nothing whatsoever. All she did was complain that she never got to see him, that he never took her out anymore, and finally yelled at him as she stormed out the door one last time, "There is more to life than just working all the time you know!"

He was actually grateful to have her gone. Her negativism dragged him down when he would return to their apartment dead tired after another 16-hour day, only to have to listen to her constant bitching.

The store did fantastic, so much so that he paid back his parents' loan completely at the end of four months. The three of them went to a small fancy restaurant to celebrate, and Ivan began to lay out his plans for the future of other stores for them to consider while they ate. He wasn't asking for more money, he just wanted their opinions, to bounce ideas off someone he could trust. They were the only souls he could confide in at this point and they encouraged him to go for it, to make it happen.

Ivan began scouting for similar locations with the same qualities and within months began opening other shops as fast as he could afford to. Each one did well with his tried-and-true system that he insisted every manager follow; he tolerated no deviation from his tried and true system. His first shop had simply been called "The Sandwich Shop," but by the time he opened the third store he renamed them all "Ivanowich." They became all the rage throughout Slovakia as he opened restaurants in every town and village that met his strict criteria for success. His best move was hiring good managers, giving them a cut of the profits, and hiring quality, college-educated individuals who were just as dedicated and hard-working as he was to staff his main office and oversee the operations as he quickly expanded. Throughout Slovakia, Ivan Tatra was soon treated with rock star status, and he began to live the lifestyle of a young good looking successful businessman with all of the benefits, distractions and vices that came along with it. He knew he was indestructible, that nothing and no one could stop him or get in his way.

IVAN LISTENED ATTENTIVELY now as his corporate attorney continued on the telephone, "They basically have you by the balls, Ivan. They control the border, so all our distribution trucks with product going into Bosnia are now getting held up with technicalities. Nothing happens when the empty trucks leave the country of course. We had one load of fresh produce spoil after the truck was held up for three days, which was a hundred-grand dancing lesson, and I personally checked the documents. They were in perfect order—the same ones we always use. They are just showing you who the boss is."

"Fuck those Muslim pricks. I made a deal with them that they get 50 percent of the net profit and the stores are doing well by the inventory turnover we are seeing. Same stores, sales continue to increase, everybody should be happy, but not these greedy bastards."

The attorney hesitated before replying, realizing the conversation was about to get real ugly at the next news he was going to spill to his best client. "Well, it only gets worse I'm afraid, Ivan. Your hunch about too much product moving through the stores turns out to be correct. We sent in an undercover driver and it appears that a lot of the product, instead of going to the stores, is being sent to the dock on the coast at Neum. Where it goes from there we don't know. I am still trying to check the registration on the tramp steamer that the loads we followed were loaded onto, but with offshore Liberian registration it's hard to get anywhere. This stuff is out of our league. I don't know where to go from here. Do you want me to go to the police with the information I have?"

Ivan knew the business better than anyone. He could feel it in his bones when something was not right at a store, and he had sniffed out this problem exactly. He remained quiet on the phone line, mulling his options, feeling vulnerable and not in his usual total control mode. He finally replied, "We can't go to the Bosnian police, they are in bed with the gang. Hell, it might be them playing bag man. They are not breaking any law, because they pay for the product, they just aren't supposed to resell it to a third party, but that's not criminal. I'm still making really good money from the eight stores in Bosnia and I don't really care where they take the product from Neum as long as I am being paid for it. The fact that those stores are served out of the new distribution center in Zagreb helps differ the costs of that place. But this is bullshit, the whole thing smells fishy. They're up to something else. Have you tried contacting the Bosnian vice president about this? Didn't we help him get elected this last time around? He owes me, and I have never asked him for anything in return."

"He got us all the permits and health certificates to open the stores don't forget," the attorney reminded him. "I have several calls in to his office already, but he's not returning them. I can go there and try and set up a meeting, but it's probably a waste of time. I'm sure he owes your partners more than us."

"I should just teach the crooks a lesson and close down the stores and pull our equipment out. I don't want to get caught up in some bullshit that they are into. The last thing I need would be bad press if they get caught doing something illegal with our trucks or our product; it would affect us everywhere. We are doing well enough now from a cash flow standpoint that we could shut them down. Then their fricking golden goose will be dead. I wonder what they will think about that," Ivan raged.

"It is certainly an option you have, Ivan, but I would be very careful about whatever you decide to do in that country—these guys are ruthless and a law unto themselves. I'm not sure how they would react to you closing their operation down; who knows, it might be tied in with something else."

Ivan was feeling full of himself now; he liked the idea of sending a message to the rest of Europe that he was no one to try and screw with. It could serve him well as he continued to expand into other countries that didn't always play by the rules.

"Keep it quiet, but see if we can get a couple of trucks and mechanical-type employees from our Croatian division who know the store setups and can unbolt as much high-value equipment as possible in one hour at each store and then drive it back across the border. The Bosnian border guards won't give a shit since they see our trucks going back to Zagreb empty every day. Make sure they bring the computers back with them also. Have the Zagreb office turn all the servers off in Bosnia after closing time there, then all the guys have to do is unplug 'em and haul ass back to Croatia with them afterwards. The stores there all close at nine, I think, so we should be fine."

"This sounds nuts. I'm not sure I can find anyone crazy enough to do it."

"There's enough Croatians around who remember the war and will be happy to mess with Bosnians for any reason. I don't care what you have to pay them, but we need to send a message to the rest of Europe that Ivanowich will not be screwed with. Am I clear?"

The attorney knew better than to question Ivan when he was in this kind of a tirade, "Let me get someone working on it immediately."

CHAPTER 2

Josip and Rocco Tarabochia, although separated by 14 months in age, could pass as twins. Their mother had actually dressed them alike after they were three and four years old and similar in size. They had been inseparable on the sports fields, excelling in soccer, basketball, and swimming. After graduation they continued their lives together after getting a once-in-a-lifetime chance to work for the up-and-coming restaurant chain called, "Ivanowich." They were the kind of individuals who thrived in the young, hip, high-pressure atmosphere Ivanowich stores cultivated for their employees, and they soon rose through the ranks. Everyone knew if you worked hard, were a team player, and were willing to work at any job offered in the company, you had a chance to move up in the company ranks. For two boys growing up in postwar Croatia, where opportunities for achievement were few and far between, this career was a dream come true.

When asked to run to Bosnia to vacate the stores, they quickly agreed to the task.

Josip drove to the fourth Bosnian restaurant they had been told to clean out with a smile on his face as he asked his brother, "How did we do? Did we get everything out that the boss asked us to snag?"

Rocco consulted the clipboard on his lap, running down the checklist, "You know it bro. We got all the good stuff from the first three stores. Now we just need to clean out the one on 42nd Street and we are out of here and back to Zagreb and a couple of cold ones."

They high-fived each other. Things were working out just as the boss had told them it would. Josip's cell phone rang, startling him in the 2:00 a.m. darkness. Picking it up he saw the incoming call was from Velko, the driver of the other truck doing the same duty on the other four Bosnian restaurants.

"Pizza Hut," Josip jokingly answered.

"Yeah, I gotch yo' pizza fo' you, bitch," Velko replied in his best gangster rap imitation voice. Josip cracked up, laughing at his friend's humor even at this time of night.

"How you guys doing? You done yet?"

"We are on our way to the last one on 42nd Street, and you?"

"Just finished the last one and heading for the border. We had to leave a couple of coolers behind, too many people around the town square for us to be emptying the whole place out, if you know what I mean. You guys better get your ass in gear or there will be no beer left when you get to the bar for breakfast."

"We'll be there. Make my eggs over easy, and Rocco says your girlfriend was great in bed last weekend while you were away."

"You can tell that fucking homo brother of yours that . . ." Josip hung up, he and his brother chuckling at getting to Velko who considered his woman to be sacred ground, where no jokes or snide remarks were tolerated, which only made it funnier when they got him fired up.

The last stop went as smooth as the others; it had an easily accessible back entrance that did not raise any eyebrows while they were unbolting small ovens, cash registers, emptying the safes, and loading the chest-type display freezers with hand trucks into the back of the single-axle delivery truck. Switching the lights of the store off and relocking the back door, Josip eased the fully loaded truck down the alley, then turned right heading for the main highway and the border, feeling content with a job well done.

Five kilometers down the road Rocco saw in the rearview mirror, the flashing blue lights of a police car speeding after them, and blurted out to his brother, "Uh-oh, we've got trouble."

Josip eased the big truck over to a wide spot on the shoulder of the highway, wondering what could possibly be wrong. The trucks were all new vehicles with all the right plates and documents, so they were rarely harassed by the corrupt police who preyed constantly on any vehicle that showed any opportunity to weasel a few bucks out of the drivers in bribes. The protection that was afforded Ivan's trucks and stores due to his relationship with his partners made this nuisance virtually nonexistent.

The police car angled in behind them, and two officers got out of the cruiser, both with pistols drawn. The one on the driver's side shined a strong flashlight into Josip's eyes.

"Passports, documents, papers," he curtly ordered.

Josip handed his and his brother's passports and a copy of the truck's registration down to the officer who reached up for them with the large menacing flashlight still in his hand. There was no doubt what this truck was for considering it was painted from one end to the other with the flashy Ivanowich logo, and every Bosnian who lived in the city was a fan of the popular shops.

The cop took the papers back to his car while his partner stood guard on the passenger side of the truck, pistol at the ready. Reading the two Croatians' passports and jotting their names down on his notepad, he spoke into the radio, and then yelled out the window to his partner, "Have the driver open the back of the truck."

Josip did as he was told and climbed down to the ground, asking the cop while he walked around to the back, "What's the problem officer? Anything I can help you with?"

"Shut up, you Catholic pig, and do as you are told," the cop shot back, giving Josip a firm shove on the back in the process.

Rocco, sitting quietly in the passenger seat heard the truck's back doors creaking metal on metal as they swung open. He grabbed for his cell phone and hurriedly texted Velko, "*We are pulled over by cops, not good, something's up.*"

Immediately he received a reply, "*Where are you?*"

"*Five clicks west of town. They opened the back of the truck.*"

"*Fifty euro should solve the problem.*"

"*No they just handcuffed Josip.*"

The guard on Rocco's side of the truck pointed his service revolver at him and ordered him out of the vehicle, yelling at him to put his hands behind his back before he slapped a set of cuffs on him also. The cop pushed him into the backseat of the police car before climbing up into the driver's seat of the truck and turning the engine off.

Josip sat in dread. He understood the gist of the conversation the officer behind the wheel of the cop car was having on his cell phone. "The truck has no food in it, it is full of equipment. You know, like freezers and machines. I don't know. Want me to ask them? No, OK. We will wait for you, yes on the main highway. Yes, sir."

Rocco chimed in after the officer hung up, "Listen men, there must be some mistake. We are taking this equipment back for repair. We're going to be late getting back and our boss is a bastard, you know. I've got a few euros in my pocket that could get you and the wives out to dinner tonight. What do you say? But we need to get going one way or the other—he's going to pissed if we are late."

The cop in the passenger seat swung his fist around, backhanding Rocco across the face, drawing blood from his split lip that dripped red onto his white shirt. The cop smiled an evil grin at him, "You think your boss is a bastard, huh? Wait till ours gets here and has a chat with you two Croatian shits. Oh, yes, and the boss lost his father and mother in the war to you assholes. He's going to love getting even with you for that also. Ha ha!"

AFAN BADZAK'S CAR raced through the tight streets of Sarajevo, able to maneuver at top speed with the streets virtually empty at this time of night, livid that he had been screwed over. No one in Bosnia messed with him, and he was insane with the thought that anyone would even consider pulling a fast one on him in his own backyard.

"Faster, we don't have all night," he yelled at his driver zigzagging the Mercedes sedan onto the main road where he could push the heavy car to well over 130 kilometers per hour.

Everyone in Bosnia knew Afan, the former general who had kept Bosnia Herzegovina from falling into enemy hands, ensuring their independence. Everyone knew him as "the General." He had personally created the economic machine that controlled Bosnia with a firm grip, both politically and in major businesses, the one that still ruled even today.

His biggest concern over the past few years of peace had been avoiding any war crimes tribunals for his own actions during the Balkan war. Getting the country's economy moving, creating jobs, collecting taxes, and making sure he and his cronies received their "fair share" of any deal while staying out of a tribunal in the Hague Courts made for a full-time job. A perfect example of his control had been the case when the Slovakian sandwich enterprise Ivanowich had come to Bosnia locking to open a dozen stores. They needed locations, building permits, health certificates, and protection from corrupt cops and bureaucratic officials who would not let any project proceed without each one of them being paid healthy bribes along the way. Bosnia, like so many other second/third world countries, made it virtually impossible for legitimate businesses to operate within their border due to the corruption embedded in daily life that served to hinder any kind of foreign investment or development. If you got pulled over by the cops, you paid them cash; if you wanted to sell a car, you paid the license department official a bribe to get the title changed. Or if you wanted to remodel a house or office, you paid a bribe—*the magic handshake* as it was jokingly referred to. The corruption was multiplied 10 times when it came to building roads, office buildings, hotels, or opening a new business venture. Nothing happened without cash going first to the local bureaucrat who was in control. Then the person seeking to open a business venture that could help the backward nation would be passed on to the next guy waiting with his hand out, and so on and so on—a nightmare most European businesses avoided, which kept Bosnia on the doorstep of the third world. Former General Afan Badzak got a piece out of every step of the transaction, or in the case of Ivanowich he became their "partner," whether they wanted one or not.

Lights of the police car flashed menacingly red and blue ahead, so the driver slowed the black Mercedes sedan as it came closer and slid to a dusty stop behind the police cruiser, dust billowing around the delivery truck parked in front of it. Afan jumped out, hustling to the truck to look into the rear cargo hold to confirm what he had been told by one of the store managers who had arrived at his sandwich shop earlier than normal to do some cleaning and found his equipment gone. The manager could not understand why anyone would steal restaurant equipment, even in Bosnia, so he called the manager who ran the Ivanowich shop in the town's main square. When that manager opened the door to his sandwich shop 20 minutes later, he found the same thing had happened to him. The phones started ringing and quickly the General was informed of what was happening to his stores. He had put out an all-points bulletin to the police to look for any suspicious trucks driving around in the middle of the night. When the local cops had seen the Ivanowich delivery truck heading toward the border and looked in the back and saw all the stolen equipment, the pieces of the puzzle began to fall into place.

The General had been getting prying inquiries from Ivanowich headquarters regarding inconsistent orders and requests to see his accounting books for discrepancies, but he thought his managers had convinced them that everything was in order. He knew now that they were not and that Ivanowich was taking back its equipment, putting his stores out of business. Besides the profits, the stores served as a perfect front for laundering money while the trucks performed well at smuggling contraband out of the country. This turn of events was going to have serious side effects for his other not-so-aboveboard ventures, and his infamous temper was raging.

"Pull those damn truckers out of the police car," he hissed at his bodyguard riding in the front seat with his driver. "Let's see what they have to say for themselves, shall we?"

The two goons grabbed Josip and Rocco roughly by the shoulders and threw them out onto the road in front of the car lights of the Mercedes, giving them each a couple of kicks to the ribs in the process.

"So where did you two think you were taking my restaurant gear?" Afan asked, giving Josip a hard kick across the back of his left leg.

Josip yelled out in pain, "Shit, we were just doing what we were told."

When Josip spoke Afan knew by the accent that he was Croatian. The General gave him another boot to the ribs as Josip and Rocco knelt on the ground with their hands cuffed behind their backs, defenseless against the beating.

"A couple of Croat Catholics, huh? What would you bastards of a whore be doing in my country at this time of night? Who ordered you to steal my stuff? Who is your boss? Give me his name!"

"Ahhgggg," Josip coughed, sure a couple of his ribs had just been broken.

General Afan's driver, Behir, stomped on Rocco's right knee, driving his heel into the space right above the kneecap and yelling, "Answer the question shithead."

Rocco had never felt pain anywhere near what surged through his ruined knee as he rolled helplessly on to his side in a futile attempt to protect himself.

Josip sputtered, "Our boss is Jakob Picinich, he told us to come. We are supposed to take these parts back to Zagreb for repairs; we have done nothing wrong. We are not stealing anything, please. . . ."

The bodyguard reached down and grasped Josip by the elbows wedged behind his back, yanking him into an upright stance facing the bright lights of the car. Afan stepped forward to deliver a much-practiced punch to the solar plexus, driving the wind out of Josip while the bodyguard held him up.

Afan screamed into his face, "No, your boss is Ivan Tatra, isn't it? You lying piece of pig shit." Josip couldn't catch his breath enough to answer the obvious, "Tell me again who your boss is?"

This time the blow was to his face, shattering his nose flat against his face, blood spurting across his neck and shirt.

Afan turned and yelled at the two cops sitting discreetly in their patrol car the whole time, hoping to be left out of the action, realizing this was going to be a long, gory night.

"You men have some rope in your trunk? Get out here and help us."

The two cops jumped out, popping the lid of the trunk before digging through the box of items they carried for occasional roadside assistance. There were flares, orange safety triangles, a bag of miscellaneous hand tools, and a 10-meter length of tow rope.

When the rope was presented to the General, he hissed at the cops, "Tie them up, back to back, standing up. Mujo, get your cell phone out. You can take a video with it, yes?" he asked his driver.

"Yes sir."

"Good, we will make a little movie to send to our friend, the great Ivanowich."

He turned back to the cops.

"You two take the patrol car 200 meters back toward town and block the road with your lights flashing, and make sure no one comes through, understand? I will tell you when you can open the road again." The cops both nodded, thankful they were not going to have to be witnesses to whatever would happen next. Stopping one of the officers, Afan continued, "On second thought, you move the truck so it is sideways in the middle of the road, then walk a few hundred meters toward the border and take some road flares and lights and block any traffic from that direction until I tell you also everything is OK."

"Yes, General."

"Wait. Take only two flares with you and leave me the rest," the General said.

"Mujo, when he gets the truck moved into place, swing the Mercedes onto the middle of the road so we can light up the Ivanowich sign on the side of the truck. I think it will make good background for our video."

Mujo smiled at his boss's ingenuity. He had been with Afan for years and never ceased to be amazed by his quick mind and ruthless demeanor. He sometimes thought the General enjoyed killing Croatians more than anything else, a seething revenge that was never fulfilled it seemed. Mujo hated them almost as much as he did Serbs and was more than willing to help his leader.

Josip and his brother stood bruised and bleeding, shaking in fear as they watched the vehicles being moved into position, not sure what was going to happen next but understanding it was not going to be good. They didn't dare move and had no way of running since they were securely tied to each other. There would be no escape.

The driver brought out two black balaclavas from the trunk of the Mercedes along with two sets of neoprene gloves. Mujo and Afan pulled the woolen masks over their heads and faces leaving only their eyes and mouth exposed before sliding the gloves on. Afan's driver backed up so he could sit on the hood of his car steady and ready to turn on the video feature of his cell phone. The two Bosniak stepped into the car's glaring high-beam headlights, the Ivanowich logo lit up with the brothers huddled back-to-back standing upright in front of it.

"Turn on the camera," the General ordered Behir.

Mujo stood in front of Rocco, and Afan took his place in front of Josip. He turned to the camera and yelled in an odd disguised voice, "This is what you get for trying to double-cross your partners, Ivan Tatra."

The first roundhouse blow from Afan to Josip's gut would have sent him to the ground were it not for the rope tying him to his brother, holding him upright. As he instinctively bent over from the blow, the next upper cut caught him on the point of the jaw, snapping it at the joint below his ear. Mujo laid into Rocco with equally devastating bows, until the two brothers reflexively tried to move, ducking, trying to protect themselves and avoid the direct shots. This only enraged Afan who clenched his fists together forming a hammer and slammed them down onto the back of Josip's exposed neck. The two Bosniak proceeded to clinically beat the Croats in a practiced rhythm, keeping them upright, making the brothers scream in pain at the bruising hits. Mujo moved like the boxer he had been before the wars, punching the defenseless young men with ruthless efficiency until the two of them finally fell to the ground where they proceeded to get kicked and stomped on. This is where Afan was an expert. He had tortured hundreds of captives during the war and knew precisely where to direct his efforts to attain the maximum amount of pain from his victims. To him a perfectly placed blow resulted in a piercing cry or yell from his targets—that's when he knew he had hit them just right.

Rocco cried out an animalistic howl when his ankle was smashed, he could feel through the dulling pain that he would never walk the same again, if he could walk at all. The thought ran through his disheveled brain: "*What am I thinking, if I walk again? I'm not going to live through this. These two goons are going to kill us.*"

Mujo halted his onslaught momentarily, reaching down to hold Josip's cuffed hands on the asphalt, making sure the camera was going to get a good shot of the General's next move. He walked around to get in position, stared menacingly at the camera through the round eerie eyeholes in his mask, and then leapt into the air, landing hard on Josip's fingers. The snapping bones were audible until the young helpless man's screams drowned them out. Mujo let the arms go, walked off camera, and returned with a road flare, pulling the packaging off the top and lighting it as he approached the prone boys.

Rocco looked up through his swollen eyes when he heard the hiss of the burning flare, the flames reaching far out of the top of the signal flare. He prayed that his wildest fears were not about to come true, but they were. Mujo swept the flare in front of Rocco's face, singeing his eyelashes and brow hair before moving it down to his bound hands. There he held the searing flare steady at the point where the wrist meets the hand, the flesh of Rocco's hand melting away, exposing nerve endings and causing him to scream at the top of his lungs for mercy.

General Afan smirked under his balaclava. This was good stuff for the camera, and it would give the Slovakian prick something to think about. He watched as Mujo moved over to the other Croat. He could tell the two were losing their fight, their will to resist any further vanishing quickly, even though he felt they had held up pretty well for civilians, much better than a lot of the men and women he had seen give up under much less painful punishment. The driver videoing the torture moved closer to the bound men to get a close-up with his cell phone of Mujo's next move, regretting it when the smell from the flesh being burned off of Josip's face with the flare wafted up to his nostrils, causing him to heave in revulsion. Both of Josip's burning eyeballs exploded from the heat, their liquid contents turning to steam in the flare's intense flame. Josip's nose disappeared as he valiantly struggled against the ropes tying him to his brother, who yelled weeping over Josip's screaming.

"I love you Josip, see you in heaven! Ohhh! Please God make it stop!"

At his yelling Mujo moved the sputtering, dying flare back to Rocco, lighting his hair on fire and letting it burn brightly for the camera. As the hair disappeared, the last of the heat from the flare was applied to Rocco's face, instantly making him unrecognizable as a human being. Mujo threw the spent flare off the side of the road before looking to General Afan for direction on how to proceed.

The General looked toward the camera that was brought forward to him for a close-up of his mask-covered face and he growled in a husky disguised voice at the camera, "Ivan Tatra, this is what you will get if you try and double-cross your partners again, you fucking pig." With that, he turned to the smoldering men, raised his pistol and shot each one in the knee before walking off camera.

The driver switched off the cell phone's video feature while following Afan to the Mercedes.

Pulling his mask off his head Afan yelled back at Mujo, "Kill the poor bastards. Do them a favor and put them out of their misery. After all, we are not barbarians."

Mujo put his Beretta 9mm pistol to Josip's temple and fired one bullet through what remained of the boy's head, ending his short life instantly before doing the same to his brother, leaving their bodies in a smoldering heap on the pavement.

When the driver pulled the Mercedes up next to the police car that was still blocking the road, Mujo spoke out the open window to the cop waiting there, "Get rid of the two bodies and back the truck to the shoulder of the road. Someone will come and pick it up in a few hours. Leave the keys under the seat. Any questions? You understand we don't want anyone finding the bodies?"

"Yes sir, no problem."

Mujo rolled his window up as the driver stepped on the gas, hurtling them back toward town. The General took the driver's phone, finding the saved video of the Croatian beating. He forwarded it to an unregistered email address he kept for untraceable purposes. Logging on to it from his own phone he quickly found the file, then forwarded it on thinking, "*This will give that Slovakian shit something to sleep on.*"

CHAPTER 3

IVAN LIKED WORKING FROM HIS HOME OFFICE EARLY IN THE morning; he had no interruptions and was able to plan his day's activities with the assistance of his personal secretary based in his main office downtown via email or phone as needed until he showed up there around 10:00. The view from his mansion's corner office was nothing short of spectacular, the old estate's landscaped grounds that he had spent a small fortune rehabilitating rolling away to the east where the sun rose this morning, bursting orange and red through a break in the cloud-kissed horizon.

Ivan opened the email that appeared to come from his Bosnian branch manager, wondering smugly what their reaction was when the store managers had shown up for work that morning and found their stores cleaned out. He was surprised it had come to him so early, thinking it might take some time for them all to communicate about what had occurred last night. He had a string of other emails, which was usual on a busy morning like this, and a half-dozen voice mails he would get to in just a few minutes. He leaned back in his leather chair waiting for the email file to upload and thinking about how he was going to word the email notification to send out to the whole company, letting his staff know that operations in Bosnia were finished. It seemed to be a large file, but since the attachment had come through his company computer servers, he didn't think twice about it having a virus attached. They had the best technology money could buy at Ivanowich, and it weeded out 99 percent of the junk.

The email finally opened, showing a dark roadside scene with one of Ivan's trucks in the background. Two men were bound together back-to-back, crouching on the pavement in the foreground, bleeding from apparent facial wounds. A man whose identity was hidden from view by the black terrorist-like balaclava spoke directly to the camera recording the event, "This is what you get for trying to double-cross your partners, Ivan Tatra."

He was stunned by the scene and watched in horror at the obviously amateur footage shot on someone's cell phone. It was like an impending train wreck, and he just couldn't take his eyes off his computer screen, knowing what he was seeing was only going to get worse. He watched terrified while the two men were beaten and tortured. Ivan began to shake violently in his chair; he couldn't believe any human being was capable of doing something like this to another human being. Then it got worse when one of the masked men disappeared for a moment but quickly returned to the screen with a flaming road flare. He started systematically burning the helpless men as they struggled uselessly to fight back or to get away.

Ivan retched, a gag reflex, feeling sick and realizing he couldn't watch anymore when one of the hapless men's faces was burned beyond recognition with the scorching road flare. Ivan lurched forward, vomiting into the wastebasket next to his massive antique oak desk. But like a magnet his eyes were still drawn to the video, watching the disgusting sight while wondering why in the hell this had been sent to him. The remainder of the light breakfast and lattes he had consumed that morning quickly found their way into the trash as the second man's hair was lit on fire. He should have turned the wretched video off, but the fact that his logo was painted on the truck in the background of the gross footage kept him wondering what the connection was, what the hell was going on. He could hardly believe it as one of the men who was torturing the captives turned to the camera and said, with an odd gravelly voice in broken English, directly to him, "Ivan Tatra, this is what you will get if you try and double-cross your partners again, you fucking pig."

The man then turned and shot the two captives in the knees before the video ended. Ivan sat horrified, not knowing the men in the video but quickly putting two and two together, realizing that his plan for getting all his equipment out of Bosnia and teaching them a lesson last night had not gone according to plan A.

He could barely hold his cell phone in his hand he was shaking so violently. He had to try three times before he was able to dial the vice president of Ivanowich who had ramrodded the Bosnian operation.

On answering the call on the first ring, his VP said, "Ivan we have a big problem. One of the trucks did not make it back to Croatia."

This confirmation of the nightmare he had just watched sent a chill up Ivan's spine and he replied, "Yes, I already know. Meet me in my office in town in one hour and contact the rest of the team and tell them to meet us there also. I want the whole upper management group, no excuses. We have a very, very serious problem."

CHAPTER 4

GREY THREATENING SKIES OUTSIDE DID NOT SEEM AS DREARY when sitting in the floor-to-ceiling window-lined conference room at Ivanowich headquarters in downtown Bratislava. All the major players in Ivan's empire sat quietly around the highly polished walnut conference table, some sipping coffee while others made notes on laptop computers or iPads, waiting for the boss to join the meeting he had called. Fifteen minutes late, Ivan burst into the room with his personal assistant hot on his tail. As Ivan took his place at the head of the table, his assistant pushed a button at the other end that slid a sculptured wooden panel into a recessed slot in the wall, exposing a large wide screen that could be used as computer monitor or for television viewing. Before connecting her laptop to the screen's control panel, she fussed with getting the screen's definition just right in her ultra-efficient manner.

No one said a word of greeting to the boss, they all just sat quietly waiting to hear what the problem was. Ivan began the meeting with, "Gentlemen, we have a problem, and we need to act now. As most of you know, we sent two teams of drivers with a helper each to Bosnia from our Croatian operation last night with the intent of pulling out the majority of our patented equipment and computers so we can close down operations there effective today. You may or may not have heard that our Bosnian partners have been ripping off our stores there, falsifying sales and inventory records. We have eyewitness accounts that some of the product that was supposed to be going to the stores has actually been delivered to the Bosnian port and put on ships to obviously be sold elsewhere, a total violation of our rules. The managers have been going along with the scam, I suppose not necessarily by choice since our partners play rough if they don't get their way, as you are about to see. The decision to pull out of Bosnia was not made lightly, I can assure you. We tried to get them to show us their records, to come clean on what the issues were, but we were stymied at every attempt. As a company, we cannot let partners in foreign countries play games with us. If others hear about us letting them get away with these shenanigans, news such as this could completely ruin our expansion plans if others figured they too could get away with this kind of thievery."

The vice president of sales chimed in, "Sir, the sales figures for the Bosnian operation were on track and quite good last quarter, I'm not sure what you mean about ripping us off. . . ."

Ivan harshly interrupted him, "Sales yes, but even though they showed profits they were not relative to the amount of sales going through the stores. Selling to another party at the docks is a clear violation of our whole program of Ivanowich being the sole supplier of all goods. We only sell to ourselves and our own restaurants. We are lucky the buyers at the docks didn't end up with tainted meat or produce. You know damn well who would have been sued if there had been some health hazard. Those lazy fucking Bosnians would have tried everything in their crooked courts to get us to pay out the ass for an issue like that. It was a good idea that we teamed up with the Bosnian Mafia, or whatever you want to call them, to get started, but now we realize our mistake since it seems they run the whole country: the judges, the cops, city hall, everything. The place is a dead end for business and they are trying to dictate to us how our business will be run and that is not going to happen," He yelled, slamming his fist down on the conference table. Ivan turned and barked at his assistant, "Mish is the video ready?"

"Yes sir."

Ivan continued, "Last night one of the trucks we sent to clear out the eight Bosnia stores made it back to Zagreb no problem, the other did not. When I opened my computer this morning I received the emailed video you are about to see from our head of the Bosnian stores company computer. We have checked with him and he confirms that he did not send the email; in fact he doesn't have a computer to send it on since our men took it last night. This means someone has been able to hack into our system and send this email. Our computer team here at headquarters has successfully disabled the Bosnian connections and we should have no more computer issues, we hope."

Ivan looked around the room, pausing to study each of the faces of the 14 somber men in attendance. He had thought about what to do with the video, whether to share it or keep it a secret, but after hashing it over and over in his troubled mind had decided his most trusted directors should witness what they were all now up against. Perhaps none of them were safe. Maybe one of them would be the next victim. He didn't know, but they needed to be aware of what had happened to two of their trusted employees on that dark highway in Bosnia last night.

He continued after he had looked each of the board members in the eye, "All right, get ready to see something you never knew one human being could do to another. I suggest you stay close to a trashcan. This is the most disgusting thing you will ever see in your life, and the two men you are about to see tortured have been identified and confirmed as the employees who are missing from Croatia, two brothers who I am told were up-and-coming managers. Jan, please turn down the lights, and Mish, run the video."

Ivan watched closely his staff's reaction to the revolting show; he knew he didn't need to ever see the video again—it was permanently imbedded in his mind. One after another, the board members turned their eyes away from the despicable scene on the screen, unable to watch the horror any longer; some did indeed vomit, while others began to weep at the sight. One vice president got up quickly from his chair and ran out of the room sobbing only halfway through the video.

When it was over, the lights were left low for a few minutes, enough time for the people to compose themselves somewhat before Ivan broke the silence and Mish returned the lights to normal.

"Those are the kind of people we have been dealing with. I'm sorry you all had to see what I woke up to this morning, but I feel it's important that you all take extra safety and security measures, just in case."

"Has this been reported to the authorities?" asked his chief operations manager while he, without shame, dabbed at his teary eyes.

"We have notified the Bosnian police and Army, not that we think we will hear anything from them. We have requested that the boys' bodies be returned to their families if they are found, praying that they are dead and not still suffering. We have reported the incident to Interpol and emailed them a copy of the video, and they will be here for an interview later today."

"Obviously we have discontinued all operations, sales, and business dealings in Bosnia. How about the equipment, signage, and remaining product? Are we just leaving it there?" the manager of inventory control asked.

"It's up to you all to vote on how we should proceed from here," Ivan said.

The company's attorney, the one Ivan had been talking to on the phone the day before, was a wise man. Ivan had placed him on the board of directors several years ago for that reason. He spoke up for the first time all morning, "I would like to make a motion that we abandon all remaining assets in Bosnia, write them off, keep the stores closed permanently, and financially compensate the two young men's families fifty thousand euros each for their loss and to prevent any future lawsuits occurring. We need to keep a lid on this and not end up in some public lawsuits."

"I recommend we make it one hundred thousand," the chief financial officer inserted.

"I second it with the change," said the head of human resources.

"All in favor?" Ivan asked.

The vote was unanimous, just as Ivan had anticipated it would be. He spoke up once more, "Right, so we will proceed as voted.

Each of you should review our security protocols and watch your backs. I would hope we are done with this affair and that the culprits will be brought to justice, but you can't be too careful with these Bosniak maniacs."

Everyone in the room nodded in acknowledgment of the tasks and threats ahead.

Ivan continued with the meeting, changing the subject quickly, "Alright then, we need to discuss the impending meeting in Hungary this weekend when I go there to meet with the countess regarding Ivanowich expanding into that market. I believe we may be able to secure the Atwood family to back us there, using their pull and connections and tons of real estate to implement a speedy and efficient expansion."

The vice president of human resources sat watching how easily Ivan Tatra had switched from the morning's deadly tragedy to a new business venture, sweeping the horror of the video and its message completely off the table and into the trash bin. Ivan, he had seen on several occasions, had a knack—as many self-made men do—of being able to focus on specific items, and then switch directions to a new subject and become completely absorbed in the new project, but in this case it seemed he was grossly insensitive. Many others in the room needed some recovery time, a chance to digest what they had just witnessed. After all, their lives may now be in a great deal of danger as well. Not sure what to say but revolted by the actions and needing to speak up, he said, "Can we adjourn for an hour and then meet up again? Each of us needs to address this problem in Bosnia in our own way and get with our people now and set the new directives in motion."

A collective sigh came over the room, and it was agreed to meet up an hour later, leaving Ivan and his assistant to continue their own private discussion.

"Do I have flights for the Hungarian weekend events?"

"Yes, I have the helicopter set up. It will be the most convenient, and I have confirmed the schedule of events and what will be happening. The dinner party on Friday night is business, not formal, so I will have your black suit and a white shirt packed. I would recommend in that crowd that you place a colored pocket square in the breast pocket, not a white one. Wear the sky blue Hermes tie. You are scheduled to spend the morning hunting with Countess Atwood on Saturday, and then Saturday night dinner is formal. Your tux will be packed and ready as well as your hunting attire and boots. There will be enough clothes packed in case a pheasant shoot happens on Sunday. The invitation says 'weather willing.' You are all set from my end."

Ivan smiled at her efficiency, "Thanks Mish, great job as always."

Mish didn't smile back, simply answering, "You are welcome, sir."

Walking back down the dark wood-paneled hallway, Ivan wondered if he could ever or should ever tell his board of directors or for that matter anyone, the rest of the story about the Bosnians. The sordid part that involved a whole bunch of tax-free cash they had paid him in kickbacks for turning a blind eye to whatever they were up to, stuff he didn't want to know or need to know. That cash cow was surely ending after this latest episode, but what could he do? He had warned them and warned them about not screwing with his company and its reputation. The cash had been nice when he was in a crunch a few years ago, when he constantly had to find new investors and small banks to fund his expansion. He had played a very risky game with cash, but he was now legitimately making more money than he could spend from his business. He would just have to find another source if he needed more under-the-table cash sent to his Swiss accounts, that's all. But at least he hoped he had that crazed Bosniak out of his way and out of his hair once and for all.

CHAPTER 5

Countess Pamela Atwood was born into money, real money, old money. The kind of money that owned large tracts of farmland for which tenants paid twice a year with a 50 percent share of the proceeds from the sale of the crops. Old money that owned buildings for more than two centuries in the middle of town where inhabitants and businesses paid monthly rent and rarely changed locations because the family owned the surrounding buildings as well. If Europe had only done one thing right as far as the wealthy of Hungary were concerned it was that most of the countries had left their inheritance taxes at zero or at very low rates, allowing families to pass on their wealth to the next generation without having to give 60 percent or more to the government, the way those wacky Americans did. The homes the Atwoods owned for summer living, winter getaways, and hunting lodges with their wooded forests nestled in the hills on the outskirts of town, manned by loyal staff whose families had been with the Atwoods for many generations, gave a feeling of unity and continuance to young Pamela as she grew up the only child of Countess Anna and Count Bella Atwood. Having bred no son, the outgoing handsome father had decided early on that his daughter would learn the ways of the man's world, while still remaining a lady. He knew that if she grew up unable to handle herself around the cut-throat business life and decision making that would be required of the eventual heir to the Atwood dynasty, the family's fortunes would soon dribble away, mismanaged by accountants and attorneys bent on milking the trusts and assets of every nickel they could. He had seen it happen to many of his neighbors, and had himself taken advantage of misguided heirs on many occasions when they would need to fire sale some real estate or other assets to maintain enough cash flow to keep the greedy lazy heirs in the lifestyle they felt they were entitled to.

Needing her to be well rounded in a multiplicity of skills, the Count brought her up to be, among other things, an accomplished equestrian. Her black Friesian warm-blood horse, Quintus, and Pamela moved through the farmlands as if joined as one at the saddle. She was able to shoot a rifle and shotgun with equal skill. Wild boar, stag, and pheasant fell in equal numbers right alongside the men and boys who traditionally occupied the shooting lines at their estate every fall, shooting lines that until the current generation had rarely seen a woman let alone a teenaged girl who could hold her own.

Her father had her filing at the office on holidays and summer breaks from the time she turned 12, working at a variety of jobs in the family's conglomerate of holdings, learning the lessons of being a businesswoman and countess from the ground floor up starting at an early age.

Her elegant mother made certain that she learned to enjoy the finer things in life as well: the best schools, clothing befitting her station in life, lessons in etiquette, and private language lessons so that by her teen years she was fluent in French, German, and English besides her native Hungarian, which was virtually useless outside the borders of her homeland.

Growing up she always figured there was a big world outside Hungary, getting her first taste of it when her mother took her to Paris and Munich on a seasonal shopping spree. She loved the bright lights, the "beautiful people," and fancy restaurants, but her family's business and social interests kept her close to home growing up where she was taught all that is Hungarian—the history, the culture, and why theirs was a history that only a little more than 100 years ago had ruled a big chunk of civilized Europe, until a Macedonian radical, who with a single shot started World War I and the eventual demise of the Austro-Hungarian Empire. She was too preoccupied with her busy life to give much thought to what the rest of the world must be like, or to pursue other travel aspirations. Hers was a world revolving around Hungary and everything Hungarian, at least until she finished her university education.

Her mother had always told her how beautiful she was, and she noticed the looks from her fellow collegiate male students, but somehow her dating was sporadic at best through her university years. Losing her virginity to a neighbor boy in the loft of the stallions barn at 18 when the two of them had been caught up in the moment had left her unsatisfied and wondering what all the fuss was about. The boy knew less about sex than she did, and it was rough and quick and hurt like hell. The coitus was not what she had dreamt it would be and certainly not like in the steamy novels some of the girls at college had loaned her to read late at night, where the sex and stimulation was said to make the earth move and fireworks go off.

Many times when she was asked out to a dance or for coffee on the weekends she already had plans back at home or at one of the farms or was meeting with her father about business. She was always busy with something it seemed. The few dates she did have were with boys who were definitely intimidated by her wealth and beauty; few of the boys' families were anywhere close to the Atwoods' money level. Her stunning good looks kept all but the boldest men from asking her out in the first place, most men not wanting to feel the sting of rejection.

At 22, Pamela graduated third in her class ready to take on the world, at least the Hungarian world she had prepared herself for. She dutifully reported to the count's main office the Monday after the graduation ceremony to begin her management-training program under the watchful eye of her father's right-hand man and longtime confidant, Franek Meszaros. They met in his elegant office to formally lay out a five-year plan, an ascension to power that would have made someone not trained her whole life to understand this was her destiny, faint at the prospect. Franek had to smile as he led her to the door when their meeting was over. This was a special person he was dealing with. Even if she were not the count's daughter, he would have hired her to run all the businesses. She was someone who could not only handle the empire down the road, but a person possessing such a natural beauty and charm that she appeared to not yet understand its depth and power, which no man or, for that matter, no woman would be capable of resisting.

Pamela was soon the talk of the town, attending all the major social and sporting events as the family's representative, accompanied by a suitable escort, a young man from an appropriate family or with her father. Her mother made sure she was always dressed elegantly, so much so that it became quite common to see her picture splashed across the social pages of the Budapest newspapers and magazines. Pamela Atwood was the most eligible bachelorette in all of Hungary, but to her there was no rush to matrimony; she had plenty of goals to achieve with lots of time to accomplish them before she would settle down and start creating her own heirs to the Atwood fortunes.

CHAPTER 6

FROST HUNG LIKE A SNOWY BLANKET ON THE WHEAT STUBBLE surrounding the stone-walled barns. Pamela rarely rode or hunted this early in the day but today was different. She wanted to check out the northern perimeter of the family estate this morning, an area rarely ventured to, and it was going to be a long cold ride on a horse. Quintus, her Friesian stallion, was full of himself this morning, prancing on the rein, steam blowing from his frosty nostrils while she saddled him in the dim light of the cold barn. Palo, the head horseman who cared for all the stock at the farm, was surprised that she was in the barn so early and rushed to help when he saw her saddling the big black steed.

"Countess, please let me get that cinch. What are you doing here so early in the morning? The boars are still asleep, and the stags will not roar for another two hours yet. Please go to the fire and warm up while I prepare Quintus for his ride. He is certainly excited and dancing today, no?"

"He knows we're going hunting; I sometimes think he enjoys it more than me! I will take the Holland bolt action today, the 6.5mm. Palo, will you get it for me while I finish saddling my Quintus?"

"As you wish, Countess," he said as he hustled off to the gun room, fumbling with the combination lock until the massive door to the walk-in vault finally swung open, revealing a row of shotguns and rifles whose total value was staggering. Reverently selecting the English-made Holland and Holland bolt action she had requested, he wiped it down quickly with a pre-oiled rag before slipping in into the sheepskin-lined leather scabbard. He selected a box of handloaded ammo and jogged back to where Pamela had just finished saddling the jet-black horse.

Quintus pranced even more excitedly feeling the scabbard being tied to his saddle until he felt the sting of Pamela's open gloved hand smack his belly, "Enough now. Settle down or I will take your brother hunting instead."

Palo knelt down and joined his hands together so Pamela could place her mirror-polished knee-high riding boot in them as she smoothly leapt up and slid onto the stallion's back.

"Where will you go today, Countess?"

"I am thinking Quintus needs a good run and I should be able to get to the border field before dawn if we ride hard."

"Shall I follow you? I can fetch whatever game you take today. Just tell me when I must be there."

"Thank you Palo, but I will be fine," she smiled. "I'm a big girl now; the boars won't get me. I will be back before lunch, hopefully with that big boar that has been digging under the fences. They say he's a monster."

"You should not be out alone Countess, you know that, I . . ."

She cut him off, "Thank you for the advice Palo, I will see you before lunch." The stirrup barely touched the steed's flank and he was off at full gallop down the dirt road toward the north border. The cold air nipped at Pamela's cheeks, and the sable fur of her elegant hunting coat and matching hat flowed with every long stride of the powerful black horse. They rode as one in the darkness on a trail well known to both of them.

Heavy white frost had formed on the grasslands and cut cornfield as dawn's rosy hue lit up the eastern sky, throwing a peach color to the whiteness while the sun crept over the horizon. Reining the stallion in when she arrived at the hidden hitching post specifically built 100 meters behind the high shooting stand, she walked quickly to it, carrying a fine leather knapsack and happy to get warmer with the exertion of the short hike. She climbed the dozen steps up to the door of the small stand, passed through it, closing it tightly behind her, and got herself settled in. Sitting comfortably in the wooden shooting house elevated four meters above the valley floor, nestled in among the trees lining the border of the 100-acre cornfield, she could easily see where the swine had been rooting in the waste of the harvest. Furrows of fresh soil lay turned up where the pigs had used their snouts to root for the remnants of corncobs after they had been combined into the farm's trucks. The rows of standing corn that the farm manager had left uncut for the wild animals to feed on over the long winter were already decimated by the red stag, fallow deer, and boar that thrived on the easy pickings.

Two fallow does with this season's fawns lingered in the middle of the field, searching for the few yellow kernels the hogs had missed. A small herd of red deer worked the brush at the end of the field, pushed by one four-year-old stag, his antlers still not up to their full potential, harassing the females in the hopes that one of them was still not bred by his much bigger cousin. It was obvious to Pamela, however, that he had missed his chance. None of the hinds were giving him any scent that they were still available.

The chill of dawn bit at her cheeks, while the rest of her was warm under her furs. The Hermes silk scarf wrapped around her dainty neck kept the itch of the woolen one wrapped tightly on top of it from irritating her neck, and the heavy woolen blanket from her saddle bag that was wrapped around her knees and feet made the morning tolerable even at these chilly temperatures. She looked out the back of the blind to check on Quintus standing patiently, steam rising from the sweat on his flanks as he waited for his mistress to finish her morning hunt. He was well trained and familiar with the routine; they had done this many times before.

A heavy black-haired boar suddenly materialized at the edge of the field, 200 meters to Pamela's right, sneaking along the tree line, wily enough not to walk into the open field in the emerging daylight. He hadn't lived this many years in a hunting area by being stupid, but the cold weather this morning made him want to feed a little longer than normal. He was too old to care about the sows anymore; he hadn't bred one in two years. He lived alone and rarely fought with the other boars now, preferring to give way to the aggressive younger males who charged and slashed at any rival on a daily basis, just as he had in years past. Now he could sometimes just flash his long heavy tusks at the juvenile boars, scaring them away if they got too close with his sheer size, chopping his jaws together to clash the tusks to remind them that he could still be formidable if pushed past his short limit of tolerance.

His tusks protruded at least 20 centimeters past his outer lip, clearly visible to Pamela through her Zeiss binoculars, even at this distance. Setting the binocs gently down on the wooden bench, she slid open the window and eased the Holland and Holland's barrel out, resting it securely. She located the mighty boar in the scope as he meandered unaware of her presence near the thick edge of the oaks and pine trees. The old boar moved with confidence, a tremendous sized boar, one like Pamela had never seen before. Her insides churned, her nerves suddenly getting the better of her while she waited for the black beast to emerge out of the shadows and into a spot where she could get a clean killing shot. The pig moved toward her up the row, now easing out into the cornfield, only to switch back and scrape up an acorn missed by the other animals inside the tree line. This boar was not the typical nervous type that hustled along in a herd. He shuffled like a bear, confident but cautious in Pamela's rifle scope while she tried to calm her jitters. The small opening 10 meters in front of the boar was going to be Pamela's only clear chance if she was going to get any shot at all on this magnificent trophy, so she slowly swung the crosshairs into position, waiting for the beast to step into the small window of opportunity.

He was facing directly at her when he emerged into her target zone, a risky shot at 175 meters, but all she had as she squeezed the light trigger of England's finest craftsmanship, immediately regretting the decision when the boar jumped to his right as the bullet raked down his left flank. Jacking another round into the action she found the boar running full speed through the trees in the direction of the property line with their eastern neighbors. She had no shot at the wounded wild boar that was crashing headlong through the thickets. He disappeared in a matter of seconds.

She swore at herself. She knew better than to take a risky shot like that, and now she had to follow the wounded animal. It wasn't that she was afraid of the beast, on the contrary, she felt bad for the injured animal, kicking herself that she had not made a clean kill like she had been taught to do her whole life.

"Wild animals deserve to be quickly and humanely killed," her father had always told her. Respecting the animals God had given them for sport and food was more important than collecting another trophy for the wall.

Gathering her binoculars and blanket into her daypack, she hurried down the wooden stairs, before striding with purpose toward Quintus who, having heard the shot, nervously pranced against the reins holding him to the hitching post, pawing the ground, frosty steam billowing from his nostrils.

"Well I screwed that up, my Quintus," she spoke, slipping the rifle into the scabbard before tying her pack to the matching hunting saddle. With no thought of gracefulness whatsoever she pulled herself up onto the saddle, and then eased Quintus toward where the boar had originally been hit. The black stallion fought the reins, anxious to get on with the hunt, but Pamela kept him firmly under control, letting nature settle back down after the noise of the shot while listening to the eerie silence that always follows one. When she arrived at the edge of the tree line where the pig had been hit, she didn't have to get off the horse to see where the boar's huge hooves had churned up the soft soil the moment the bullet raked his side. Easing her black steed forward at a walk, following the spoor on the frost covered leaves, detouring around the heavier thickets where the horse could not follow, she came to the three-strand barbed wire fence that separated the Atwood's estate from the neighboring Pushkas land. She had to follow the wounded animal; there was no second thought as she searched for a gate, but seeing none in the area, swung Quintus around, high stepping backwards 20 meters, giving him the chance to size up the fence in front of them, then nudging his flanks and pushing the reins forward to his neck.

"Hayah," Pamela commanded into Quintus's ear.

The mighty horse charged forward through the gap in the trees toward the wire. Seconds later the two of them were airborne, only barely clearing the fence, touching back down on the plowed earth with a practiced grace. Quintus let out a mighty whinny, proud of himself, before Pamela directed him back onto the boar's clearly visible tracks on the frost-crusted open field. Pamela had never been onto this field before; actually it was strange she thought, watching the trail in front of her, that she had never met any of the Pushkas family members other than the matriarch of the family once whom she learned a few weeks earlier had passed away almost two years ago. The family members were reputed to spend most of their time in Switzerland, with this farm used only on rare occasions. She could see several shooting stands scattered around the perimeter of the fields so she assumed they must hunt it, if only rarely. She would have Palo let the manager know she had followed a wounded animal onto their property later that day, she thought. They would understand; they would be expected to do the same if roles were reversed.

The old boar had run out of gas, the searing pain down his flank might not be fatal to a younger animal, but at his advanced age he could not tolerate much blood loss. After crossing the open grass pasture, he rolled in loose soil and leaves in an attempt to sooth the wounds and stem the blood flow. Instinctively, he searched for the thickest part of the brambles and lay down to catch his breath and see what followed his trail, because some unknown assailant had caused this and he had no choice but to make a stand now, running would only weaken him further. The wily old boar heard the horse approaching before he saw it.

Pamela could make out fresh droppings of blood in the frosty pasture sprinkled on top of the boar's distinct prints, confirming she had hit him. Still, she was mad that the blood flow was not stronger, which would indicate a mortal heart or lung shot.

"The boar will run a long way with only a superficial wound like this," she thought, keeping her eye on the tracks as they approached

the next tree-lined border. Seeing no opening to go through the heavy brush she cautiously pulled the Holland and Holland from its scabbard and jacked a fresh shell into it, cranked the variable scopes power down to the lowest setting and flicked on the safety. The rifle sat comfortably across her lap while she rode slowly up to the tree line to find out where the boar had run to.

The charge of the wild boar caught Quintus off guard. The wind was not blowing in his favor so he couldn't smell the pig and hadn't noticed the massive swine's location five meters in front of him until it was too late. The boar lunged forward as if not wounded at all. Pamela, realizing she could not get the rifle up in time, watched as the massive boar charged into Quintus at full speed, his slashing tusk catching the Friesian's left fetlock and ripping the muscle to the bone. Quintus's natural reaction was to rear back, kicking his right hairy hoof at the boar's head, connecting solidly and sending the boar rolling onto his side. The sudden attack combined with Quintus's rearing back caught Pamela completely off guard, sending her tumbling over the horse's flanks, the rifle flying out of her grip and smashing into the dirt field. She hit the ground hard, landing flat on her back, the wind knocked out of her lungs while she struggled to escape the enraged horse's flailing hooves. It was all she could do to roll once onto her side, and then roll one more time out of harm's way. The boar let out a deep bellowing squeal as it recovered from the horse's kick and bravely came for the black steed once again. The horse spun his rear end around to use his back hooves to protect himself from the onslaught, his balance almost lost as the incredible pain from the wound on his lower left leg surged up his flank. Quintus kept one eye on the boar and the other on his master, stepping over her prone body and barely missing her while he kicked out viciously at the black fury trying to gore him again. The porcine terror dodged away from the flailing hooves, jigging to his left, jagging to his right, the horse screaming, the pig squealing, and Pamela scrambling on the ground to try and get up and find her rifle. She saw it two meters away from the spinning horse who was keeping the 240-kilo boar at bay temporarily. From her lowly vantage point she saw in the melee the bloody carnage of Quintus's leg and it made her gag at the sight. The boar now saw the human on the ground crawling in front of the horse, and suddenly everything made sense. He had seen in his many years what these two-legged creatures had done to his ilk in the woods. Without a second thought for his own safety, the enraged wild boar backed away from the horse to find a clear way to charge at the human on its hands and knees, scampering away from him. When the horse spun awkwardly to the left, he gave the boar the opening he needed and he began his vicious charge.

Pamela looked over her shoulder just as the enraged wild pig locked onto her, coming in a low rush, jaws snapping, the long cream-colored tusks glimmering like deadly daggers in the sunlight while the boar closed the short gap between them. As suddenly as the boar began his charge at her it collapsed in a heap as if poleaxed two short meters away from her. The report of a heavy rifle rang out a millisecond after the boar fell. Quintus kicked out savagely two more times into the dead beast's side before he himself limped out of harm's way once he saw the boar was finished. Pamela struggled to her feet now that she had the rifle in her hands and pointed it at the boar, just in case. Her hands shook as she stood wondering what all had transpired in the last few seconds.

"He's dead, you won't need that now," came a booming man's voice from her right side. She quickly turned, surprised and suddenly embarrassed to see anyone else in the field.

The man dressed in expensive hunting togs emerged from the woods 30 meters away and strode confidently toward her, his rifle casually resting against his shoulder.

"Are you OK, madam?"

Pamela self-consciously looked down at herself, taking a quick inventory, and realized that other than some sore muscles and bruises she was going to be fine and replied, "Yes it seems I was tossed by my horse when the boar charged." She looked into the handsome man's dark brown eyes as he came closer to her and felt like a little girl in his dominant presence. Her cheeks flushed crimson knowing that someone had witnessed her being awkwardly thrown from her horse and that she should have known better than to approach the thicket not prepared for the wounded boar's charge. She was better at this than anyone else she knew, and her pride was damaged much more than her body.

The man strode right past her, slowly getting Quintus's reins in his hands, stroking his neck, gently speaking to her horse, "Easy boy, there's a good horse, take it easy."

Quintus held his head steady and stopped his nervous painful prancing at the man's touch to his muzzle, realizing he was safe from the boar now.

The gentleman spoke to the horse as much as to Pamela, "We need to get this horse to a vet as soon as possible. I think it's only a gash—the muscle and tendon seem to be still attached. This is a very brave horse you have here, and I would hate to see him crippled."

Pamela walked over to Quintus, bending down to look closely at the damage, softly touching the edges of the gash.

"Here, wrap this tightly around the wound while I hold him," the man said, handing her a silken scarf from around his neck.

She did as he instructed and the bleeding stopped almost immediately from the applied pressure to the wound. She stood back up straight, within half a meter of the middle-aged handsome gentleman standing uncomfortably close to her, and said, "Thank you, sir."

"No problem . . . ," he was replying, interrupted in midsentence when she suddenly embraced him and held him close, laying her head on his chest. He could feel her shivering underneath her luxurious hunting garb, but did not break the moment until she slowly pulled away from him after regaining her composure. He looked closely at her now, seeing that she was an exceptionally beautiful woman, much younger than him, but with a confident sense of maturity for her age.

"I owe you a debt of gratitude. I will never be able to repay you, sir. Thank you once again."

"Don't give it another thought. I had to make sure I could catch the beautiful poacher who was trespassing on my land." He laughed, making her instantly feel at ease and diffusing the uncomfortable situation.

"I am Anton Fushkas," he said, removing his glove and offering her his hand. "And you are?"

"I am Pamela Atwood. My family owns the land over there," she replied, nodding back over her shoulder at the fence she had crossed.

"Ah, the famous Countess Atwood. I have heard about you, seen your photo in the magazines but have never had the pleasure of meeting you in person." He bowed deeply, kissing her hand in an exaggerated gentlemanly gesture, continuing when she smiled at his action, "We need to go and get your horse fixed up. I believe it is much closer to my house than yours, and the less walking your horse does the better. May I?" he asked as he took the reins to lead the horse while she walked at his side, warming instantly to this stranger who had just saved her life.

CHAPTER 7

Pamela and Anton's worlds collided on that day in the field and were never the same again for either of them. Pamela had found a man mature enough to understand her desires and not be intimidated by her wealth, while Anton had found a young, vivacious woman who made him the envy of all his friends. Even more, she was a woman of her own substantial wealth who would not run off with a big chunk of his if things didn't work out as planned. Even though 20 years separated their ages, at the time of their marriage it didn't seem to matter. They had agreed on having children right away. Anton had been a bachelor his whole life but felt a need to finally settle down and create heirs for the continuance of his family's inheritance. If he didn't produce male heirs, his brother's boys would take the lot. Pamela realized that with Anton and his age she would need to start having children perhaps sooner than she had planned, but was still excited at the prospect. Being the only child, she kept her last name rather than change it when they were married and made her father weep for joy when she told him she was doing so. Anton didn't seem to care; it was not that unusual among the landed gentry to do so.

Everything proceeded in their lives according to a storybook schedule, Anton receiving not one, but two male offspring, and nannies were brought in immediately to help raise them so that Pamela could continue keeping her hand on the tiller of the Atwood Empire, steering it expertly to new heights never dreamed of by her father.

Anton's single life of so many years was hard for him to give up, though, and after a couple years of domestic bliss he was soon back to his old ways, spending time with his cronies, traveling, staying out late at night if he came home at all, taking on a full-time mistress at his villa in Nice, France, and playing the role of father and husband when it suited his needs. Pamela kept herself busy with her work, social life, and family, avoiding the temptation to rein in her husband. When they made love it was good, very good as far as Pamela was concerned. Anton had lots of experience at how to please a woman. As time wore on, however, it was not lovemaking anymore. It was only sex, and it didn't happen very often, certainly not often enough for Pamela, who was now in her sexual prime. It seemed to always be on her mind. Most of the women who ran in her circle of friends were content with having time away from their husbands as they grew older, so Pamela bit her tongue more than once when she wanted to confront her husband about his vagabond ways. By the time she was 36 years old, she and her husband basically led two completely separate lives. She continued to mother the children, enjoying the outdoors with her boys, teaching them the ways of nature and hunting at the family estates. She was as close to them as she could be with her very busy schedule. Her father, when he passed away at the too-early age of 72, left everything to Pamela with a hefty stipend for the care of his wife's needs, knowing full well that Pamela would make sure her mother's lifestyle would continue unchanged, as the two women enjoyed a relationship as best friends in addition to being mother and daughter.

Although not living the life she had dreamed of as a young woman, Pamela felt blessed to have what she had, so she kept herself busy and avoided too much free time to think about making any drastic changes in her life, such as divorce. However she was alone, and she was a vivacious woman who had her own needs . . . craving needs.

CHAPTER 8

For Matt Simmons, his hectic life had finally fallen back into a routine that allowed him some semblance of peace of mind. His wife Bianca had made a miraculous recovery by all the doctor's accounts, from her physical and emotional trauma while being held captive in the Sudanese wild lands for almost a year by the Janjaweed rebel Rashid. Matt had gone back to find her and their miraculous rescue and escape from Darfur to South Sudan in the stolen King Air plane Matt had piloted was the stuff movies were made of. They were all lucky to be alive. Matt's African Banda tribe tracker Zumbula and his new woman Djuri, who had also been a prisoner of Rashid's and who had also escaped with Matt from Sudan, lived with Matt and Bianca at his estate on the outskirts of Portland, Oregon. The CIA, at Matt's insistence, had made last minute arrangements to get Djuri and Zumbula legal immigration status while they were all being debriefed in Italy after the Darfur affair was finished.

Zumbula, who had met Matt originally while he was on safari in the Central African Republic a couple years earlier, had been at his side ever since the moment their lives were inextricably entwined when Bianca was originally kidnapped. Residing in the United States and feeling for the first time in their lives after living in African turmoil and war that they were safe and could plan a life together free from kidnapping, disease, and famine, Djuri and Zumbula had fallen deeply in love and were looking forward to and hoping for a bright future. Djuri had taken to wearing American clothing and worked hard at her English lessons, managing the vast household for Bianca and becoming Bianca's closest confidant. The two of them loved shopping together, preparing meals, and making the best of their fortunate circumstances; however at the end of the day, Djuri knew, and rightfully so, that Bianca and Matt were her employers. So she left Bianca to all the free time she needed and kept herself from being jealous if she was left out of any social event.

Bianca's physical injuries from barely surviving as a captive in Africa were disappearing rapidly, but the psychological ones were not fading as fast as Matt might have wanted. Having just celebrated her twenty-seventh birthday, Bianca was able to handle life's little ups and downs on a day-to-day basis pretty well; however there always seemed to be some niggling issues that would not go away. Having been raised in the dangerous bush of East Africa, Djuri on the other hand was able to cope better than Bianca with the nightmares of their incarceration.

Bianca had a social life once again, but her close girlfriends knew better than to ask too many questions about Bianca's mysterious year of absence and the goriest details of her kidnapping. She kept herself busy redecorating Matt's mansion in an attempt to rid it of the trappings of years of bachelorhood that prevailed at the estate. She had exquisite taste, and Matt loved the changes she made to their home. But more than that he really loved having a woman around the house again; she had made it truly a home. After his divorce 10 years earlier Matt had sworn to remain a bachelor for the rest of his life. That is, until in his late forties, he had met the young and vivacious Bianca and fell head over heels for her. Truth be told, their marriage had not been perfect—far from it—before he had taken her on safari to Central Africa where she had been kidnapped and held for almost a year before he rescued her. Since then though, they had been inseparable. Perhaps Matt had matured. Perhaps Bianca had as well. But from Matt's perspective, for the first time in his life, he really wanted to take care of someone, to give love beyond any level he had even dreamed of in the past. A friend, one night after several cocktails in a downtown bar, counseled Matt it was not love he was feeling but that he figured Matt was just wracked with guilt and that's why he had changed and thought he was so much in love.

"After all if you hadn't taken her to that shithole of a country, the Central African Republic, your wife would still be normal," his inebriated friend had told him.

"Not that she isn't improving," he continued, backtracking after he realized he might have pushed the issue too far. "But what happened to the good ol' Matt that used to be so fun and ready to party and go hunting and fishing at the drop of a dime?"

"I'm happy and I'm doing what I want to now. I don't miss those days. I'm a different guy now, you know, things change," Matt replied and he meant it.

MATT WORRIED CONSTANTLY about Bianca's mental health because even though the nightmares and screaming in the middle of the night were less frequent, they still rose to the surface, taking sometimes two or three days for Bianca to return to normal after some of the most severe memories returned to haunt her. The psychiatrists Matt had hired were doing everything they possibly could and were the best money could buy. They had Bianca on several prescription drugs meant to stabilize her, which seemed to work as well as advertised. Overall, day by day, Matt saw improvement and prayed for a normal existence in their lives in the near future. Hopefully the horrific memories of her year away would end real soon. He alone knew what was really going on and that she was far from being fully recovered.

CHAPTER 9

BIANCA DROVE HOME FROM THE DOCTOR'S OFFICE GIDDY with joy and a secret she couldn't wait to let Matt in on. She knew he would be so happy, overjoyed at the news, embrace her and swing her around in his arms when she told him the big news.

Before they had been married Matt had told her he did not want to have any more children and that was going to be part of the arrangement, just like the prenuptial agreement, and it was not negotiable. However, after all the events surrounding the kidnapping and getting her back home safely, he had changed his mind. It was the one thing she wanted more than anything, and he had changed his mind and agreed with her that he too would like to have kids when she recovered. Bianca was not sure she could even conceive children after the punishment her body had been through in the past year. Between the malaria, the internal parasites teeming in her digestive system and blood stream, and the pure lack of personal hygiene available while in captivity, she was lucky to be alive, never mind capable of becoming a mother. It took several months after her return to America for Bianca and Matt's love life to return to the passion they had once enjoyed before the safari, but it was back now and was the one place they could escape to together, pushing away the world's and Bianca's issues at least until the morning. All her prayers had been answered this morning when the ob-gyn gave her the great news that she was at last going to be a mother.

Hearing the news, Matt did indeed hold her in his arms and swing her around in circles in the kitchen, tears of joy filling his eyes when he let her down, telling her as he stared deeply into her beautiful green eyes, "I love you so much, thank you for making me so happy."

"I love you too Matt. I'm so excited. Should we tell Zumbula and Djuri?"

"Yes, of course, it's party time!"

Matt went to the intercom keyboard on the kitchen wall, pushing the number for Zumbula's wing of the house.

"Jambo, Bwana," Zumbula replied in Swahili, not in his native Banda, which Matt couldn't speak.

"Hey, can you and Djuri come down to the kitchen? Bianca and I have something we want to tell you."

"Us too, Bwana, we will be right there."

WALKING INTO THE kitchen five minutes later, holding hands with Djuri, Zumbula surprised Matt. The African was not known to be outwardly affectionate, and Matt couldn't recall seeing his friend ever hold a woman's hand before.

Bianca couldn't wait to tell their friends the great news, blurting out as soon as they walked into the room, "Guess what, I'm pregnant!"

Djuri smiled meekly, then looked at Zumbula for support, receiving a squeeze of her hand before replying, "We are very happy for you, and we too have news. I am also with child."

Bianca rushed into Djuri's arms squealing with joy, the two of them dancing in a circle like two 12-year-old girls and yelling, "Yahoo, this is going to be so much fun. We're pregnant together! We're going to have babies! Ha ha, how wonderful is this?"

Matt walked up to Zumbula holding out his hand to shake it, and then giving his trusted friend a man hug, asking, "When did you find out, old man?"

"Yesterday Bwana, but I was not sure how the news was going to be received in your house, since we know you have been also trying to have a baby. We were not necessarily trying, but when the gods decide it is time, it is time. May our children be men of power and great hunters like their fathers."

"May they be healthy, my friend," Matt answered, his statement not meant to be as profound as it sounded, but both he and Zumbula stood staring at each other for a moment, pondering their futures, before Matt interrupted the solemnity shouting, "It's time for some champagne!"

"Not for us mothers-to-be. I guess we are on the wagon now," Bianca cheerfully replied. "But we will have some Martinelli's, won't we?"

She gave Djuri another hug before skipping down the hallway to the wine cellar. Matt turned from watching her skip away to find Zumbula standing alone with his arms folded sternly across his chest, staring at him, searching behind Matt's icy blue eyes in the soul-piercing way the scar-faced coal-black man could. Matt stared back until he broke the intimidating gaze, knowing what the African questioned and realizing he didn't have the answer.

THE TWO BABIES' rooms were soon outfitted, one in the south wing next to Zumbula and Djuri's room and one upstairs next to Matt and Bianca's bedroom, with the paint colors being put on hold until the doctors eventually determined that they were both going to have boys. Both men swelled with pride at the news and budgets for the redecorating were thrown out the window.

As spring approached and the Northwest weather improved, Zumbula was thankfully able to spend more time outdoors, working on various landscape projects, keeping the Mexican gardeners who tended the manicured estate grounds on their toes. Even though there was obviously no hunting allowed in the exclusive neighborhood the estate stood in, it didn't mean the African could not spend time trapping feral cats, coyotes, and raccoons that sauntered onto the estate from the surrounding woods, hoping for an easy meal from the gardens or chicken coop he kept in a far corner of the grounds.

Zumbula was bored out of his mind, he had never had extra time on his hands like he did now but he kept himself busy to avoid having to face the misery of thinking about the land and the people he had left behind on the Dark Continent. He could never return to his birthplace now even if he wanted to. The war between the rebels and the quasi-government in the Central African Republic continued with none of the superpower nations giving a damn about that God-forsaken corner of earth. All of his family and children had been killed or had scattered to other somewhat safer locales. All contact with them had been lost, forever it seemed, with no cell phones or email where Zumbula came from, no communication at all. He had a new family now and his life had changed forever and he had no choice but to make the best of it.

The hot weather of summer allowed Zumbula to wear his traditional sarong-style wrap he loved, the one Djuri had made for him from colorful fabrics she brought home from one of her and Bianca's shopping excursions. He went pants-less and shirtless around the yard, tribal scars etched across his torso and back showing his manhood shimmering purple when he sweated in the heat.

The neighbors had become accustomed to the scary-looking black man in their midst, especially after meeting him at a neighborhood party Matt had thrown to introduce everyone to each other. The neighbors enjoyed the uniqueness of his simplistic perspectives on the world especially as his English continued to improve with daily use. The tall three-foot-thick stone wall encompassing Matt's estate became the place to meet and chat—about current events, the weather, and kids—for the neighbors who took their dogs out for an early morning walk or worked off calories after dinner and saw Zumbula working in the yard and stopped to catch up on the latest.

MATT ALSO HAD children in his past life; his were not dead like Zumbula's, just gone. Matt's children rarely came to see their father. He made every effort possible to see them whenever they were in town, which must not be very often, Zumbula thought, because he had only seen them twice in two years. It hurt Matt deeply that they refused to be a part of his life. He reached out to them; he invited them to every event, birthday, and holiday. He tried his best to keep the family together but the impact of his divorce and hateful rhetoric from his ex-wife had worked as she had planned on swinging the kids to her side of the family. Matt could only hope and pray that with maturity they would see both sides of the story. He felt he had no choice but to wait patiently, reach out to them whenever he could, and bite his tongue about their mother. He swore to himself that his participation in the upbringing of his and Bianca's son was going to be a lot more involved than the first time around.

THE BIG DAY arrived for Bianca, but it was a long, drawn-out labor that took more than 12 hours. The doctors and Matt were extremely concerned with the length of time it was taking and the pain it was causing to Bianca's body and mind. Besides her ob-gyn, Matt made sure her regular physician was in attendance; he was fully aware of her past physical issues and could assist with any complications that might arise during birth.

Finally at exactly 10:22 p.m., Tyler Mathew Simmons entered the world, a healthy 8-pound, 10-ounce child with the world at his fingertips. The baby was cleaned up quickly and brought to Bianca to snuggle in her welcoming arms. His first few moments of life were shared with his mother while Matt sat in awe at the side of the bed watching the two people he loved more than anything in the entire world. It was obvious that after the long labor Bianca was wiped out and needed rest, so the nurses whisked Tyler away to the nursery giving Matt and Bianca a few moments of time alone.

Matt brushed her hair away from her face, leaning over her and whispering, "I am so proud of you, you did great, sweetie."

"Thank you darling, I must look horrible right now, can I have a mirror?"

"You look beautiful, prettier than I have ever seen you before. You are glowing. Thank you for bringing our son into this world."

Bianca smiled up at this man she had been through so much with in such a short time. She felt lucky and thankful at that very moment to have so much support and love.

"You need to sleep now, honey. The doctors said everything is perfect with Junior, so sleep well. I am going to run to the house and pick up some goodies for you. Zumbula can't bring your bag over here because he said Djuri feels like she may go into labor any time now also."

Bianca smiled at the good news about the woman who had helped her survive while she was in captivity and now helped her at the house and had become so much more than just a friend.

"Tell her not to take so long when her time comes," Bianca laughed softly.

"I will. Sleep well, and I'll be here when you wake up."

Bianca's eyes closed and she fell soundly asleep as Matt finished by telling her how much he loved her.

DJURI HAD THOUGHT long and hard about the name of her first child. While Zumbula had pushed for a traditional Banda name, Djuri knew the child would be growing up in America and needed an American name. She had seen some African men who played basketball and were treated like stars on television, so at the appointed hour Michael Kobe Zumbula popped out for the entire world to see. A solid healthy child whose first cries could be heard 10 rooms down the hospital corridor. No one was prouder than Zumbula as he lifted his new son to the light of the hospital window, the morning sun streaking into their room, he showed an unseeing world that a new life was beginning: one of hope and promise, one that would surely be filled with success. Djuri watched the proud papa, thankful she had such a man in her life, the man who had saved her from a life of slavery, of being a harem wife to that Janjaweed bastard Rashid. Why the thought of him crossed her mind at this moment she didn't know, but try as she might, her past was never very far behind her.

"LET ME HOLD our son and his father also," she asked.

Zumbula gently laid the baby in her arms before leaning forward to hug the two of them at the same time, holding them closely, longer than planned, not wanting Djuri to see the tears of joy filling his eyes. He couldn't remember ever being so incredibly happy in his entire life.

THE WORLD SEEMED to be on track once again for Matt, finally. It was as if all the pain and suffering over the past few years had somehow been worth it and now he could live a more normal life, perhaps one like everyone else.

CHAPTER 10

BIANCA COULDN'T STOP CRYING. SHE DIDN'T KNOW WHY SHE was crying, she just was. She should be happy and she knew it, after all she had everything any woman could want: a beautiful home, a handsome wealthy husband who devoted more time to her than any other husband she knew, a happy, healthy baby boy, friends, and family. But even with all that, she was depressed most of the time and couldn't stop it.

Her mother and father had flown in from hot humid Texas and spent the first two weeks after the birth of their only grandson at Matt's mansion, helping Bianca and Djuri, thrilled with the two precious little boys. Matt and Bianca's father Dr. David Johnson got along well, spending quality time together in the evenings, out by the pool, having a beer or two, letting the Northwest cool down from the hot summer days. Chatting about life and politics was easy since both of them had the same conservative values and morals.

Thankfully for Matt, Bianca's father had long ago gotten over that fact that his daughter had married an older man, and he never blamed Matt for his little girl's disappearance in Africa. He had inevitably resigned himself, just like everyone else had, to the fact that she was dead after her apparent drowning in Kotto River, until Matt had called them by satellite phone to tell them he had found her alive in Sudan and rescued her. David and his wife Doris had been waiting at Matt's estate when they arrived home. They did all they could to help, which didn't seem to be much, but being there for support was good for all of them. Matt had been humble about the details of the rescue, and were it not for a follow-up phone call to Bianca's father from CIA agent Dennis Anderson, who was Matt's handler in the covert operation and checking in with him to see how Bianca was doing and telling him what has transpired, he would never have heard the real story.

To say Bianca's dad was impressed would be an understatement. It was more that he wondered how Matt had ever summoned the courage and the balls to go back and take a chance with his and Zumbula's lives in the first place, to seek revenge and then stumble across his daughter in the clutches of the Sudanese rebel. Luck, skill, no regard for his own life, insanity—however you wanted to tell it—Matt had pulled off a miracle, and Bianca's father was eternally grateful.

IF ONLY THE doctor had been 20 years younger, he would have loved to join Matt in the adventure, or so he proudly told himself after a couple of scotches.

After life had settled into a routine, and Bianca and the baby were getting at least six hours of straight sleep per night, Bianca's parents decided the time was right to go back home and let the Simmons and Zumbula families get back to normal.

They all stood together on the sidewalk in front of the departure area of the airport saying goodbye, getting in some last-minute hugs, until Bianca's father casually pulled Matt aside to have a few private words with him away from the women, "Matt, thanks for everything you are doing for Bianca and Junior. If you ever need a break or if I can help in any way, you just call me, huh? Her mother and I are always available."

Matt started to respond but was interrupted by her father, "Matt, she's not OK yet, you realize that, right?"

"Yes sir, but the doctors say she is progressing, and I have seen a lot of improvement. She doesn't have as many nightmares as she used to, for what that is worth."

"Yeah well, I'm a doctor too, remember, and we don't always see everything that's wrong with people, especially when it's in their heads, trust me. But I can tell you her mother and I see a different person behind those green eyes than we used to see. Keep an eye on her for us, will you?"

"I will, I will. You have my word on it that I will keep doing all I can for her." They shook hands and walked back to the women who had one last hug before making their way to the check-in counter.

Matt pulled his burgundy Maserati sedan away from the curb, while Bianca waved out the window one final time to her parents, then turning back to Matt she asked, "What did Daddy have to say?"

"Oh, he wants to come along on that dove hunt in the fall at the farm. He wants to bring your uncle. I told him it would be great if they both came."

Bianca turned from looking at her husband and stared at the freeway in front of them, wondering what he was lying about.

BIANCA KEPT THE daily crying fits to herself, using the excuse she was going to lie down for a nap whenever she felt the major doses of depression setting in. Through the closed bedroom door Djuri heard her sobbing alone again in her room one day when she had come up to ask Bianca if she wanted some lemonade or sweet iced tea, since it was such an unusually hot and muggy day. Djuri stood quietly outside the door, wondering what was wrong, why she would cry in the middle of the day so much, but didn't want to barge in on her privacy. So she turned and walked back down the stairs to the kitchen, assuming maybe Matt and Bianca had a small squabble or something. After all, what else could Bianca possibly have to weep about?

The next week Zumbula noticed Bianca walking in the garden at midday with her baby in his favorite English-style pram. Bianca was softly crying, her shoulders heaving forward a little as she wept in the warm, soothing sunshine. Zumbula stayed hidden in the shadows of the old rhododendron bushes where he was pulling weeds just to keep busy. He did not want to interfere with Bianca and the baby, and she could not see him so he remained still and quiet. He watched as she left the buggy, slowly walking to the vegetable garden where she stood in front of it as if counting the tomatoes and zucchinis that thrived there. After five minutes of staring blankly at the garden, she bent at the waist and reached for a large ripe tomato, picking it gently with her manicured hands from the trellised lush green plant. She held the fruit in her palm, chest high as if admiring its texture and red beauty. Zumbula noticed there was a sudden and very strange change in her demeanor. Bianca was no longer sobbing, simply staring at the tomato until an odd tension built up in her muscles and a look of hatred, a kind of meanness Zumbula had only seen in the eyes of killers. Intrigued by the performance he watched her squeeze the tomato in her fist until its contents squirted out through her fingers, red watery juice and seeds running down her arm while she remained stiff and watched the juice flow. In a new rage, she violently tossed the smashed pulp aside and reached for another one, once again admiring it as she held it aloft then crushing the life out of the hapless tomato. She repeated this until all eight of the red ripe ones were picked from the plant in front of her, leaving the green tomatoes. She walked back to the pram and Junior who had napped throughout the whole episode and pushed it back down the gravel garden path toward the mansion, as if nothing out of the ordinary had happened.

Zumbula diplomatically passed on what he had witnessed to Matt that night, but rather than confronting Bianca with the issue, Matt called the psychiatrist's office the next morning and let the doctor in on the whole story. The doctor said he would deal with it and check on her medications, perhaps upping the dosage a little. Matt was frustrated, what could he say to her that wouldn't cause another issue or a denial. He had tried before when he had observed strange behavior from his wife, but was always met with crazed denials and heated arguments. Bianca had acted as if nothing in the world was wrong at the dinner table the night after the tomato incident; she was fully engaged with the children, happy, bubbly, even feeding Djuri's baby some pureed veggies while Djuri served the dinner. To the unknowing, nothing seemed out of place with her.

TWO WEEKS LATER Matt woke as usual just after 5:00 in the morning, softly kissed Bianca on the forehead without waking her, slipped on some old jeans and a grey tee shirt and a pair of old cowboy boots. He made his way quietly to Junior's room and gave him a peck on the cheek after admiring him for a few minutes sleeping soundly in his crib. Matt loved him so much, more than anything he had ever known. The little boy in front of him made the future seem bright. Sneaking back down the hallway and descending the main staircase, he found Zumbula waiting for him in the kitchen drinking tea, the smell of coffee wafting from the pot the African had just made for Matt.

"Thanks, my friend, I need a caffeine fix right now."

"You will need your strength at the farm today. The cattlemen will like to see you helping gather the beasts; they think you spend too much time in the office now and that you are getting soft."

Matt laughed, "We will see about that. With 300 of them to move off the farm, they are going to need our help today for sure, even if you just get in the way."

EVERY YEAR MATT participated in the annual roundup at his ranch near Medford with the cowboys who managed his herd of Angus cattle. He liked to play cowboy with them, riding horses, cracking the bullwhip, chewing some tobacco, and being in the outdoors. He and Zumbula were quite a sight together. Zumbula, with his bullwhip and his two-meter-long African hunting spear, jogged along next to Matt's horse, dressed in his bright red sarong draped cockily over his shoulder and a pair of safari shoes protecting his feet that had lost some of their toughness now that he lived a "civilized" existence. The African refused to dress like a cowboy or a westerner while outdoors working with livestock. The cowboys had come to respect Zumbula's prowess with a whip and his total lack of fear of the headstrong cattle when he packed his spear deftly, herding them boldly toward the holding pens.

The day went well; the cattle drive pushed most of the heifers and calves to the waiting trucks. While they were being directed up the loading chutes by the drivers, the cowboys rode back into the far pasture to gather up the few belligerent veteran stragglers that never wanted to be pulled in with the rest of the herd. Matt and Zumbula had done their part and were talking about leaving for home when Matt's cell phone rang, the number on the screen he saw was his house calling. Figuring Bianca was calling to see when they would be home for dinner, he cheerily answered, "Hey Baby, what's up?"

Matt listened in dread as the person on the other end of the line explained to him that he was with the Portland Police Department, calling from Matt's land line and that Matt needed to rush home immediately.

"I will explain everything to you when you arrive, Mister Simmons," the officer had said, not answering Matt's specific inquiries as to what exactly was wrong.

CHAPTER 11

THE DAILY EPISODES OF DEPRESSION HAD BEEN GETTING worse and Bianca knew it, but today she was feeling a deeper more ethereal depression than usual, almost as if she were slipping into the mentally protective trance that she had fallen into during her year in Rashid's grip of terror. She had not bothered to tell the psychiatrist about all the increasing episodes she was having; there were too many for her to recall at her twice-weekly visits to the expensive offices in downtown Portland's financial district. Last week the doctor had asked her about the tomato-crushing incident. She was surprised and felt threatened when he questioned her about it because she assumed no one had seen her do it and had not given it a second thought. She wasn't sure who had told on her, but she suspected it had to have been Zumbula.

"*That sneaky bastard is always creeping around, spying on me and telling Matt what I'm up to,*" her deranged accusatory brain told her.

She had lied to the shrink that day as she had many other times, telling him it was her nerves that had caused her to crush them rather than any kind of hate or psychotic episode—just nerves, that's all. The doctor asked his usual, prying questions about her and Matt's relationship: how was it, did they make love, how often, did she enjoy it, would she like to have another baby, was she happy with the baby. The doctor was also concerned about issues related to any postpartum symptoms that may also be affecting her, probing her with leading questions on the subject. Bianca told him the truth, that Matt was very good to her now, a better husband than he had been before they traveled to Africa and she had been abducted. He was affectionate to both her and their son, while tolerating her recovery process and devoting all his time and efforts to her getting better. She really loved him. They made love at least once a week and it was fine.

Yes she enjoyed it, she lied to the doctor.

The truth was she did not enjoy the sex at all anymore, rarely reaching a climax, certainly nothing like the sex she craved before her incarceration, but now faking an orgasm just to satisfy her husband's ego. Ever since she had returned from captivity, sex was not the same as she remembered it before. She did not know why it was no good, but thought that it was probably better if she didn't dwell on it too long.

"How are you and Tyler getting along?" the doctor asked.

"He is doing super, growing like a weed and is sleeping through the night. I couldn't be happier with him, doc."

"And are you taking your medications as I instructed? Any side effects? Depression, nausea, cramping?"

"Yes I am. The pills don't bother me one way or the other and I'm sure they are helping, thanks."

Bianca had kept the memories of her time in Rashid's harem locked away in the dark corners of her mind, where they would not ever see the light of day, only emerging in the middle of the night, usually waking her and the rest of the household from their sound sleep when she screamed at the top of her lungs in sheer panic at the brutal depraved remembrances coming back to haunt her once again.

Bianca realized that if she wanted her life to have any semblance of normalcy, she had to keep up the façade that she was improving, not going daily into deeper depression. No one, including the doctor, had any business prying into what was happening to her. If they wanted to help her they should have saved her from Rashid's clutches sooner. Bianca knew she could clear her mind of the evils without pills or these twice-weekly time-wasting question sessions and had not been taking them at all She simply threw them in the toilet each day so that if anyone was checking on how many she was taking they would think she was following the doctors stupid instructions. It had scared her when her mother had a frank talk on the telephone with her one day about working with the doctors, trusting them, reminding her that they were there to help. It was almost as if her mother could sense that she was not following the doctor's advice and it could have ramifications if she did not do what she was told to.

"Sugar, you know you can always call on me anytime of the day or night. Just pick up the phone. Don't you go and get yourself all worked up over something and let it get to you now, you hear?" Her mother had gone on and on that day counseling her, "You have a good man who loves you, and you have two wonderful people in Djuri and Zumbula who are there to help you also. So you get yourself better, OK?" She cooed in her Georgian drawl, "And you be sure you take those prescriptions they tell you to take. They are for your own good."

Everyone loved her. They told her she was beautiful. They told her she was lucky to have such a great life and to live in such a beautiful home, and she realized sometimes that they were right. But knowing they were right didn't make it any easier for her to keep the demons imprisoned in her brain chained up and under control.

Unfortunately the memories of her past were becoming clearer to her the longer time went on and the more the doctors probed. Memories were brought up to the forefront; protective clouds of traumatized memory lost were blown away. Today, standing in front of her closet's full-length mirror, completely naked, she could recall as if it were only yesterday, Rashid's filthy hands upon her once more. She could feel him stroking her lily white breasts, pinching her nipples, moving his rough hands down across her belly and onto her vulva where they probed roughly into her vagina as she stood defenselessly naked in front of him in his smoky Arabic-style quarters in the wilds of Darfur. She shuddered at the memory.

Bianca's deranged mind snapped back to reality. While she had been running the faucet to fill the big tub earlier, she had heard Tyler Mathew fussing in his crib in the room next door. She decided, spur of the moment, to bring him into the tub with her and give him a bath while she soaked her demented miseries back into hiding where they belonged. She locked the bedroom door and the bathroom door behind her as she carried a giddy Tyler to the tub. He loved the warm water, willing to happily play and splash as long as he was allowed to. Wrapping him in a large luxuriant towel and then laying him gently on the floor next to the tub, Bianca turned off the faucets when the water level reached its perfect depth and went to Matt's top drawer where he kept his shaving kit. Finding what she needed she stood staring once more at herself in the tall polished mirror. There was a time when she used to spend hours admiring the reflection of her firm young body, but not anymore. Now she stared at herself in disgust, at the physique that had been violated by the terrorist and for that matter she thought, by all the men in her life. That body was the filthy vessel that made men crave her for only one reason.

"*We women are looked upon like the lowest life forms on earth. All they want to do is fuck us,*" she thought as she looked disgustingly up and down the length of her reflection. "*Men treat us like shit. God, if there is one, put us on this earth to be used and abused worse than goats or donkeys, yes like an animal only worse. Fucking bastards, I'll show them.*"

Gathering Tyler up in her arms she slipped one leg into the water to test the temperature, making sure it wasn't too hot for her baby. It was just right as she slid down the polished marble side, Tyler smiling and waving his arms, laughing and splashing water all around the tub when his bum was submerged. He looked up in wondrous curiosity at his mother when she turned his body around so his face was looking away toward the wall and not at her. With one hand on his belly and one on the back of his head, she pushed him under the surface, holding him there firmly while he fought helplessly back, the last bubbles of life-supporting oxygen finally gurgling to the top a few moments later, the struggling mercifully coming to an end.

"*He's in a better place now, in God's hands. Where no one will be able to hurt him like they did me, where everything will be safe and full of love, a place where people will treat each other with love and dignity. He is all yours God . . .*"

She let go and Tyler's lifeless body slowly sank to the bottom of the tub while she reached for the razor blade that she had removed from Matt's drawer. This would not hurt and it would only take a second she felt. With the blade in her left hand she moved her right arm under the warm water and pushed the blade deep as she ran the razor across her wrist, the sting of the slash stopped almost immediately when the ruby red blood began to flow into the tub, dispersing like sunset clouds across the marble bathtub's surface.

She switched the blade to her right hand, but it was hard to grip with her weak wet fingers and she had to hurriedly slash at her left wrist. The cut was ragged but blood flowed quickly from it. Letting her body slip down into the warm bloody water she closed her eyes and relaxed, but her ravaged mind would still not give her any peace as old memories flooded her senses, another chapter in the never-ending nightmare coming forward in her last dying moments. She was back in the Kotto River's rapid current again, floating among the explosion strewn helicopter wreckage while flaming fuel raged in pools around her, treading water looking for Matt, looking for Mikhail, looking for anyone to come to her rescue, but no one came. No one was there to save her then, and no one was here to save her now in the bathtub.

She screamed out Matt's name just like she had in the river, "Help Matt, help me, please! Save me, Matt I'm over here. Pleeease save me, Matt!!!"

Then in her nightmare she saw him swimming toward her, treading the flame-covered water, pushing debris from between them, panicked words yelled from his mouth, but she could not hear the words over the roar of the ignited fuel.

"Matt, my God, please help me. I'm going to drown. Hellllllpppp meeeeee! Maaaattttt, help me!" She screamed one last time before her head slid under the rosy water, into another world, a better world, one she remembered slipping into once before on the Kotto River bank, before she had been brought back from the brink of death, back to life by Rashid's men.

"This time though, Rashid will not find me. No not this time, it's too late."

Bianca felt a contented aura engulf her knowing she would soon see her little boy in that better place, just beyond the darkness, on the other side in the afterlife that called seductively to her. She would wait for Matt there.

CHAPTER 12

DJURI HEARD THE SCREAMING EVEN THOUGH SHE WAS IN the kitchen while her son napped contentedly. She had heard some screams before in the middle of the night but realized those were from Bianca's recurring nightmares and were not this loud and never during the day. Taking the stairs two at a time, Djuri turned right at the top of the stairwell, running as fast as her legs would carry her to Matt and Bianca's master suite doors.

She yelled at the top of her lungs through the door, "Bianca, Bianca, are you OK? What's wrong, can you hear me? Bianca!"

Getting no answer from the other side of the door, she tried to open the doors, fidgeting with the handles finding them locked from the inside. An eerie sensation came over her when it dawned on her that little Tyler was not awake, surely the noise of the screaming would have woken him from his daily midday nap. Djuri ran farther down the hall to the open door of Tyler's room, bursting in and feeling a sense of dread upon seeing that the crib was empty.

"There must be something wrong with Tyler. That's what the crying and yelling was all about," she thought, scampering back down the hall to Bianca's door, banging as hard as she could, yelling, trying to get Bianca's attention. Still no response from behind the door made the dread in her soul compound itself and panic taking over, Djuri kicked at the double door. It did not budge, the solid wooden doors impenetrable to the pounding from her 100-pound body. She backed away a meter or two then ran full tilt into the door leading with her shoulder which only sent her crashing backwards onto the carpeted floor. Djuri yelled and pounded on the door several more times with both fists until she decided to change tactics and ran for the garage

to find some kind of tool or axe to help her smash her way in. She returned to the bedroom door a few minutes later with a long-handled shovel, the first thing she found in the gardener's shack. Jamming it between the gap where the matched set of doors came together, she pried back and forth while chips and pieces of wood broke away scattering on the hallway floor. Seeing one door move slightly she put her shoulder into it again. Thankfully this time it popped open.

She ran across the spacious master suite to the bathroom door encountering the same locked door issue, while still yelling out Bianca's name, but getting no response from her or the baby. It did not take Djuri as long to break through into the bathroom and when she did, she was surprised to see no one there. The room seemed to be empty until she noticed steam coming from around the glass block wall surrounding the Jacuzzi bathtub. Djuri had a gut-wrenching sense that she did not really want to look any further, that she should not look around the corner of the opaque glass wall, but she had to.

Her hand went to her mouth when she gasped at the site of the bathtub filled with blood, only the flowing hair and part of the top of Bianca's head showing above it. Instinctively she reached down to pull Bianca's face above the water line, but knew immediately she was too late. The color was gone from her face; her lifeless eyes stared blankly straight ahead while Djuri struggled to hold her face out of the water. She had seen the look of death many times before during the famine and wars in her African homeland. She knew this look; it was all over for Bianca, and reluctantly she let go of her friend who eased slowly below the surface once more. She ran to the phone, calling 911 and telling the dispatcher as calmly as she could the home's address and what she had discovered. Just before she hung up she realized there was something else wrong.

She told the female police officer, "And another thing, the baby is missing."

"Say again, ma'am?" the dispatcher responded.

"Bianca, the woman who drowned has a baby, a boy, Tyler Mathew, and I can't find him."

"Don't touch anything. Officers are on their way and will be there in a matter of minutes. Do you understand?"

"Yes," she replied, hanging up and then running from room to room, calling out Tyler Mathew's name, searching every nook and cranny in the house for the baby boy.

CHAPTER 13

Matt sat in his office with the big walnut doors closed, his chin resting in his hands while he stared blankly at the computer monitor again, not giving a damn what the impressive figures told him. Even though profits for his vast integrated business holdings were doing well, he could care less. Ever since Bianca's suicide and the drowning of his son he had been a shell of the man he had once been. The quiet funeral for the two loved ones was attended by only Bianca's family and a few close friends. Neither his ex-wife nor his two children from that marriage showed up to support him in his grieving, but he had not really expected them to. The funeral service had not brought any closure in his life with Bianca, just the opposite. Now he questioned everything about his very existence: who he was, what he had become, and what he was going to be in the future. He lived with a guilt that ate away at him 24 hours a day, seven days a week, even wondering why he should continue to live on after all that had happened.

Why had he taken her on that safari to Central Africa in the first place? He had been warned it was not a safe place. He should have got her more help after he rescued her, more professional help. He had hired the best that money could buy, but maybe there were others who could have done a better job. Should he have moved her parents to Portland to create a bigger support network? Why had he not read the suicidal signs ahead of time? He should have seen this coming. He should have confronted her about her problems himself, instead of relying on the doctors to take care of everything, like they were supposed to. They had let her down and so had he. It was entirely his fault that Tyler and Bianca were dead.

Deep in the middle of most nights he woke from nightmare after nightmare, mad at the world, mad at himself, mad at the doctors, crying out in the blackness of his lonely room, sobbing like he had never cried in his whole life, wondering where exactly he had gone wrong and what he should have, could have, done differently.

Sleeping pills did nothing for him other than knock him out for a few hours, but never giving him any real relaxing sleep. Matt ran to good old booze for a few weeks and it made him pass out after enough of it coursed through his body, which was slipping further and further out of shape every day he continued pining for his lost wife and child. The liquor hurt him worse than anything, the hangovers kicking his ass so badly that he eventually quit on his own, other than having a beer or two every once in a while. The hangovers from drinking too much had always been the thing that kept him from being a raving alcoholic: he hated being hung over, ruining another day and feeling like hell after a night of heavy boozing. The payback just wasn't worth it and luckily he still possessed a tremendous amount of willpower.

It was never in Matt's makeup or DNA to seek help from a psychiatrist. It never even crossed his mind to contact one. He had always been able to handle life on his own terms; his inner toughness had guided him through many a tough time in years past. Matt was a rags-to-riches guy who had taken his life from being nothing to a multimillionaire. He had done it all the hard way, making major decisions every day about the lives and fortunes of hundreds of people in his employ until he had hired managers to run it all. He would handle this crisis also, no problem, he just had to toughen up. He waited for that toughness to emerge and save him once again; however, this time it seemed it was not going so quickly or smoothly, not at all.

He and Zumbula would speak of past adventures at the dinner table some evenings, his friend keeping the spirit of the house bright and positive, Djuri making the house a home as best she could. Seeing their growing baby boy tugged at his heart strings daily, but Matt enjoyed playing with him, holding him, giving him love and affection as if somehow the little man was part of his own family.

ZUMBULA WAS WISE in so many ways and he knew when to counsel Matt, when to question him, when to give him a positive nudge, and when to tell him to get his chin off his chest. Matt would sometimes use Zumbula as a sounding board, chatting about any subject, reasoning with him, venting to him his innermost fears, and he truly appreciated him as the great friend he was. Whatever cosmic collision had put the two of them together in life was hard to fathom, but without him, Matt was not sure he could have made it through each and every day after all that had transpired.

BUSINESS, THE CHALLENGE of it, the struggle to keep growing had always driven Matt onward, while at the same time being an enclave where he knew he was safe, where he controlled all the daily moves and decisions if he so chose. He had hired a great team to run the logistics empire, and he was not needed day-to-day but he had come back to work full time now that he was alone in the world once again.

His latest problems at work had started when he began sitting in on several high-level meetings only to find that he was not engaged in the subject matter whatsoever. He did not care what was going on. His mind wandered off to distant places, places of sorrow and despair where money and profits and beating the competition had no meaning for him. Several of his top-level executives had approached him to see if they could help out or to engage him in new projects, but none of the projects caught his fancy, and the executives soon slipped back to business as usual, ignoring his presence as if he was not even in the building. After all, they had a thriving consortium to run, even if the boss was not interested.

Sitting all alone in his well-appointed private office, the view of the emerald green Cascade Mountains covering the horizon in the distance, Matt hit a couple of key strokes on his computer, scrolling to the emailed proposal from the German shipping company showing a real interest in purchasing his company. The price they offered was good, a higher multiple on earnings than he had ever seen before for a company such as his. Even though he seemed to get legitimate offers at least once a year from potential buyers, the company had never been for sale. He had always loved to participate in the business world, every aspect of it even if now he was not engaged in the day-to-day operation of it. On paper it made sense for the two companies to merge, the synergies were significant, making the resulting profits tremendous, giving the buyer the ability to pay Matt top dollar, multimillions of top dollars.

Matt knew that what the Germans really wanted was his management team to assist them in their aggressive expansion plans, since they had been watching as his company had continued to grow into new innovative arenas even during tough times. Matt and the CEO of the German company had always stayed in contact through the years, dining together if they were ever in the same city, golfing at industry functions, shooting driven red-leg partridge after an industry convention and meetings in Spain, so it was no surprise to Matt that they could smell his weak state of mind and were trying to pounce on him while he was down and out, lonely and depressed after losing his wife and baby only a few months ago. Sadly, in a way, he knew they were right, and he really had been thinking it might be the right time to sell and get away from it all.

The email he was reading was an invitation to join Herr Gunther A. Schneider on a combination wild boar, pheasant, and red stag hunt in Hungary at the fabulous estate of the Countess Pamela Atwood. The invitation listed each day's scheduled events, the appropriate attire required for each of the activities and dinners along with the names of the confirmed guests. Ten men showed as confirmed, and Matt knew three of them and the rest by reputation. Several were bringing wives or girlfriends, however Herr Schneider would be coming alone, which made sense to Matt: it would allow no interruptions if the opportunity presented itself to discuss details of the deal they were contemplating. The invitation was even more enticing, knowing he would have more time alone with the potential buyer to potentially parlay the price to an even higher level in a casual, relaxed atmosphere, which was where he worked best. Matt was a maestro at befriending customers, competitors and suppliers, putting them at ease. His good looks and wit endeared him to them, along with his honesty and masterful deal-making skills.

Even though he loved his business, after all he had started it from scratch and it had always been his passion, he sat in his office and felt deep down that it was time for a major change in his life, a time to go down a different path for his future. Maybe his calling would be helping others in need, charity work, working with villages in disadvantaged countries, conservation projects in Africa, helping inner city youth get a break in life. He wasn't sure what he was going to do, but there was certainly a lot to do in the world that was good, that his energy and resources could help with and make positive changes in other people's lives. The money from the sale would go a long way to help others through the foundation he would set up with the proceeds.

"Let's see what old Herr Schneider has up his sleeve," Matt said to no one in the room as he forwarded the email to his assistant Diane with a note telling her to let them know he would be attending. Leaning back in his leather armchair with his hands nested behind his head, Matt suddenly felt a new life spring into him, a cause, a reason to push forward with life, an immediate goal that would keep him occupied and give him something else to think about besides pain and sorrow. First thing he needed to do was get to the gym, start running at home on the treadmill, get back to eating right, and get himself back in prime shape once again.

Yes, he was going to start today!

Just before he hit send, he added to the email instructions to Diane, "Let them know my guest will be Zumbula."

Why not? He figured Zumbula was just as bored and grieving as he was and needed a change of pace and a getaway as well. Some hunting was always guaranteed to get them both excited. Matt would have to find his tracker-friend the appropriate clothes for the fall European weather and laughed to himself when he pictured the Central African with his tribal facial scars and dour demeanor dressed in a tuxedo or Wellington rubber boots and a tweed shooting jacket.

This will give them something to talk about in Hungary!

CHAPTER 14

THE LOOK ON THE FACE OF THE SNOBBY SALESMAN AT THE high-end hunting and fishing store they walked into was worth the trip to Seattle to get Zumbula outfitted for the Hungary hunt. The salesman was obviously used to dealing with well-dressed white men from the city who liked to wear the British plaid-patterned togs while going to "shoots" in civilized locations such as Scotland or England or Germany, and in all his years as the main salesman at the exclusive shop, he had never seen a "negro," as he referred to them, enter his store, never mind a 6-foot, 2-inch one with lateral welted scars across his cheeks encasing a permanent scowl. When Matt jokingly told the salesman that he needed to have his friend "Prince Zumbula" from the African Kingdom of Bandu dressed appropriately for an upcoming jaunt to Europe, the salesman's prejudices soon melted away at the prospect of the $5,000 sale he was about to make. After all, one could not attend a civilized shoot in Europe dressed inappropriately!

Zumbula played along with Matt's fictitious role for him; the two of them conversing in Swahili to keep the proprietor's interest piqued and making jokes about him that he did not understand, right in front of him. It was all Zumbula could do to not crack up laughing at some of Matt's jibes at the man helping them. After four hours they finally had the African decked out with everything a gentleman needed, including knee-high rubber Wellies and fine leather shin-high boots that would need some breaking in.

ON THE THREE-HOUR drive back to Portland Matt gave Zumbula tips on how to act in Hungary, how the hunts were conducted, who was in charge, what the species would be, and that it would be cold in the mornings, something Zumbula had still not gotten used to, living in Portland.

"It is good that we have the clothes made from the sheep wool then," he simply responded. Silence fell over the two of them as they drove through the small town of Centralia, halfway home to Portland from Seattle.

Zumbula broke the comfortable quiet between them saying, "I believe it is best if I am your tracker and guide, patron. I am not made for these formalities and people who have rules on how they hunt."

Zumbula always called him *patron*, the respectful title he had used on safari even though Matt had insisted on many occasions that he simply call him Matt. Matt knew what the African was thinking, that he wouldn't fit in, that he was not an equal to the others, at least not financially or by education, and his role should be one of assistant or a more subservient role in front of the other participants.

"Naw, you should kill a stag or two while we are there; you are getting pretty good with my rifle. You'll like it, I promise. It's like killing a kudu or a giant eland, the stag is a very beautiful creature, trust me."

"Can I use my spear or assegai? That would be more 'sporting,' as you say, than a rifle. Otherwise no, I will track for you after you wound the animal and cannot find it, just in case you do not shoot well, patron. Then there is the skinning and butchering and making sure I get the best parts of the beast for our dinner. We all have a job, you do yours and I will do mine, patron."

Matt laughed out loud but knew better than to argue with Zumbula when he got in these moods. He would just play it by ear once they got there. But at least Zumbula would be dressed appropriately!

THE TWO OF them worked out at the house and gym over the next month, going to the shooting range on a regular basis to get Zumbula practice with different weapons, and at the same time breaking in Zumbula's new clothes and boots in the early chill of the fall mornings.

On the one hand, Djuri was jealous of the men going off on a trip and leaving her behind, but seeing the change in Matt and the positive effect it had brought to his and her husband's demeanor, she felt it was well worth it. The nights she heard Matt walking around the house when he couldn't sleep were becoming less frequent and he would not fall into the trance-like depression after dinner like he used to. He did not talk about Bianca every day anymore, although Junior's name would come up occasionally, but typically only in a positive way now. Djuri had acquired a small network of friends to hang out with and never had to worry about money or buying what she and the household needed since Matt gave her free rein to manage things as she saw fit. She was the woman of the house now. She had nothing to complain about in life and knew she would be able to handle things while Matt and Zumbula were away.

CHAPTER 15

Former General Afan waited for the answer to his pointed question directed at the manager of the four Ivanowich stores that had been cleaned out by the Croatians the week before. The manager was a nervous wreck, not sure if he was going to live to see the end of the week, even though none of the problems had been his, but he was still watchful of the General's well-known temper and sometimes deadly discipline.

"I'm sorry General Afan, but the headquarters of Ivanowich will not return my phone calls or my emails, nothing. They are obviously ignoring us. I can't open the stores with most of the machinery missing and no product to sell coming in from the distribution warehouse."

"What about the trucks, have there been any more coming into or through the country? I need a couple of them. The one we were able to get our hands on is not enough."

"Nothing sir, no one has seen anything."

Afan had his contacts at the border crossings keeping an eye out for any Ivanowich vehicles that might cross back in again. Above all else he wanted to get his hands on a couple of the ones that had been converted to suit his special trucking needs, needs that most of Ivanowich management was not aware of, only the handful of insiders he had handpicked to carry out his assorted smuggling tasks.

"Stay vigilant and keep me informed if anything new comes up," he said, leaving the shop by the front door and climbing into the backseat of his waiting black Mercedes sedan.

Frustrated and not used to not getting his way he barked at his driver, "Get the men organized, and I want a meeting for tonight set up. Tell them it is time to put plan B into action against Mister Tatra."

CHAPTER 16

ARRANGEMENTS HAD BEEN MADE BY THE COUNTESS TO HAVE Matt and Zumbula picked up at the Budapest airport in one of her forest green-colored Range Rovers so that when Matt's Gulf Stream jet taxied to a stop at a clean, well-maintained hangar at the south end of the private strip, it was waiting for them. He walked down the stairs to the tarmac and was met by the driver, who introduced himself as the Atwood's assistant gamekeeper, welcomed them to Hungary, and told them the drive would take approximately two hours before they arrived at the Atwood estate.

The fall colors of the rolling hills reminded Matt of home, tall oak and cottonwood trees with an occasional elm mixed in were all beginning to turn a rouge hue against a vivid clear blue sky, swept clean by the recent rains. The smell of the countryside wafted through the partially open window as the crisp air brushed at his silver hair. The ancient farms dissected the streams and valleys, inhabited by tenant farmers whose job was to protect the land and the wildlife as much as produce income for themselves and the landlords from farming and raising livestock.

Over the centuries these European land management practices had paid huge dividends in sustainable renewable trees and wildlife for hunting and for domestic meat production. While some in the New World might argue that the system of land ownership, the passing from wealthy generation to wealthy generation of vast estates with no inheritance tax penalty, was not fair for the masses and only perpetuated a wealthy nobility class, one had to admit that the masses of peasants who had taken over control of land through other means in other countries had not been renowned stewards of the forests and wildlife.

"Sir, I need to stop for petrol if you wouldn't mind," the driver asked in heavily accented English, looking to the backseat, interrupting Matt's daydreaming.

"No problem, I need to stretch my legs. How about you old man?" he ribbed Zumbula who unfolded himself out of the backseat when they stopped at the fuel pumps in a village with a name on a sign Matt couldn't pronounce.

The small town consisted of a dozen or so stone-walled houses, vines twisting and clinging to the 300-year-old walls surrounding them. Each large yard had a vegetable garden, chickens scratching for a meal among the brambles, some pigs or a few sheep and a ribbon of smoke wafting out of the rock chimneys. The gas station attendant put out his cigarette as he opened the creaking door of the repair shop, lazily shuffling toward the new Range Rover to pump petrol for only the second customer he had seen since noon. Admiring the shiny vehicle he knew belonged to the Atwoods, he jumped back in fright when he came around the back of it and discovered a tall muscular black man, his cheeks scarred in a horizontal tribal fashion, but dressed in dapper attire stretching his arms and torso.

Zumbula gave the startled local a stare guaranteed to intimidate before turning away and smiling at Matt as he walked to the end of the gravel parking lot, stretching his arms and bending at the waist while the attendant went about fueling the SUV, cautiously looking over his shoulder and keeping an eye on the sight he had never, ever seen in Hungary before.

Thirty minutes later the driver pulled to a stop in front of two grand stone-and-stucco pillared entrance walls supporting two massive black wrought iron gates that opened automatically when he pushed a button on the Rover's dashboard and announced, "Here we are sir, Palikroso Castle."

The view down the long winding driveway leading to the centuries-old stone country mansion took Matt's breath away. Cypress trees lined each side of the boulevard, while giant oaks stood sentinel along the low grassy ridges paralleling the road. A bevy of pheasant scattered off the right side of the road when the Rover passed; a dainty roe deer doe casually lifting her head from eating oak acorns to watch the known safe vehicle continue past. The driver eased to a stop under the portico where a man dressed in a traditional European green woolen hunting jacket and breeches greeted them, "Mister Simmons, welcome. And you sir must be Zumbula, the man that we have heard so much about."

Zumbula simply nodded in reply as the man hustled to retrieve their bags from the boot of the Rover.

"Please follow me, gentleman. I will show you to your rooms," he said in heavily accented English.

Leading through a grand entrance with twin staircases curving upward to the second floor, huge paintings of ancestors and Flemish tapestries hanging on the walls, the butler turned back to them as he wheeled the bags, "You are just in time. Countess Atwood has requested your presence at dinner tonight. All the guests are meeting at seven in the drawing room for cocktails, followed by dinner at eight in the blue dining room. Coat and tie tonight, gentlemen."

At the end of the hall they turned right and proceeded another 30 meters down a grand hall with full-length windows on one side and doors to guest rooms lining the other, before stopping at the third door from the end.

"Mister Zumbula, this will be your suite," he said, swinging the door open to show a high-ceilinged rose-colored room superbly decorated with antique hutches and a hand-carved headboard taller than Zumbula highlighting the massive bed.

Matt stuck his head in to the room to check it out and said, "Just like Bangui, eh?"

Zumbula thanked the man and closed the door behind them, a broad grin plastered on his face.

Matt's suite was even more opulent and was located right next door to Zumbula's. As the butler left Matt's room, Matt noticed that at the end of the hall were two fabulous 4-meter-high doors and asked the man, "Where do those lead?"

"That is the countess's private quarters sir. No one is allowed in there, and no one disturbs her. I'm sure you understand."

"Of course," Matt responded, closing the door. Looking at his watch, he realized he had better get unpacked and organized right away if he was going to be on time for the cocktail party.

FORTY-FIVE MINUTES LATER he emerged from his room dressed in a dark blue Armani suit and cream-colored silk shirt, a blue tie knotted perfectly to highlight his eyes. The tie was Bianca's favorite and his as well; it was the one she had bought him for their last Christmas together.

Zumbula's door opened just when Matt was passing by it and out stepped the African in a black Hugo Boss tailored suit with a pale cream shirt and red prep-school patterned tie.

"Looking good man."

"You too, patron. How long must I keep this tie on?"

Matt chuckled. "Until we come back to the room. You look sharp, seriously."

Zumbula nodded down the hallway, tugged at his cuffs the way he saw actors do it on television, exposing the cufflinks Djuri had bought him and led the way to the drawing room.

Walking through the drawing room's elegant entrance, Matt and Zumbula were introduced around the room to the other guests by the butler. A waiter discreetly brought Matt a Crown Royal and ginger ale, and an orange juice, no ice, for Zumbula without even asking them what they wanted—the well-prepared staff already knew. Besides Herr Schneider who was in fact attending the event alone, Matt also knew from past business meetings John Charles Gordon and his wife Susan from London, and Simon Comstral and his Swiss wife Ingrid from Munich. They had all spent time together at a charity fundraiser three years before. Thankfully no one brought up Bianca's name, Matt guessed they all knew what had happened but possessed the common courtesy to not mention her.

After briefly catching up with the latest with them, Matt excused himself to mingle with the others, working his way over to a knot of people he didn't know yet and introduced himself. The cocktail party was suddenly interrupted by the whine and racket of a helicopter's rotors rapidly approaching the estate's manicured grounds, barely skimming over the trees. As it grew louder a well-kept middle-aged woman Matt had not been introduced to yet, leaned over and said into Matt's ear, "Ah, here comes our missing guest finally. I assume you have never had the pleasure of meeting the infamous Ivan Tatra?"

"Can't say as I have, ma'am."

She dramatically rolled her eyes replying, "Well then I guess today is your lucky day."

The shiny black French-made SA 341 swept smartly onto the front lawn in front of the drawing room's floor-to-ceiling windows, fashionably late, making a grand entrance for everyone in attendance to see. The cocktail party's participants watched in wonderment, some in disgust, while the pilot hustled around the front of the chopper, snatched the latch on the passenger door free and swung it open. A tall, thin-built black-haired man sporting a jet-black goatee stepped out first, and then turned to assist the next person out of the chopper.

The woman standing next to Matt leaned in even closer, uncomfortably close, resting her hand on the small of Matt's back, hissing over the rotor noise into his ear, "Yes I was right, that there Monsieur is the sandwich king of Europe, Ivan Tatra. He has a new friend with him I see. We've never seen this one before."

Matt couldn't believe his eyes when a beautiful auburn-haired woman descended from the helicopter's passenger compartment, holding her short skirt down with one hand and her other hand trying to tame her red mane as it swirled against the updraft from the helicopter's blades. Matt glanced over at Zumbula, who was already smiling back at him, before sensuously whispering back to the woman at his side, "I've seen her before."

CHAPTER 17

TATRA AND HIS GUEST'S LUGGAGE WERE RETRIEVED FROM THE rear compartment as the chopper idled on the lawn while they were led around to the front entrance of the house and to their suite by the countess's staff. Once they had cleared the prop wash and the luggage hatch door was locked shut, the pilot deftly lifted the chopper into the sunset, and the clinking glasses, spirited conversation, and laughter soon returned to the drawing room.

Matt mingled with the guests and introduced himself and Zumbula to the others at the party, answering the repetitive questions about Zumbula with a practiced story, "Yes, nice to meet you as well. Let me introduce you to my friend Zumbula, originally from the Central African Republic. We work together on a variety of projects. He now lives in Portland also." Matt had this standard line and Zumbula followed it since it made things easier to explain. Several of the guests spoke French, which put Zumbula at ease since that was his second language after his tribal tongue. Sometimes he would switch between one guest and another in English, then French, impressing them all while holding up his brief story about being a businessman.

Matt could tell by the way the people would talk to each other and stare at Zumbula from across the room that the tribal scars and the tough look etched permanently across his face made them nervous. But in today's world of tattoos and piercings it seemed that anything goes, so they were probably thinking "what the hell." It was his eyes though that made it hard for many of the people to hold Zumbula's stare. The boldness, the depth of his soul, the "I could kill you in one heartbeat" look that he radiated made many—the women especially—nervous in his presence.

At a quiet moment away from the others, Zumbula smiled and leaned into Matt to speak softly, "The woman with the red hair could be trouble, patron. She knows and has seen many things. I felt we would never see her again and that all the problems we had in Sudan were long behind us and we would never speak of them again."

"I think she'll be cool. Remember she was as involved as we were in the whole affair. I have thought about her many times since we last saw her, but have avoided contacting her; you know, letting bygones be bygones, as we say."

"Yes, I know the meaning, patron. You think she is still working for the Foundation?"

"No idea, but I guess we will find out."

Just then, into the drawing room strode Ivan Tatra with the auburn-haired gorgeous woman, wearing an expensive-looking, perfectly cut emerald green cocktail dress, on his arm. He first loudly apologized to everyone in the room for being late, and then began introducing his date to the other guests one by one, working the room with a practiced confidence. A waiter brought them each a glass of champagne and asked if there was anything else they would care to drink.

"I'll have a double Grey Goose on the rocks with a lemon and the lady will have . . ." Ivan asked when he turned to her.

"Irish whiskey on ice if you have it, please," she spoke with a distinct Irish accent.

"Right away," the waiter replied, backing away to fetch the drinks from the bartender working in the corner. She took a sip of the cold crisp French champagne, smiling at the guests, subtly surveying the room over the top of the glass. Freezing in midsip, she couldn't believe her eyes. Her breathing stopped and her senses went numb, dropping her champagne glass onto the Turkish travertine-covered floor when she saw the tall black man and the incredibly handsome silver-haired man staring back at her from the far corner of the room.

"Matt Simmons," she whispered before realizing everyone in the room had turned to see what the crashing glass was all about. The room fell silent for that awkward second that occurs after someone drops their drink or a plate onto a stone floor but they all quickly resumed where they left off once they saw Caitlin fumbling to gain her composure. A waiter hurried over with a towel and tray to mop up the glass shards and spilt champagne. Another waiter bailed her out when he appeared at her side with Caitlin's Irish whiskey over ice.

"Are you OK? What happened?" hissed an impatient Ivan.

"I'm sorry. It just slipped out of my hand. I don't know how it happened. I'm sorry," Caitlin replied as her pale cheeks blushed in embarrassment.

Ivan was taken aback by the accident. His dates were typically well-behaved and well-mannered, and this was not a good way for him to impress the cultured crowd gathered at the event he had longed to attend for many years. These people were the kind he had always wanted to be associated with, powerful men and women who could perhaps help him in the future in some way.

"The Irish, they have no class," he thought to himself as he eased away from his date to mingle with his soon-to-be friends.

CHAPTER 18

Dzevad Malkoc's life had been one of hardship and heartbreak for as long as he could remember. Growing up on a dirt-poor Bosnian farm in the northern border region, the son of a single mother who gave birth to him out of wedlock after she became pregnant while working illegally for and sleeping on demand with a Hungarian farmer, he had struggled and scrounged for every meal he ever ate until he joined the army during the last Balkan war. At the beginning, the Bosniak controlled the ebb and flow of the battles and the living was good, pilfering every village they conquered, raping the Serb women to teach their hated neighbors a lesson about purity of race, and eating three square meals a day, life was pretty good overall. It was actually the only happy days in his life that he could recall.

When the Bosnians were finally reined in and forced back within their borders, times became tough once again for Dzevad. He couldn't return to the shame of the village where he had grown up a bastard by a Christian father, despised by his hardcore Muslim kinfolk and unable to find work after the war. Finally, at the end of his rope, fate stepped in and he heard from a cousin that there were jobs for farm laborers in Hungary. Illegal immigration was spreading across Europe as the borders fell in the European Union. Hungary was facing the same labor issues that most countries were—no one wanted to stay on the farms and work.

Ambitious young people all wanted to move to the cities as soon as they could, leaving family farms behind with no workers available to work the crops and tend the herds of sheep and cattle that supplied Europe's cities. The void was filled by willing hard workers from poor countries with massive unemployed labor, such as Macedonia, Turkey, and the Balkan States. From his cousin's lead, Dzevad found a good position at the Atwood farms where he was provided with a place to stay along with three meals a day and a small payment of cash every two weeks. Soon he was promoted, due not only to his hard work but also his ability to speak the Hungarian language, which his mother had learned when she worked there and had taught him as a child.

It was during his last trip back to Bosnia to visit family one week ago that he had ran across some of his old cronies from the war. These were guys who had treated him as an equal, guys who didn't care who his father was, they only cared about his loyalty to the Bosnian cause and how well he followed orders and fought, and he had done both very well.

It had been a strange coincidence when he had run into them at the local bar where they all used to hang out before he had left for his job in Hungary. Strange indeed, but he was glad to see the old gang and have a couple of beers together and get caught up on what they were all up to. His former colonel, Fikret Imamovic, did not seem surprised when he told them that he was still working in Hungary, but simply asked who he was working for. When he told them, they all nodded as if they knew who the family was. True, the Atwoods were somewhat famous for their wealth and philanthropy, but hardly anyone that he knew had heard much about them in Bosnia, that was for sure.

As the bar crowd began to thin out, the patrons heading for their meager homes that sat waiting for them within walking distance, the cigarette smoke dissipating, it was then that he realized their meeting was no coincidence at all. The former colonel quietly asked him, "Dzevad, you were a trusted and loyal soldier to General Afan during the war, and he passes on his regards to you."

"I am honored that he even remembers I ever existed," Dzevad humbly replied.

"Oh he remembers you well. You know that here in Bosnia the war has not ended for many of us. The fight goes on, but now it is a fight every day trying to keep a free and independent Bosnia, one not meddled with by our former enemies."

Dzevad knew full well of the struggles the current government was involved in and felt his patriotic vigor swelling just talking about it with his former soldier buddies. "Yes I know, it is a tough road."

"You are a true patriot, Dzevad," he said, glancing at the other two men who nodded in agreement at the statement lifting their beers in a mock salute. "That is why the General has asked me to personally make a small request of you, a way for you to help your homeland in our struggle against outsiders who mean our country and economy harm."

Dzevad's patriotic zeal surged, he fought back the urge to cry with joy he was so happy to be included in his country's plans. He, a lowly house staff worker for a Hungarian farm, was being asked to help his nation.

"Tell me what I can do to help, please," he begged.

The colonel handed him a cell phone, a brand new one with email and texting capabilities, a much nicer one than he could afford and was instructed, "Only use this phone for contacting me, understand? It has prepaid minutes that will work from the Atwood estate. Simply push 11 for auto dial and it will ring to my cell phone." The colonel had him try it once to confirm that it rang through to his cell phone.

He then went on, "In one week's time there will be a big event at the Atwoods, have you heard anything about it?"

"Of course, we are already preparing for it. The countess is hosting meetings and has a big hunt organized each day. Some very important businesspeople are said to be attending. But I don't think any of them have any interest in Bosnia do they?"

The colonel smiled at the news that it was already public knowledge who would be attending, "You would be surprised how some of our enemies hide behind facades of being 'businessmen' and yet are working behind the scenes in an attempt to ruin Bosnia's economy through shady backdoor channels."

Dzevad didn't care what it was they wanted from him, he was ready to help his friends, his only friends, with whatever they requested of him, so he listened intently to the rest of their instructions.

CHAPTER 19

MATT COULDN'T HELP BUT SMILE AT THE RED-HAIRED woman's reaction to seeing them. He and Zumbula casually went back to debating with the septuagenarian Greek ship owner and his twenty-something Italian girlfriend about the depressed prices of Mediterranean tariffs due to unregulated tramp steamers from Turkey plying the ports. Matt had to smile as the old man continued with his rant, after all the Greeks and the Turks had been blaming each other for their internal problems for a thousand years, and if it wasn't the Turks they were ranting about then the Greeks were complaining about the cheap labor in Macedonia screwing things up. Matt bit his tongue rather than bringing up the fact that maybe if Greek society ever considered a work week of more than 30 hours and lazy workers did not expect three months' paid vacation every year, then perhaps the economy of the stifled nation would improve.

He paid as much attention to the Greek as was possible but his mind was racing now that the auburn beauty from his past had walked into the room. The Italian woman who was getting bored with all the business talk, softly squeezed the Greek's arm and cooed, "Darling, would you please get me another vodka and soda?"

THE SHORT, STALKY Greek, antsy and not waiting for a waiter to come and take the order, predictably replied, "Sure, I will be right back, my love. You gentlemen want anything while I am going?"

"No, we are good, but thanks," Matt answered.

No sooner had her date walked toward the bar than the Italian girl had her delicate hand in the crook of Matt's arm, staring into his eyes with a look that had "I'm all yours to do with whatever you want," written all over it. She leaned in close and asked, "Tell me about yourself Mister Simmons. I see you are not married? How can a handsome devil like you not have been tied up by now?"

"I was married but not now. And you, when are you and your boyfriend tying the knot? You seem so in love," Matt quipped with a smirk of sarcasm across his face.

"Aha, you play games Mister Simmons, but you know and I know what fireworks could happen if we were able to get away some weekend, no?" Her lips were brushing up against Matt's ear lobe as she spoke, not even attempting to hide her advances until they were interrupted by Zumbula clearing his throat from a meter behind them where he stood sentinel-like, back against the wall, observing the goings on in the room. Matt stepped deftly a foot to one side to halt her advance just as Ivan Tatra and his date appeared in front of him, the Slovakian holding out his hand in introduction.

"Mister Simmons, I am Ivan Tatra and this is my date Miss Caitlin O'Shea. It is a pleasure to meet you finally."

Matt stood silently staring at Caitlin, flashbacks of their adventurous, near-death experiences in Sudan bringing back emotions he had been trying to keep buried for the past two years. He reflexively shook Ivan's hand, then turned to Caitlin, recovering some of his wits about him and spoke, "A pleasure to meet you both, um, ah, let me introduce you to my, ah, business associate, Zumbula."

Zumbula stepped forward and shook Ivan's hand, before taking Caitlin's and bowing slightly and kissed the back of it.

"My, what a gentleman," she quipped to Zumbula, who grinned slyly as he backed away from the conversation once again.

Caitlin smiled from ear to ear at the sight of Matt so nervous and out of character. Here was the man who had saved her and several other people's lives without any regard for his own life and had been cool as a cucumber under fire, but was now stammering and edgy in front of her. Not wanting to punish him anymore she held out her hand to shake his, feeling the dry warmness she recalled when he had held her in his arms and kissed her passionately in the hallway of their hotel in Khartoum. A thousand times since she had wondered what it would have been like to have made love with him that night. In the long run she was glad that they had not, since only a week later they discovered Matt's wife—who everyone thought was dead—was being held captive in the terrorist camp in Sudan. Neither one of them said a word for a fleeting moment while they both stared, transfixed, into each other's eyes. Matt remembered the beauty of her vivid dancing green eyes and Caitlin melted at the icy blue stare of Matt's.

"Nice to see you," Caitlin said.

"Do you two know each other?" Ivan asked, sensing some sort of connection between them.

Matt let Caitlin reply, not sure what to say and having no idea what the hell was going on.

"No, but I have certainly heard of his business ventures and of course his hunting exploits. You know Ivan enjoys hunting just like you do Mister Simmons, only not as much of course."

Ivan chimed in, "I do love it, but I am so busy with my restaurants. I have no time for it, at least not as much as I would like. What a pleasure it is to be here with the countess for the weekend though, eh?"

Just as he finished his sentence, Countess Atwood made her grand entrance into the room, dressed in a floor-length burgundy-colored silk gown, the neck line plunging to reveal her substantial cleavage, the cut at the waist showing off her shapely hips perfectly sculpted into the breath-taking dress. All eyes turned at the sight, everyone gathering around her to greet and thank her for hosting the event. The countess glowed in the adoration but humbly thanked each and every one of them for attending. As the crowd took turns chatting with the countess, Ivan got in line waiting for his turn to schmooze her, leaving Caitlin standing next to Matt.

Matt discreetly leaned forward and whispered to Caitlin, "You look fabulous. Thanks for not saying anything."

Without turning Caitlin quietly replied in her lilting Irish accent, “We will talk later; I can’t wait to hear what you have been up to.”

Matt and Caitlin followed Ivan toward where the countess was holding court, while Zumbula eased along behind them, soaking in the whole affair, enjoying the irony of the evening.

“Good evening, Mister Tatra, and you must be Caitlin O’Shea. A pleasure to meet you both,” the countess greeted them before turning to Matt.

“And you, sir, have to be Matt Simmons from America. I have heard so much about you from Herr Schneider. He says you lead quite the adventurous life?” The countess’s eyes locked onto Matt’s, the depth of her beauty holding him mesmerized, his rugged good looks and piercing blue eyes holding her breathless for a brief second too long. Caitlin bristled jealously at the contact between the two of them, her woman’s intuition letting her see that the countess was flirting with Matt.

Matt leaned forward giving the countess a cultured kiss on each cheek, just like a European gentleman would and replied, “So nice to finally meet you, Countess. Thank you for hosting us in your beautiful castle.”

Turning to Zumbula he continued, “May I also introduce you to my colleague and friend, Zumbula?”

Zumbula stepped forward and when the countess extended her hand to him, Zumbula bent gracefully at the waist and lifted the back of her hand to his lips giving it a peck before saying, “Bonsoir, Madam, enchanté.”

The countess smiled at the gesture and without missing a beat at the dramatic overture replied in perfect French, “Merci beaucoup, Monsieur Zumbula, welcome to my home. I have heard many stories about you as well.”

Matt stifled a smile at his friend’s graciousness, wondering to himself where in Hell’s name he had picked that move up? It was the second time tonight, and he had certainly not learned it growing up in the Central African jungle, that was for sure. Perhaps he had been watching too much television back in Portland.

The countess excused herself from them for one minute, nodding at the head waiter who rang a silver bell to get everyone's attention after which the countess announced to all gathered, "Would you all please make your way in to the dining room and take your seats; dinner is served."

The crowd eased toward the large double doors that were swung open at that very moment to reveal a long baroque-style dining room with gold leaf trim framing a hand-painted ceiling mural, two matching Murano crystal chandeliers hanging from it, lighting up the massive hand-carved table that spanned the length of the room.

The countess slipped in seductively next to Matt, resting her hand on his elbow and asking, "Would you mind escorting me to the table Mister Simmons? I am afraid I have no dinner date tonight."

"Only if you call me Matt, Countess Atwood."

"Of course," she smiled, walking toward the doors lightly holding onto his elbow. "You may call me Countess," she joked. "No, please, call me Pamela."

"OK Countess," Matt jibed back, feeling like the king of the world with this gorgeous, refined woman on his arm.

Everyone took their assigned seats at the table once they found their name cards, the couples getting to sit together but seated intentionally to interact and meet new people. The countess was seated at the head of the table, to her left sat the Greek and his Italian girlfriend, then Sergio and Paloma Villarreal from Spain, next to them Herr Schneider and the McAllisters from Scotland. On the right side of the table starting at the end farthest away from the countess sat Caitlin and Ivan, Susan and Charles Gordon, Ingrid and Simon Comstral, and next to them Zumbula with Matt at the seat directly to the right of the countess.

A yellow squash soup garnished with a decorative cream swirl and chopped green onions was brought to the table immediately once everyone was seated. The waiters, dressed in matching green Bavarian-style lederhosen, hustled the steaming bowls around the table.

Champagne was poured for all before Herr Schneider stood to make a toast in English, “Ladies and gentlemen, I would like to thank Countess Atwood for inviting us all to her fabulous estate and hosting this event.” Turning toward her he continued, “Your generosity is only surpassed by your grace and beauty. To the Countess.” He held his fluted glass high as the other guests did the same.

“To the Countess!” echoed all the guests.

She rose to her feet, replying, “Thank you all for coming. I hope we all shoot well and that you enjoy your time here. It is a great honor for me to be able to host this gathering of such distinguished personalities and, how do I say this politely, hummm, *characters*, I believe is the word?”

Everyone chuckled at the description and Matt thought, *“That will be the understatement of the weekend, characters indeed.”*

Matt glanced down the table to where Caitlin sat and received a wrinkled-nose “I’m mad at you” look in return and wondered for a moment what he had done wrong.

The countess continued, “Please everyone enjoy your dinner. My chef Francois Bouvier has prepared a little something special to welcome you all, and I hope you enjoy it. We will have the drawing for stands for the boar hunt tomorrow as soon as we finish dessert. Welcome once again, and bon appétit.”

Everyone clinked glasses with others close to them, and Matt finished his toast with the countess who gave him a long sensual look as their glasses met, holding them together just an instant too long, long enough for Matt to realize what Caitlin was mad about. The countess’s lips parted in a devilish little smile as the glass of champagne came to her rosy lips and she took a small sip before setting it down to start with her soup.

Zumbula waited until he saw the ladies near him begin to eat, and then used the same style spoon they did to eat his soup. All the different variety of eating utensils was confusing. Even though he had been schooled over the last couple of months on etiquette, he still wanted to make sure he was doing it correctly. He was dipping his spoon into the soup, tipping it away from him before lifting it to his mouth, just like Matt had shown him and feeling pretty proud of himself when he felt something rubbing the inside of his upper leg and it made him pause with the spoon halfway to his mouth. He looked up from his soup as he realized it was a foot stealing its way closer to his crotch, but stopping just short. Directly across the table from him the Greek's Italian girlfriend was chatting with Senor Villarreal as if nothing was happening. Zumbula watched her acting job while her foot attempted to get higher, but he understood quickly that she was not tall enough to reach all the way under the table and get to his manhood, nor did he slide down in his seat to give her a chance to succeed. Their eyes met when she turned back toward the Greek tycoon, a fleeting look that even Zumbula understood was full of lust and invitation. Her foot seductively slid slowly back down to the floor a few moments later giving him a chance to finish his soup in peace.

He glanced to his left when Matt looked over at him and asked, "Everything all right my friend? You look a little rattled about something."

"Everything is good, patron," he softly replied, quickly glancing over at the Italian out of the corner of his eye.

Matt smiled and returned to the conversation the countess was having with Herr Schneider about the pros and cons of being in the European Union. It seemed to Matt that this was the hottest topic going on in Europe these days, and he could not for the life of him understand why any country would want to join this now-failed socialist idea that had no hope of long-term survival. He decided to keep his mouth shut and just listen, especially after the Greek got into the discussion and became louder with each heated sentence. Surveying the rest of the room and the table's occupants, he saw everyone happily immersed in conversations with each other. The countess had done a good job of mixing the personalities and couples to get a wonderful gathering of different, yet sympatric cultures.

As the main course arrived, Countess Atwood leaned in toward Matt, rested her delicate hand on his forearm and quietly said, "Thank God the servers interrupted the debate about Europe. You are very quiet about the subject, or is it that you are just a nontalkative man in general?"

"There are times when I believe I should stay out of a debate in which I have no business being involved and don't want to choose sides," Matt said, out of the corner of his mouth, smiling at her.

The countess giggled in reply, "A wise man. Tell me more about yourself Mister Simmons; it seems you are into all kinds of adventure and business deals. From what I have been told you are a very busy person and not just the international playboy people say you are."

"Hardly Countess. I'm not sure where you heard that—what a bad reputation I must have," Matt laughed. "I try and keep myself busy. You know what they say, idle hands are the devil's workshop."

"Yes, I'll bet," the countess cooed, staring deeply into his steely blue eyes, mesmerized by the man sitting next to her. She could feel a stirring inside her, one she had ignored and subdued for so long, too long. Her married life was a shambles; her husband hadn't made love to her in so long she did not even recall when the last time had been.

She had been a good wife even if he had not been a faithful husband, not even looking twice at another man, avoiding any possible scenario where she might be caught up in a situation where she could be tempted. Not that men had not tried. Plenty of them who knew the story with her missing husband had made it clear to her that they were available to take care of any needs she may have. However, this Matt Simmons man was making her feel like a schoolgirl once again. She was giddy, ready to dance, ready to give affection, and receive it in return, something she had done without all these past lonely years.

Ever since she had read the dossier on Matt that told her of his adventurous side, the rumors that he had rescued his wife from some sort of kidnapping, that he was independently wealthy so she wouldn't have to worry about him wanting her for her money, she had been drawn to this man. There was something about his looks as well that made her crave making love with him. He was older than she was, but she had always been attracted to that look. He looked to be in superb physical condition, and he carried himself with a bit of a confident swagger, not cocky, just confident in his abilities.

Countess Atwood thought to herself, as she was finishing her dessert, that she would love to find out how good his abilities really were. She had to find a discreet way to get him alone, and she knew she had to quit acting like a teenager in front of the other guests. She smiled seductively at Matt one last time, before asking the head waiter a couple of questions in Hungarian, sending him rushing away. He returned five minutes later with an assistant helping him carry in a large whiteboard that listed all the guests' names with boxes and lines drawn in a graph next to them. Across the top were listed Stag, Boar, and Pheasant.

When the board was placed on a large easel stand made for just such an occasion, the countess announced, "All right, everyone; please may I have your attention? Thank you, now we will have Franek our head gamekeeper draw names for the stands for the wild boar hunt tomorrow and then the pheasant shoot the next day. We will have two people drawn for each stand and we will have individual and team prizes for the most boars and the biggest tomorrow. We will hunt in the morning in one stand then after lunch your team will go into a different stand. We will draw both stand locations now. There will be one gamekeeper's assistant with each team to assist you and keep count and keep you honest."

"Good way to do it," Matt thought. *"Keeps anyone from complaining about not getting a fair chance or being put in a bad blind."*

"Any questions?" the countess continued.

No one asked any, so Franek went to two cloisonné pots sitting on a table in front of the whiteboard and reached into the left one and withdrew the first name and read it out loud.

"Miss Caitlin O'Shea." Everyone clapped at the announcement as Franek drew out her partner's name and announced, "Herr Schneider. You will be in stand five in the morning and stand one in the afternoon."

Herr Schneider stood and walked around the table graciously and greeted Caitlin with a big hug and announced to the room, "Not only will we be the best team at shooting, we will be the best looking!"

Everyone laughed at the old German who, it could be said of, was not in any way good looking and he knew it. A few good-natured jeers got thrown in toward them while Franek drew the next lot.

"Team two, Senor Villarreal and Sir Ian McAllister will be in stand one in the morning and stand two in the afternoon."

More applause while Matt realized they would be the team to beat, both of them were excellent shots and had their own shooting estates back home.

"Team three, Ivan Tatra and Paloma Villarreal in stand six in the morning and stand four in the afternoon."

Ivan continued the tradition the German had started and went around the table to Paloma, bending at the waist and kissing her hand in gentlemanly fashion while clicking his heels together, standing stiffly at attention and announcing to the room, "The Senora will have to shoot well for the two of us I am afraid, since I am the amateur in this crowd. I hope you are up to the challenge, Senora."

"It is a heavy burden to have to carry our team, but I will do my best," she laughed to the other diners.

Matt noticed that Ivan seemed a little too drunk for such an occasion. He looked over to Caitlin at the end of the table and saw her watching Ivan's every move, but not in what could be described as a loving way, more in a cautious way, like a cat watching a mouse to see what its next move might be.

Matt was looking around the table to see who his partner might be from the remaining attendees when he heard his name announced by the gamekeeper.

"Team four will be Matt Simmons and," he hesitated as he pulled the next name out of the pot, "Countess Atwood in stand four in the morning and six in the afternoon."

Everyone graciously clapped while Matt stood and followed Ivan's lead by dramatically kissing the countess's outstretched hand while bent at the waist like a true gentleman.

The rest of the teams were selected and stands assigned with Zumbula and Susan Gordon in the stand next to Matt and the countess. The two of them made a strange couple when Zumbula continued the hand-kissing routine with Mrs. Gordon, her being the classic British well-groomed stately woman next to the black African nattily dressed, yet still somewhat scary-looking to those who did not know him.

The crowd began to disperse once the drawing was completed. Some guests made their way to the bar for a nightcap while others excused themselves and retired to their rooms. Ivan and the Greek and Spaniard stood at the bar talking politics, the volume getting higher as the alcohol flowed. The countess diplomatically worked the room telling each of the guests good night and that she would see them at breakfast at 5:30 sharp. She crossed to the hallway door where Matt stood and gave him a brief goodnight kiss on the cheek and whispered, "I can't wait until tomorrow to hunt with you."

"Sweet dreams Countess, I am really looking forward to our hunt."

Letting her hand slowly slip from his grasp she walked down the hallway feeling Matt's eyes on her and turned to look back and confirm it, sure enough catching Matt watching her. Matt smiled, embarrassed that he was caught, but happy to see her smile back before she disappeared around the corner to her suites.

Caitlin took her cue that Matt was now alone and approached with a fresh Crown Royal and ginger ale for him in one hand and an Irish whiskey on the rocks for herself in the other.

"Same old Matt I see. Can't keep the women away from you, eh? You better be careful with that one, you know she's married?"

While Matt could sense she was trying to make a joke, it certainly didn't come out that way, and Matt could hear the edge in her voice. He jokingly replied, trying to lighten things up, "Wow, don't tell me you're actually jealous of another woman? You of all people, who shows up with a rich Slovak for dinner? No wonder I never hear from you, although I must say I don't think he's really your type."

Caitlin sneered back at him while her cheeks turned a rosy hue, "We need to talk, but not now. Please do not take things for what they appear to look like from the outside, OK? Promise me you will keep an open mind?"

"Sure," Matt responded, puzzled by the way she put it, but willing to give her a break on any more of a hard time.

"No one told me you and Zumbula were coming here. What is your role? Who are you working for?" Caitlin asked.

Matt hesitated at the remark, his curiosity piqued. "I'm an invited guest, and I brought Zumbula along. We are just here hunting. How about you?"

Caitlin stared into his eyes, looking for a spark of lying hiding in there but found none, before understanding he was telling the truth and responding, "Ah yes same for me, I was invited by Ivan as his guest. I suppose he needed a shooter since from what I have heard he can't hit the broad side of a barn."

"He seems a little creepy to me. You actually like this guy, Caitlin?"

"If you only knew how hard this charade is for me to pull off, it would make you laugh, Matt." Caitlin thought before answering, "How about after the shoot tomorrow we go for a walk and I'll fill you in on what's happening in my life. Could we do that?"

She pulled Matt into the hallway, away from prying eyes, then quickly leaned up onto her tiptoes and gave him a quick kiss on the lips and whispered, "It's really nice to see you again Matt, I've been worried about you. I heard about Bianca, and I'm really sorry about what happened. See you tomorrow."

With that she walked quickly to the left, down the long hallway toward her room, hoping she could get to sleep before Ivan arrived in their room and decided he might want to fool around. The thought made her shake her head no as she hustled to their room.

CHAPTER 20

THE BAR AT THE COUNTESS'S PARTY WAS DOWN TO ONLY THE drunken Greek, the famous sandwich king who was also slurring his words, and the Spaniard keeping up a steady argument about European Union woes. Dzevad discreetly took a slip of paper from his pocket and set it and a pencil on the dining room table where he was removing the dirty silverware and dishes. Seeing no one else in the room he quickly wrote down the hunting stand assignments as he had been instructed by the colonel to collect. On the board Ivan Tatra's name was paired with his partner Paloma Villarreal and the chart showed the morning and afternoon assignments. He hurried and wrote on the slip of paper "morning" and "afternoon" and was just about to fill in the numbers when the chef came into the dining room and barked at him.

"Hey, I need you in the kitchen now. We have pots and pans piling up and you need to wash them first. Let's go. We have lots to do before breakfast; cooking starts in six hours."

"Yah, yah, I'm on my way. I'll bring in a load with me; how's that?"

"Just hurry up. I'd like to try and get a couple hours of sleep before breakfast, damn it."

When the cook turned to go Dzevad grabbed the piece of paper, stuffing it in his front pocket, filled his hands with a stack of plates, and then looked over his shoulder at the board. He had to look twice to see the right line then memorized the numbers.

Morning six and afternoon four.

He would call in five minutes and give the colonel the news. Why they wanted it he didn't know and didn't dare ask, it was not his position in life to question why an officer told him to do something. As he dialed the cell phone, the numbers nagged at him but he let it go, "*Was it six and four or four and six? Four and six I'm quite sure.*"

CHAPTER 21

Sitting alone in her room at the castle hoping she had a little time before Ivan showed up, Caitlin looked at her watch to see that while it was late in Hungary it was still business hours in the United States, so she dialed the secret number to Washington, D.C., to report in on her status and give her handler an update.

The phone was answered on the second ring, "Advanced Technologies."

"Sixty-seven Tango Bravo reporting in," she spoke, giving them her code. If she used the number sixty-nine anywhere in the code her handlers would know she had been compromised and disregard anything she told them. If she was in serious trouble she would give them another series of numbers, a mixed code revealing the threat level she was at and hopefully her handlers would be there to assist her, quickly. But in this game she was playing now, you never knew if help would ever be on the way, that's just the rules of the game.

She had been given instruction in this and a litany of other lessons in covert espionage during her two months of intense training at the Langley CIA headquarters beginning two years ago. After returning to Ireland after her escape out of South Sudan with Matt Simmons, when he had rescued his wife and Djuri from their enslavement at the terrorist encampment of the Janjaweed warrior Rashid, she had immediately quit her job with the Helvig Foundation. What had started out as a simple business trip to Khartoum for the philanthropic Helvig Foundation had turned into a nightmare and taught her lots of things about how the world works and how Africa doesn't. Her approach to saving the world had taken a sharp turn away from working for NGOs who gave money to causes hoping to save everyone while lining the pockets of the powerful rulers and bureaucrats who ran the corrupt poverty-stricken countries into the ground while filling their Swiss bank accounts with most of the foreign funds they received.

UPON HER RETURN home she had worked at the estate her father had willed her, getting the place ready for the spring plantings and keeping a low profile while wondering what she was going to do with herself now that she had quit the Foundation. She didn't have to work, she didn't need the money, after all she had a trust that came with the land from her father that kept her comfortable. She was not one to sit around and waste her life though; she was the kind of person who needed a cause, a reason to get up every day, some way to show the world she could make it on her own, that she mattered.

She thought about Matt all the time it seemed, but tried her best to keep those dreams under wraps, after all he was a married man and obviously deeply in love with Bianca his beautiful young wife. She heard through friends who checked for her that he and Bianca had brought a son into the world and it made her cry when she heard the news, maybe not tears of joy, however.

After three months of getting settled back in at her Irish farm, she received a call one day out of the blue from the U.S. government agent, who had debriefed her and Matt and the rest of the entourage when they had returned from Sudan, "Hey Caitlin, this is Dennis Anderson from the U.S. government. How goes it?"

Caitlin recognized the cranky but loveable man's voice immediately, "All is well, just working my butt off here at the farm in Ireland."

"So I hear. Have you got time for lunch today? I'm only an hour away from your place and would like to run a proposal by you about a project I'm working on. Of course it's hush hush, you know."

Caitlin let the idea swirl in her head for a few seconds. She could feel her pulse rising at the thought of her getting back to work for some sort of cause.

"Why don't you come here? I can have something ready by the time you get here. Do you know how to find my place?"

"Oh yeah, no sweat, I'll see you in about an hour. I assume no one else will be there? Can I bring anything?"

"No, we are fine. See you then. No one else will be here."

She immediately yelled for Mary her maid to put a nice lunch together for one other person and then take the rest of the day off. Caitlin ran to her bedroom and stripped out of her working clothes and climbed into the hot shower to wash off the morning grime and be ready to see Dennis once again.

Over lunch on the stone patio, the two of them enjoyed a rare sunny Irish spring day for a half hour of small talk until Dennis eventually came to the point of the meeting, "We talked during your debriefing with us after the Sudan episode that perhaps we could work together in the future. I have spoken with my team about you, and we think you would be a good fit with a new program we are working on."

"Go ahead, Dennis, I'm all ears."

"First of all, and I probably don't have to tell you this, but I have to say it anyhow, what we are about to discuss is top secret and no one can know anything about it. The agreement you signed during the debriefing is still in effect, just to be technical."

"OK, no problem. I assumed after the Sudan episode that you weren't really in the technology sales business, nor was Matt. So yes, I am OK with that," Caitlin laughed.

"By the way, speaking of Matt, he is not working with us at the moment. He has become a civilian once again, so don't relate anything to him if you speak to him, OK?"

"I haven't spoken with him since the debriefing after the rescue."

Dennis noted her eyes drop when she spoke of Matt, something else must have been going on between them that he wasn't aware of. He made a mental note of that for future reference.

"All right, good then. You heard they had a baby?"

"Yes," she answered, and the look in her eye told him even more about whatever it was that he had missed earlier.

"The bastard Matt must have been fucking her. Damn, the lucky son of a bitch," he thought as he continued. "Anyhow, here's what's happening. First it shouldn't be dangerous, nothing compared to your experience in Sudan, that's for sure. Mainly gathering info, undercover, posing as someone you are not, we will set you up as needed with fake I.D., credit cards, et cetera, for the assignments. We need someone with your stunning looks and ability to manipulate other people, especially men to garner info and report back to us. Once we have the intel we need, I will send in the bad boys to do the dirty work as necessary once you are out of harm's way. The pay is good and you get all your expenses covered. You will be treated as an independent contractor, that's the way we do it to keep things clean with no trail back to us. Secondly, you will need to come to America for some training. There is a course that will be essential for you to take and some intense training in a variety of fields that you will do just fine in. It should take about 12 weeks total. I know you can already handle a rifle and a shotgun expertly. How about your pistol skills?"

"I like the small nine millimeter Berretta. I do OK with it, but it's hard to practice here in Ireland, all these stupid UK gun laws and all."

"Yeah, I hear ya, not like in the good old USA, eh?"

Caitlin let the whole concept sink in while she sipped her tea in the sunshine of a glorious day. The idea intrigued her. She liked adventure, but this was something way out in left field. A spy? Her, Caitlin O'Shea working for the U.S. government undercover? This was crazy—she should be looking for a man to settle down with and raise babies peacefully at the farm in Ireland, not gallivanting around the world playing life-or-death games. She thought about her father, the man who had taught her to be independent. What would he have to say if he were here right now?

She smiled to herself and thought of him in one of his moods when the two of them would sit by the fire in his office at the farm while he would give her another lesson regarding their business holdings, or tips on how to run a meeting when you are in charge, or how to watch out for the lawyers and accountants who were going to sock it to you. Him with his pipe and Irish Whiskey in a crystal glass, her sipping tea sitting across from him in the matching Chippendale armchair, absorbing every one of his words as if he could die at any moment and she had better pay attention. And die he did, sooner than he should have, but thankfully not before teaching her the rough-and-tumble ways of the world. Her mother had passed away years before and suddenly she had been all alone.

"What would Dad have said about this situation? He would have told me to go for it! What was it he used to say? 'Caity my lass, you only get one chance at life on this rock we call earth and I'm not too sure about heaven and hell. However, I'll tell ya this, I know there's too many people who spend their life in hell right here on earth and you shouldn't be one of them. Dearie, when you get the chance, promise me you'll go for it, will ya? Make your old man proud 'cause I'll be watching ya from up above when I'm having a we dram of Ireland's best with Saint Peter himself don't ya know?'"

Dennis said nothing as he watched her look around the farmyard, lost in her thoughts, gazing over the peaceful rolling green hills, ancient stone walls cutting through them, creating checkerboard patterns of emerald green and grey stone that made Dennis wonder how anyone could leave such a beautiful place for the grungy city life he had endured his whole life in urban America. But he knew full well that people like Caitlin were always on the move. They needed, no they craved, adventure and risk and that's why it was so easy for him to recruit them to do his dirty work.

"Maybe I'll retire to Ireland when the time comes. Yeah, that's it and I'll marry Caitlin and we will live happily ever after," he laughed to himself. *"I'm sure she's looking for a sixty-year-old balding man carrying a few extra pounds around his belt to be her boy toy!"*

She interrupted his thoughts when she answered him in her lovely Irish accent, "I'm going to need a couple of weeks to get things organized here and then I can go to wherever you want me. I'd like to hear more about what we are going to be doing though first. Make sure it's something I want to be involved in."

"Hey, before we go any further there is something else you should know about Matt, because you have apparently not heard about it yet," Dennis said.

"What, what is it?"

"In case you do talk to him someday, I think you should know that Bianca committed suicide last year."

Caitlin's hand went to her mouth to stifle a cry, "Oh no, oh my God."

"That's not the worst of it I'm afraid. She murdered Matt's son before she killed herself."

Caitlin could not help herself and she began to weep softly, at the same time suddenly feeling guilty that she had not stayed in touch with them after their ordeal together in Sudan. Her head was bowed and her hand covered her eyes, and Dennis gave her the time she needed to compose herself, before going on, "I didn't want you to be blindsided and not know. I know you two were close in the past."

Collecting herself, she dried her tears with a napkin and keeping a stiff upper lip in the face of such devastating news said, "Thanks for telling me. I had not heard a thing about it." She hesitated another full minute while staring off over the verdant green fields, her mind racing with a thousand questions before turning back to Dennis and saying, "So you were about to tell me about what you want me to do for this project you are working on."

"Right," Dennis replied. "There is this Slovakian guy named Ivan Tatra, ever hear of him?"

CHAPTER 22

MUJO WALKED INTO THE HOUSE WHERE GENERAL AFAN AND a clan of rough former military types dressed in civilian hunting clothes sat smoking cigarettes and drinking stiff black tea. Well-used weapons leaned casually in the corners of the living room and against the furniture. An AK47 here, an Israeli Uzi there, and a scoped Remington 700 sniper rifle left over from the failed U.S. Vietnam War effort lying across the mantle of the old farmhouse's fireplace. The house and surrounding 200 hectares had been leased for the fall season by one of the General's cohorts under the auspices of using it for rough shooting of pheasant and wild boar.

General Afan was in a foul mood. He had been for days after he realized that the partnership he had enjoyed with the Slovak Tatra had come to an abrupt end and was not going to be resurrected.

Calling it a partnership was probably wrong he knew. The General had imposed his needs on Ivan and his company when they approached him for the rights to open the restaurants. It was a take it or leave it deal he offered but would be a lucrative deal for both of them. When he first heard the request from the sandwich king Tatra that he needed help in opening restaurants in Bosnia and Herzegovina, General Afan took a look at the operations, saw how he did his distribution of product and was impressed with the Slovak's efficiency. Sensing immediately how this could help his "other more lucrative businesses," the General had called a second meeting with Ivan and made a proposal to him regarding partnering on the restaurants as well as on the transportation. Afan assured Ivan that he could find Bosnian drivers to keep the stores supplied from the Croatian warehouse and that there would be no customs hassles if they used his drivers. Ivan had jumped at the opportunity.

The General needed transportation and distribution to get his products to market, Ivan needed the general's blessing and connections to open his shops. The goods that were to be shipped didn't take up much room in a truck, they needed to be moved to a variety of locations around Europe, the profits were very good, and the General was not a fool, so he was willing to share in the wealth even if the idiot Tatra did not realize how much or exactly what he would be involved in.

As Europe had evolved into the Euro zone and borders disappeared, it had helped moving his products, but he still had to be careful with the larger shipments of drugs such as the 1-kilo marijuana bales. Using commercial trucking companies had worked occasionally but too many people were involved and the risk was too great. Opium he could move in small quantities with junkies or students willing to put their lives on the line by swallowing a few balloons of the stuff and fly it in from Turkey or Iran, but here again the failure rate was high and the *mules* as they called the carriers were undependable just by their very nature and willingness to do the job.

Smuggling women destined for prostitution roles around Europe was made a lot easier when he had some of his trusted men reconfigure a few of Ivanowich's trucks and construct a false compartment to hide them in. It had all worked well and he had found that shipping the dope and young girls mixed with other legitimate products was the answer and that none of the authorities expected them to move around Europe that way. Due to the enormous volume of big trucking rigs on the highways and roads of the European Union, it was virtually impossible for the authorities to bust him.

It had all been working very well up until Tatra had screwed things up.

"General," Mujo interrupted his thoughts, "I received the call; we know where the Slovak bastard will be in the morning, we have the information for which stand he will be hunting from."

"Is he going to be by himself?"

"No our contact says he will be with a local guide and a woman, some Spanish senora. They will be in stand number four."

The General hesitated before answering, "Collateral damage I guess, unless we can avoid killing the woman somehow. Listen men, if possible do not take the woman's life, but if she gets in the way, so be it."

A murmur of recognition of the situation rose from the four men, all of whom had killed plenty of women and children in retaliation against the Serbs during the genocidal Balkan Wars of the 1980s and 1990s. It would be without conscience or second thought, and the General had given them their orders. He trusted this group of men to do whatever it took to get the job done.

"OK, so here is the layout of the Atwood estate," the General began as he unfolded a large topographical map that covered most of the dining room table. The men all stood up and gathered around to find out the details of the plan the General had cooked up, which seemed simple enough.

"Here are the locations of the various hunting stands on the property, they are each numbered. You can see our inside source shows which way they face into the fields. This is the way the hunters will be looking for animals to come toward them. Here is number four. You can bet the rich arrogant scum will still be very sleepy when they arrive at their designated spots an hour before dawn, but the guides and gamekeepers with them will have good eyes and know the farm very well; some of them have grown up on the estate. Be cautious if you are approaching from the front of any of blinds, understand? Remember, others may be able to see you from number five and number six."

Everyone nodded before he continued, "In and out, that's it, make it quick. We need to send a message to anyone else who may be thinking of double-crossing us in the future, but I don't want anyone at the event to know that we are involved. I will let the word leak out later. They will all know in due time, once we are all back in Bosnia."

CHAPTER 23

An eerie mist hovered just above the plowed fields, giving Matt and Pamela some additional cover as they eased quietly toward the hunting stand they had drawn. The guide assigned to them for the morning's hunt waited behind in the Range Rover as he had been instructed to do at the last minute by the countess. Matt trailed her by three steps since it was her farm, courteously letting her lead the way in the still pitch darkness of the frosty fall morning. Matt watched her confident stride with great respect, the way she carried herself in the field and the experienced way she toted the custom built, gold-inlaid Mauser rifle as if she were a pro. Matt couldn't help letting his eyes linger a moment longer than he should have on her perfect derriere, the tailored moleskin pants fitting her perfectly and highlighting her physical attributes. Sensing Matt's eyes on her, Pamela turned to look at him, catching him looking at her behind and giving him a wide-eyed wicked little smile, which made him smile back.

She silently wagged her gloved finger at him, wrinkled her nose at him then turned to continue on, smiling and thinking, "*You have no idea what this weekend has in store for you, Mister Simmons. No idea at all.*"

Leaving the guide behind at the SUV had been her idea at the last moment, it would give her free time to spend away from prying eyes, a chance to test the waters with Matt. She could tell by the way he looked at her that he was just as interested in her as she was in him. She just needed a little time alone with him, but it was difficult for her to conjure any up with all her people working at the estate.

Matt carried the small leather rucksack containing a thermos of tea and some snacks, as well as extra ammo for both of them and a small spotting scope. A pair of Zeiss binoculars with a built-in range finder, capable of giving them exact distance readings to 1,000 meters hung around his neck. His hunting belt containing a leather ammo pouch, multitool, and skinning knife was strapped around his waist under his insulated Barbour oiled cloth field coat. The only sound in the foggy morning was the squish of their Wellington rubber boots in the muddy field. An owl called to its mate from the tree line in front of them, dawn would soon be approaching and their night-time hunting foray would come to an end. The headlights of another vehicle sweeping the horizon on the distant border of the property caught the countess's attention, and they stopped to watch until the lights disappeared.

Pamela leaned in close, letting her warm lips brush against Matt's cold ear and whispered, "One of the hunting groups must be lost, or going to the wrong blind, they should not be coming in from that side of the property."

Her closeness and breath in his ear stirred Matt's manhood instantly and placing his free hand on her waist and pulling her closer he replied in hushed tones into her ear while his nose tickled from the fur of her sable hat, "Will we be OK? Or should I walk over and have them move, Countess?"

Feeling her knees get weak at his closeness, her womanliness stirring, she smiled at his sensual use of her title and almost silently answered, "No we will be fine. Let's hurry."

She grabbed his gloved hand from her waist and led him the last 100 meters hand-in-hand until they arrived at the elevated hunting stand built into a small grove of oak trees and brush. A stand had been in this location for as long as hunting had been conducted on this land, Matt's experienced eye could see. Its location on a slight ridge with a 180-degree view of the open fields and small bush- and tree-filled thickets along the babbling brook made it an ideal place for spotting wildlife. Even in the dark, Matt could make out the distant black forms of three wild boars rooting up the newly planted winter wheat field. The four rungs of the steep stairs leading up to the enclosed 2-meter by 3-meter blind had a brown metal railing to hold on to. Matt waited for the countess to climb up them and open the door. He then handed her his unloaded rifle and she placed it safely in the gun rack before reaching for her own unloaded weapon that he held up to her. Matt climbed quietly into the stand behind her, placing the rucksack on the floor between the two comfortable chairs, and then turned back and latched the door shut. Pamela slid the interior lock off the wooden window cover at the front of the blind, allowing a small amount of moonlight to light up the otherwise pitch-black interior of the hunting stand. Matt then did the same to the window cover in front of him. On a shelf behind them were several woolen blankets. Pamela handed one to Matt, and then grabbed two for herself. As she tucked herself into the padded chair she gently slid the chair over so it was touching Matt's without making any sounds that might scare away the game. Getting the hint Matt laid his blanket over the two of their laps and smiled a dimpled grin at her in the dark.

"Now, we will be warmer while we wait," she whispered, gazing up into his eyes.

"Oh yes, much better. How long till shooting is legal?" he questioned.

"Does it matter?" she asked, leaning in, softly putting her hand on his chin and drawing his face to hers. Matt met her passionate kiss with one of his own. Her lips were soft and warm and full and needing as he explored her sensuous mouth. It was as if some unseen power had been unleashed upon the two of them, the power to give everything they had into one long kiss, to release from each other the pent up frustrated lust they both craved. Their cold noses soon became hot before they broke apart to catch their breath

"Mon cheri," the countess whispered, as she stared into Matt's blue eyes, visible even in the dim light.

"Oh baby," Matt chuckled back, shaking his head in wonderment of the situation, then leaning back into her and changing his position so he could get a better angle on the chairs as he began kissing her once more, their tongues meeting in frenzied desire.

Pamela couldn't believe what she was doing with this man—a stranger until yesterday, but a real man with whom she felt some kind of connection. And now she knew just how badly she missed having a man, a man to share her passion, and she had a tidal wave of it built up she realized. She slid her hand onto Matt's crotch, brazenly stroking him through his pants while he did the same fumbling with the zippers and buttons of her awkward layered hunting clothes. The two of them could not even separate long enough to undress in an organized fashion, they just kept up the fiery embrace while at the same time struggling to rid themselves of the layers of garments, their passion boiling over in the morning's chill.

CHAPTER 24

THE SNIPER WAS NOT HAPPY WITH THE SETUP HE FACED. IT wasn't the fact that the target was 400 meters away—for him that distance was a chip shot. He could put three rounds in a golf ball from that distance in five seconds. He had a solid rest in a well-camouflaged position in the tree-lined thicket along the brook. The other three former Bosnian soldiers were still creeping along the tree line in the darkness, trying to shorten the distance to the elevated hunting stand so they could follow up on his shot if it was needed and to confirm his kill. What he didn't like about this setup was that he was going to have to make a shot through the 25-centimeter-high open window in the hunting stand at the target's head. He had been told in the pre-attack meeting that this blind would have bigger openings where he could see the target as it moved around inside. With this setup the sniper would have only a few fleeting moments to nail the Slovak bastard when his head appeared in the small opening. The first shot would be easy, but the second one could be extremely difficult. If he failed, then it would be up to the other three men to sort it out. The General's goal was to get the shots off at dawn and get out of there before full light. That way, anyone hearing the shots from his Remington would think it was simply one of the guests shooting a stag or boar. The Bosnians would all be gone from the property long before anyone knew what was really happening. It was a perfect plan.

Watching the wraithlike fog lift from the field, waiting patiently for shooting light, the sniper wished that they would have arrived at the estate much earlier in the morning. They had taken a wrong turn on the unfamiliar country road and had approached the field an hour later then they should have. The sniper was the only one of this crew who was still a professional; the others worked at a variety of odd jobs for the General these days, busting heads, roughing up potential rivals, doing the goon jobs the General required in his new line of work. They were out of condition and not the fighting machines they used to be when they were gallantly defending themselves and their villages against the dreaded Serbians. He didn't remember now exactly how many Serbs he had personally killed from rooftops and tree stands and other secretive positions during the war, more Serbs by far than Croats, far too many to remember each and every one. Civilians, as in this mission, were usually a piece of cake because they typically had no idea they were about to die; so he was relaxed but still not pleased with the setup.

Looking through his high-powered rifle scope he did not yet see anyone in the stand through the two open windows. The wooden covers had been lowered so he knew someone had to be inside. He saw the blind move back and forth a couple of times, perched as it was on its four legs it was not totally stable, but no face had showed yet to look out through the glass for wild game.

"Maybe the lazy Slovak pig is sleeping, or maybe he's fucking the Spanish bitch. It will be the last time he does either," the sniper thought, patiently waiting for dawn to provide him with enough light to complete his mission.

He looked at his watch and then toward where the other men would be hiding by now, thinking, *"Five more minutes and it's all over Ivanowich, you prick."*

CHAPTER 25

MATT ROLLED OVER, PULLING TWO MORE BLANKETS OFF THE shelf above him in the process and laying them gently over the countess's half-naked body, lying in a jumbled heap of coats and sweaters on the floor of the stand. The temperature inside the blind was still almost as cold as outside but the two of them were soaked with sweat from the past half-hour's frenzied lovemaking. Pamela reached up and pulled his head down to her breast where he laid it softly, listening to her breathing and rapid heartbeat.

"That was unbelievable," Matt said, forgetting to whisper but not really caring.

"You are a wonderful lover Matt, really fantastic," she answered, then paused for a few seconds before continuing, "I'm sure you will now always think of me as some sex-starved tart. I apologize but you must understand . . ."

Matt smiled, interrupting her by saying, "No, I wanted it more than you, trust me."

"I don't think that is possible, my darling," she said. Looking at the window above them she sighed, "I could lie here all day or, better yet, make love once more, but people may wonder why we are not shooting at something. The guide will be coming to check on us to make sure we are all right if he doesn't see us in here."

As much as he didn't want to, Matt got the point and knew she was right. He rose up on his knees, but as she tried to get up and put her clothes on he leaned forward pinning her down and ran his tongue from her navel up to her lips.

"OK, let's get to hunting, Countess. We wouldn't want to start any rumors now, would we?" He joked, letting her up and gathering his clothes and putting them back on while she discreetly did the same while facing away from him. Matt stood upright and stretched his lower back, remembering he wasn't 20 years old anymore and glanced out the window, the rosy emergence of dawn giving him plenty of light to see the big nine point stag feeding in the field with six hinds following him. Two big male boars with three sows and a passel of piglets trotted toward the center of the field while he watched. Matt turned slightly to tell the countess what he saw, but dropped his belt in the process, quickly leaning down and grabbing for it as it hit the wooden floor of the blind. Just as he did, the Plexiglas window shattered and the wood at the back side of the stand, right where his head had been one second earlier, exploded sending shards of shattered wood flying wildly around the insides of the stand.

"What the . . . !" Came out of Matt's mouth just as he heard the report of a rifle from somewhere on the other side of the field.

The countess cursed at the shot, "Some damn idiot missed something and hit our blind? Has to be that son of a bitchin' Greek. He wouldn't know a stag from a cow." She pulled on her coat, getting madder by the minute.

"Stay down please in case he's not done, Countess."

She got to her feet to look out the window while Matt buckled his belt, raving, "Where is he, he's not even supposed to be over there, the bastard. Bloody Greeks! I'm telling you they don't listen when they are told . . ."

"Ahhhhh!" the countess yelled, spinning around at the sound of the rifle once again and hitting the floor clutching her hands to her neck, blood oozing out from between her fingers. Matt rolled her onto her back to get a good look at the damage and saw that she had been shot on the side of the neck, more than a scratch, but the bullet had luckily not hit the spine. It had cut a swath just centimeters below the surface of her skin. The bullet's impact had been hard enough though that it knocked her unconscious. Confused at first, but now understanding that this was certainly no accidental shooting—not two bullets in a row into the same small windows, they were definitely being shot at—Matt reached for the countess's silk scarf still lying in a heap next to her fur hat and placing a bandana from his pocket on the exit wound, wrapped the scarf tightly around her neck to stem the blood flow to a trickle. It was probably better that she was out for the count, Matt knew as he tied a knot tight enough to hold the makeshift compress in place, but loose enough to let her breath normally. Reaching for his rifle he jacked a shell into the chamber while contemplating the situation. Using an old trick to see if he could draw more fire without getting his head blown off, Matt picked up the countess's fur hat and stuck it on the end of his gun barrel, then lifted it up to the window and held it there for a count of three before another bullet blew the hat off the end of his rifle barrel. He wanted to stay low next to the countess until he took a quick look around the inside of the blind in the emerging light and realized how precarious their situation really was. The only door, their only means of escape was to his right and would be easily seen when he opened it by the person shooting at them. The windows in the back of the blind were all far too small for him to slip through.

"Why the hell is someone shooting at us? Why does this shit happen to me? I wonder who the countess has made into such an enemy," Matt thought, looking down at the still unconscious countess. Reality told him he had to do something and it better be quickly because they were sitting ducks, trapped as they were in this wooden blind. If he could get back to the truck or get the guide's attention and have him drive over he might have a chance. The guide would not be coming their way soon though Matt remembered, because the countess had told him to stay where he was until she came back to the truck and got him.

"Surely he must hear the shots, but he probably thinks someone is just shooting at some boar."

If he could get to cover away from the blind he would have a chance to fight back and draw fire away from the countess. Remaining calm, feeling as if time was slowing down, like the world was moving in slow motion and he could analyze the situation in a methodical crystal clear way, a plan began to percolate. Staying low so the shooter couldn't see his movements in the blind, Matt got his feet underneath him and leaned against the door. He would have to hope that the shooter would be focused on the windows and not the door and when the door swung open toward where the shots came from Matt would be shielded by the plywood for a nano second until he landed on the bottom step and lunged into the cover of the trees. The brief time it took the shooter to reposition the rifle was all he would hopefully need.

"This might just work," he thought while he took three deep breaths and slowly unlatched the door making sure no movement of the door would alert his enemy, then pushing with his left shoulder, the rifle in his right hand, he swiftly swung open the door.

A bullet smashed through the plywood just behind his head as he leapt down the length of the stairs hitting the soft dirt at the bottom, diving into the brush and finding safety behind three ancient oak trees. Crawling forward to get behind a fallen tree he took a chance and raised his head above the log to see where the sniper was shooting from. He had enough branches and leaves in front of his face to offer a good deal of cover while he scoured the opposing edges of the field for any signs of movement. Searching the far side of the plowed field he was surprised when he saw movement only 100 meters off to his right along the tree-lined brook. That was not where the shots had come from. That meant there must be more than one shooter.

Matt felt the odds slip, no longer in his favor when out from the cover of the creek bottom, crouched over and hustling across the field toward the blind, came three armed men in camouflage, submachine guns held out menacingly in front of them. Matt knew he only had one choice and that was to stop them where they were and not let them get any closer. Distance was his friend when his adversaries were armed with rapid fire, but inaccurate machine guns. Matt used the log he was hiding behind as a rest, found an opening in the bushes to fire through and squeezed off his first round when the lead man showed clear. He intentionally aimed low to hit the assassin in the legs, the 160-grain 7mm solid copper bullet breaking the man's left leg mid-thigh and sending him spinning to the ground, screaming out in pain.

The other two men were now caught out in the open field and had no clue where the shot had come from that hit their comrade, but retaliated by opening fire with their AK47s at the blind, riddling it with holes. Matt worked the bolt on his hunting rifle and realizing he had to respond with brute force now, no more wounding and shot the man closest to the blind squarely in the chest, a fist-sized hole appearing on his back where the expansion bullet exited after taking out the would be assassin's heart and most of his lungs. Blood splattered onto the one remaining shooter who smartly dove to the ground, rolling toward where Matt lay tucked behind the log, sending another burst of bullets in his direction.

Matt saw that the man had spotted him when he shot but ducked quick enough behind the tree before the spray of automatic weapon fire splintered the rotten log to pieces. Matt slipped two more rounds into the magazine while he lay hidden, then jacked another bullet into the rifle's chamber. The shooter caught out in the open in a suicidal position suddenly lost his nerve and jumped up, sprinting back toward the shelter of the trees along the creek, while flipping the banana clip magazine of his AK over and clicking a fresh one taped upside down to it into place. He slid the bolt back, letting it slide hard into place before twisting around and spraying Matt's hiding place with another volley of bullets to cover his retreat.

Matt crawled forward to a different location five meters farther away where he could take another shot, but when he cautiously peered over the top of the log he was too late, the shooter had already made the cover of the woods. Matt watched him running in a zigzag pattern, realizing now that the man had plenty of military experience by the way he covered his retreat. Matt tried a running shot at the shooter anyway, his shot grazing a scrub oak tree, peeling bark off it, barely missing. He watched another man Matt assumed was the original shooter join up with the escaping assassin, and they shortly disappeared into the woods.

The first man he had shot still yelled out in pain in a foreign language Matt could not understand as he lay bleeding profusely in the field clutching at his leg with both hands. Matt heard a vehicle speeding toward him from the direction he and the countess had walked in from, relieved when he saw that it was the gamekeeper driving full speed toward him in the Range Rover. Matt stood up quickly; jumping out from behind the tree, then ran directly at the wounded man, rifle ready to shoot if he tried to defend himself. The assassin's AK was lying two meters away from him, allowing Matt time to get to it and kick it even farther away. The heavy-set bearded shooter had tears running down his cheeks and quit jabbering when he saw that Matt had him cornered. Matt stood menacingly over him with the 7MM aimed perfectly between his eyes. The would be assassin looked at the blood pooled next to his shattered thigh then up at Matt's cold deadly face.

The Bosnian had seen and been the cause of plenty of death during the wars, and by the tremendous amount of blood still spurting from his severed femoral artery he knew he had only minutes to live. Matt stared at the leg realizing the same thing; the man was going to bleed completely out in a matter of moments. The Bosnian regained his dignity and stared at Matt, studying his face and then it dawned on him that the man he was looking at was not their intended target. The gang of killers had all studied Ivan Tatra's photos to make sure they killed the right guy, but somehow things had gotten screwed up. This man had longish grey hair not jet black, no goatee and did not look anything like the target. He could barely keep his eyes open now as darkness took over his brain, he was going to die and his final words hissed out of his mouth when Matt bent down close to him, "No Ivan? No Tatra? No?"

Matt heard the words but they made no sense to him at the moment. It was all over a moment later when the assassin's head lolled over to one side, his hollow cold eyes staring into space, the last steamy breath escaping in a rush from his spittle edged mouth.

The gamekeeper's Range Rover skidded to a stop at the edge of the field next to the blind. He jumped out; yelling in Hungarian and

Matt couldn't understand him. Matt ran over to him grabbing him by the arm to haul him up the stairs of the blind where he showed him the countess lying on the floor. Matt made sign language to show the guide to get on his two-way portable radio and call for help saying to him, "Doctor, doctor!"

The guide understood and jumped down and ran back to the SUV, snatched a Motorola radio off the front seat then proceeded to excitedly let everyone listening on the system know what was happening. From the top rung Matt first heard, and then saw a silver BMW SUV moving fast through the trees less than a kilometer away, escaping from the direction where the first sniper shots had come from. He turned to look behind him and seeing another one of the countess's matching Range Rovers high-balling down the dirt road toward them, he jumped to the ground, ran to the guide's Rover, pushed him out of the way and threw his rifle into the passenger seat before he slammed the transmission into drive and sped off across the field after the escaping Beamer.

The Rover's all-wheel drive system kicked in automatically giving Matt plenty of traction across the loose soil of the young winter wheat field. Matt swore at himself that he hadn't grabbed his rucksack from the blind with his cell phone in it as he rounded the far edge of the field, loose dirt flying in a wave behind him, ecstatic that a small wooden post and wire gate showed him where the field road led off the plowed portion and into another fallow field of dew-covered grass. The wire gate snapped like twine when the grill of the Rover hit it at 90 kilometers an hour, the posts scraping down the polished metal sides of the vehicle before they broke away.

All the crop fields at the countess's estate were surrounded by groves of trees offering shelter and food for the wildlife, and now giving Matt some cover to try and catch up to the guys who had shot at him, but the trees also forced him to have to follow the two track roads paralleling them since he couldn't short-cut across the fields without running into another row of impassable trees. The driver of the BMW knew what he was doing; he was an experienced driver Matt could tell, watching the vehicle slide gracefully around each obstacle it encountered. The BMW approached a small wooden bridge crossing a wide irrigation canal where the banks of the canal rose a meter above the fields on each side and without slowing down climbed the bank at full speed and jumped over the bridge, landing hard on the other side but speeding unhindered onward.

Matt was closing on them now. He had made good time crossing the open grass field and was within 200 meters of the shooters when he saw two of the men in the backseat looking back toward him and wildly gesturing at the driver to let him know they were being followed. The man on the passenger side rolled his window down, stuck his shoulders and arms out so that he was facing backwards and let loose a burst of AK47 rounds at Matt's Rover. The first burst missed Matt completely, the shooter not having much chance at that distance firing from a bouncing vehicle going 100 kilometers an hour down the rough road. Steering the Range Rover slightly to the left so the shooter on the right wouldn't have a clean shot at him gave Matt some safety but was slowing his pursuit down since he only had one tire in the road, the other running in the open field. The 120-kilometer speed they were now traveling at was insane for the conditions. All it would take was one pothole or muddy spot and the vehicles would be out of control.

The shooter fired several more blasts, getting lucky when one of the rounds hit Matt's windscreen, shattering the passenger side section into tiny diamond like chunks of glass that flew onto the front bucket seat. The hunting rifle on the front seat was useless to Matt since it required two hands to work the bolt and shoot it, so all he could do was avoid the incoming rounds as best he could and keep gaining ground. What he was going to do once he caught up to the BMW had yet to occur to him, but he flew after them in a vengeful rage anyway. Perhaps pent-up fury or a chance to get even drove him crazily onward, gaining on the SUV when it had to slow down and take a sharp right turn toward the paved county road.

The shooter hanging out the window now had a clear shot at the Rover, but just as he squeezed the trigger, the BMW hit a deep pothole that smashed the shooter into the door's window frame, painfully forcing him to drop the machine gun onto the road. Matt was tempted to stop and grab it but he was closing fast when he made the same turn, barely avoiding the same pothole the BMW had hit. He was less than 25 meters behind now, pushing the gas pedal all the way to the floor in a suicidal race to catch the bouncing, fleeing vehicle. The passenger in the backseat on the driver's side had his window rolled down now, the first shooter appearing to be out of commission, bent over and clutching at his side where he had surely broken several ribs when they hit the pothole and he dropped the AK.

Rather than hang out the window as his partner had, the second shooter simply stuck the barrel of his weapon out the window and let go with a blast of bullets at Matt's SUV. Matt saw the move coming, swerving to the right to avoid the onslaught. Closing even tighter he was within 10 meters when the BMW took a sudden hard left onto a small bridge crossing the same canal they had a crossed a few minutes earlier. The abrupt turn caught Matt off guard; he was not going to be able to make the same turn onto the wooden bridge, so he aimed the front bumper of the Rover at the left rear tire of the BMW, smashing into it, forcing it into a slide and tipping it up onto the two right-side wheels. The Bosnian driver kept it balanced precariously on the bridge, struggling to keep the car from rolling over at high speed across the rickety wooden farm bridge. The BMW driver managed to make it to the other side, balancing on two wheels until the SUV slammed back onto all four tires and continued on its way across the muddy field to the paved road at the end of it.

Matt was not so lucky. At the speed he was going when he hit the rear corner of the BMW, he had no time to compensate and make the sharp turn onto the short bridge and Matt was completely out of control when the Rover launched over the bank of the canal. As Matt flew helplessly through the air, time seemed to slip into slow motion again. He was fully aware of what was happening, it was like a dream sequence where he knew he was not going to make the other side of the canal and the Rover was twisting on to its right side as it sailed heavy through the air. Suddenly the elegantly sculptured SUV was nothing more than a shiny and very expensive steel missile.

"I guess this is how it finally ends," he thought living in slow motion. "*Damn I'm not ready to go quite yet. I've got so much more to do in this life.*"

The last thing that went through Matt's mind before the SUV crashed into the far bank was an angelic vision of his baby boy smiling up at him from his crib, reaching out for him.

CHAPTER 26

FOUR DAYS OF UNCONSCIOUSNESS MAKE DOCTORS WORRY that maybe the patient has slipped into a long-term coma, after which they have no idea how long the patient could be out of commission. The human body will quite often shut down various parts it doesn't need in order to heal the damaged ones after massive trauma, so the Hungarian doctors kept their hopes up that their American patient would come back to a conscious state when his mind and body were ready, but there was nothing more they could do for him except be patient and let him heal on his own. Nothing was broken as far as bones went, but Matt was covered with a variety of deep purple and reddish bruises and had slammed his head hard into something in the vehicle. The doctors were positive he had massive internal bruising and a major concussion, but no signs of internal bleeding had showed up on the scans they ran on him. The doctors would have to determine the full extent of his injuries once he woke up and his bodily functions tried to get back into a normal routine. They did all they could for him with their limited equipment that dated back to the Soviet occupation days, but there was not much they could do except keep him stable.

Caitlin sat at Matt's bedside, just as she had for the last four days, hoping and praying the same thing. It had occurred to her that perhaps she should have Matt evacuated to another more modern facility somewhere else, but her contacts back in the U.S. had told her, after reviewing Matt's medical records, that the Hungarian doctors were doing all that they would, so it was better not to take a chance moving him at this point. Zumbula sat in the opposite corner of the room, facing the door, acting as a guard, out of habit, just in case. He and

Caitlin rarely spoke to each other the last few days; he just sat stone-like waiting for his friend to waken.

Caitlin had spoken with her CIA handlers in Washington, D.C., while she waited and filled them in on what had happened the day of the shooting.

Agent Anderson had found it humorous when she first told him that Matt Simmons was involved, chuckling as he responded, "That son of a bitch is a magnet for trouble. What the hell was he doing there to start with? Does he know what you are up to, why you are there?"

"No, I haven't told him anything yet. Should I? The tracker from the CAR, Zumbula, is here also."

"Wow, that's kind of strange. I don't think it would do any good to let him in on anything yet; he won't be able to help us considering how messed up he is. I'll pull his file just in case though. What is our friend Ivan up to? Did he leave the estate?"

"Oh yes, he flew out on his helicopter that afternoon after the shooting, the minute he heard about it. It's as if he knows the shooters were not intentionally going after the countess or Matt, especially when the dead guys were identified as Bosnians by the police who showed up to investigate."

"Why didn't you go with him and keep an eye on him?" Agent Anderson quizzed her.

Caitlin hesitated, knowing she should have gone but not wanting to leave Matt alone in the hospital, she lied.

"He took off without inviting me along. He was in a big panic when he heard what happened. I think he has had more than one run-in with these guys before. He was definitely rattled by the whole affair. We should maybe dig deeper into the whole Bosnian connection with him and see where that leads. Something is fishy in the way he overreacted to the shooting. I'm telling you, he knew those shots were meant for him."

"I'm sure you are right. None of the other guests are likely targets, the countess has very few enemies, no one knows Matt over there, so I'm sure with all we know about the sandwich king, he must have been the target, but how could they have mistaken him for Matt? I've got a man inside working with the Hungarian police and as soon as we get more info on the dead Bosnians, I'll research any connections. Doesn't Ivan have restaurants in Bosnia, if I remember correctly?" he asked, shuffling through the papers in the file on his desk.

"Yes, he does, or rather he did. I'm pretty sure he closed them down a month or so ago, though. I'll confirm it."

"OK, maybe there is something there. Why would he close them all down? I'll check it out, and you do the same on your end. Say hi to Matt when he wakes up. No, I'm just kidding, don't say anything to him yet. Let's see how he comes out of it. You better make contact with Ivan today and see what he's up to; this might be the missing piece of the puzzle we couldn't figure out. If he's in bed or was in bed with the Bosniak, he is in way over his head. Those guys are a nasty bunch of clowns, with a chip still on their shoulder from the war. Stay close to him but you be careful, kid."

"Righto," Caitlin replied, hanging up and feeling a little embarrassed that she had stuck with Matt at the hospital instead of staying close to Tatra as she had been ordered to do. She had for once let her emotions override her typically tough Irish resolve.

"I can always renew the relationship with the sandwich king later in the week," she reasoned, when she noticed that Matt was suddenly stirring in the hospital bed next to her for the first time.

She stood up and gently wiped a cold wet cloth across his bruised and skinned-up forehead, quietly reassuring him, "Matt, can you hear me? It's Caitlin. Everything is OK. I'm here with you. You're safe."

Matt's blackened eyes slowly opened a fraction. He squinted at the bright hospital room lighting, blinked his eyes a couple of times, then closed them and made a small smile. He tried to say something, but his tongue felt like it was too big for his dry mouth. His lips moved but only a hoarse grunt emitted from his throat when he tried to communicate. Caitlin held a glass of ice water up to his face, placing the straw sticking out of it between Matt's lips, encouraging him to take a sip of water. Joyously, Caitlin watched when he responded, sipping softly at the fluid, before slowly opening his eyes halfway once more.

"You want me to turn the lights down? Are they hurting your eyes?"

Matt nodded in agreement, so Zumbula walked over to the entrance door and flicked off the light switches, leaving only the daylight from the window to illuminate the hospital room. With less overhead light Matt could open his eyes more, smiling a crooked grin at Caitlin, his eyes as focused and blue as ever, taking her breath away.

She smiled back at him, leaning forward to whisper with her flowery Irish accent into his ear, "You had me worried there for a minute, laddie. I thought I might have to slap you around a wee bit to make you snap out of it."

She kissed his cheek, feeling warm all over when he responded by doing the same to her when she tried to pull away, and he simply whispered, "Thank you."

Zumbula stood in the corner, simply nodding at Matt when their eyes met, an acknowledgment that he was there making sure everything would be all right.

The head nurse walked into the room just then, interrupting their reunion, and said in broken but intelligible English, "You wake finally, hello. I am nurse, I call doctor." She fussed over him, rearranging the bed, smiling the whole time, and with Caitlin's help propped Matt up, stuffing another pillow behind his head.

"You drink water. I bring you ice." Looking over at Caitlin she continued, "You be nurse until I return, yes?"

Caitlin smiled warmly and said she would be glad to and the nurse left the room in a hurry, returning 10 minutes later with the doctor who ran through a series of tests and checked all Matt's vital signs, reviewed what the monitors were saying on their green-lined screens, and made notes on his clipboard. When the doctor pulled his Matt's hospital gown to the side to inspect his torso, Caitlin noticed that more of Matt was black and blue than not. He had to be in unbelievable pain. The doctor poked around at Matt's sides and legs for five minutes to determine the pain level Matt was at, making Matt wince sharply a couple of times when he touched a bad spot and finally said, in lightly accented English, "I'm sure you hurt all over, but anywhere worse than others?"

"Kind of sore all over, doc," Matt replied.

"It looks to me that you have some severe bruising and a couple of cracked ribs to go with your concussion. I would like you to spend another two or three days here under observation to make sure you have no internal injuries we have not discovered. We will get an MRI set up and another full body scan tomorrow afternoon. If you need anything for pain, just ask the nurse here and she will get what you need. I want to leave you on the IV until tomorrow afternoon and keep your fluid levels up."

The doctor turned to the nurse and gave her instructions in Hungarian, then smiled back at Matt and said, "Please rest and I will see you tomorrow after lunch. I am glad to see you are conscious. You had me worried for a couple days—these car accidents and injuries kill most people. You are a lucky man."

"Thanks, doc," Matt whispered, his throat still dry and hoarse. The nurse followed the doctor out of the room, leaving Zumbula and Caitlin alone with Matt.

"How is the countess?" Matt asked Caitlin.

"She is fine; she's back at the estate with lots of security around. The bullet just grazed her and didn't hit anything vital. Some muscle damage but she will be OK. I think some plastic surgeon is going to make a lot of money fixing the scar on her neck though. How much do you remember of what happened?"

Matt let his mind focus for a few seconds, ran the events around, and figured they were in order then answered, "The last thing I remember is the Rover flying through the air and then crashing. I remember the guys shooting at us when we were in the blind. I think I recall everything up till the crash."

"You did some shooting of your own. Do you recall that?"

"Sure, but they were shooting at us, and they had wounded the countess. What else could I have done?"

"I know. I heard the whole tale from the countess. She's quite enamored with you by the way and is telling everyone, especially the police, that you saved her life. You are the hero of Hungary this week, Mister Simmons."

Ignoring the joking sarcasm, Matt questioned Caitlin as all the events started coming back to him in clear detail, "Why the hell were they shooting at her to start with? Anyone answered that question yet? 'Cause I don't get it."

Caitlin remembered her conversation with the CIA earlier and lied, "The authorities think it was a case of mistaken identity, that maybe the shooters were after someone else. The police and Countess Atwood can't come up with a motive for someone to kill her. Kidnap her for ransom sure, but these guys were shooting to kill from what the countess said, and kidnapping is very uncommon in Hungary. It's not like we are in Mexico or something. What do you think?"

Matt considered the overall situation for a few minutes before replying, "This was not an attempt at a kidnapping. The sniper was very good from that distance. We were just very lucky, I think, that he didn't kill us both."

"Lucky that the countess was just putting her clothes back on," Matt thought deciding to leave that part of the story unsaid, since he assumed the countess would have left that part of the event out as well when she told the authorities what had happened.

Matt got his elbows under himself and tried to ease up on the bed, stopping short when a searing pain ran over his broken ribs, taking his breath away.

"Aghhhh, whoa," he cried, lying slowly back down.

"You should rest now, you need to heal up," Caitlin said.

"I'll be all right. I just need some pain pills. Where's my clothes?" he asked, looking around the hospital room.

"They had to cut them off you, you were a mess."

"Do me a favor and bring me some tomorrow morning, will you? I have to get out of here."

"You will still be here a couple more days, doctor's orders, I'm afraid. You heard him."

"No way. If you don't get me some clothes, I'll have to escape from here naked and that might cause a stir, eh?"

Caitlin giggled, happy Matt's humor was back.

"So where is your boyfriend, Ivan, or whatever his name was? Is he at the countess's place still? Was there any other shooting? Who were the guys I shot, did they ID them yet?"

"Whoa, easy Matt, one step at a time. The two guys were Bosniak, Muslim Bosnians, some former soldiers is all we know. No one else was shot at. Ivan Tatra went back to Slovakia the afternoon of the shooting, and I haven't heard from him since. The police found the getaway car abandoned near the Croatian border. They figure they ditched it and were hauled through Croatia in a different vehicle back to Bosnia, assuming they were all Bosnians."

Matt lay silently soaking the story up wondering before asking, "What would they want here? I don't get it. If the countess had no interaction with Bosnians, and I sure as hell don't, why would someone want to shoot us?"

Caitlin wished she had the answer for him but didn't, "I don't know Matt. Who knows? I'm sure the police will be looking into it. They want to talk to you and get your side of the story."

Looking at her watch she continued, "I'm going to go now and let you get some rest. You stay put until I come back tomorrow morning, you hear?" She turned to look at Zumbula standing with his arms across his chest, statuesque in the corner telling him, "Will you stay here and keep an eye on our lad, Zumbula?"

"The patron will be OK. I will stay."

Caitlin wanted to tell Zumbula to go back to the estate and freshen up and sleep in a bed but knew it was useless. She leaned in and kissed Matt gently on the lips then whispered, "I'll let everyone know you are OK, and I will see you tomorrow morning. Do you want me to bring you anything besides clothes?"

Matt stared back into her emerald green eyes replying, "No, but thanks anyhow."

Caitlin gave Zumbula a hug as she walked toward the door, waving to Matt as the door closed behind her. Zumbula watched Matt after she left the room, marveling that he was so alert after almost dying in the car wreck four days earlier, watching the wheels turning in his head and sizing up the situation. After 10 minutes of silence, Matt began to nod off, so Zumbula walked over to sit in the chair next to his bed for the first time, reaching over and grasping Matt's hand dangling on the edge of the hospital bed. He felt a firm squeeze of acknowledgment from Matt before his friend eventually fell into a deep healing slumber that his tattered body still required.

ZUMBULA WOKE FROM his own sleep slumped in the chair next to Matt four hours later. He stood up and stretched and, seeing that Matt was still sleeping soundly, decided to walk down to the lobby to catch a taxi back to the countess's estate where he could clean up and grab a small bag with a clean set of clothes for Matt and himself, because he knew that when the morning dawned, Matt would be leaving the hospital, one way or the other and he was sure that Caitlin would not bring all the accessories that they were going to need.

CHAPTER 27

IT WAS 1:00 IN THE MORNING, A COOLING BREEZE WAFTING IN from the Adriatic Sea onto the rickety pier protruding from the only Bosnian port city of Neum, where General Afan Badzak stood, the collar of his black wool coat pulled up around his neck against the wind. He personally and very cautiously supervised the unloading of his precious cargo from the rusty tramp steamer that had just arrived right on schedule. The ubiquitous ship had just finished a long circuitous route after its initial cargo had been taken on in Bushehr, Iran. The raw opium delivery came packaged in small yellow waterproof bales. An entire multimillion-dollar shipment like this one would all fit in the back of a Toyota pickup truck; however the entire ship had been chartered to bring it to Bosnia. After the opium was carried off the ship to the waiting trucks, enough one-kilo marijuana bales to fill four pallets two meters high by one meter wide were then unloaded onto the pier from a secret hatch below the waterline, ready to be distributed to the assigned trucks that would carry them far and wide throughout Europe. The rest of the legitimate cargo space on the rust bucket of a boat was filled with a large heavy shipment of Turkish travertine stone cut into half-meter-square pieces, six centimeters thick, picked up in Istanbul on the way to Bosnia. The General had a sale for the travertine to a broker before it had even departed Turkey along with all the documentation paperwork to prove it just in case the ship was delayed by an overanxious customs boat crew as the ship passed through various nations' sovereign waters in the Mediterranean. The statistical odds of that happening were slim to none considering the thousands of small ships that plied the Mediterranean and Adriatic Seas every day; however, the General was thorough if nothing else.

The risk of shipping the lucrative drugs around Europe was greatly diminished once the small bales were dispersed at the dock in Neum. Being the only tiny port carved out of Croatian coastline that Bosnia had been granted when the boundaries of the Balkan states were redrawn, he was able to utilize a variety of modes of transportation from Neum to the rest of Europe. The carriers of his precious goods were always trusted workers of Afan's and could be relied upon to perform as instructed, no questions asked. Most had been soldiers working directly for him during the war and their loyalty was unquestionable. The fact that he had lost two of his best men in the failed killing of the Slovak Tatra in Hungary last week still rankled him and made his life even more difficult and dangerous than it already was. Another huge irritation was that now he didn't even have Ivanowich trucks to use for shipping his cargoes. He had yet to replace the two trusted men who were killed, and had to resort to some new staff. He had to be cautious in his line of work; he could not simply run an advertisement in the newspaper looking for a new employee willing to do drug smuggling and the occasional killing as part of a job description. It took time to groom his forces, to test them in lesser duties but today he was running out of time.

His blood boiled just thinking about the losses as he supervised the ship's Lebanese mates. Walking the length of the small pier in silence, the captain of the vessel approached him, quietly asking, "What shall we do with the women?"

"We will deal with them after the other product is gone. I have three trucks they will go in. Separate them so there are not too many who speak the same language—it makes for fewer escape attempts if they can't communicate with each other."

"Already done General."

"How do they look? Have you been keeping an eye on them?" Afan asked with a wry smirk on his face.

"We did as instructed: they are well fed, they beg for their daily dose of heroin, and they are all young and beautiful. They have been locked up below deck. Four or five have been seasick a lot of the voyage, but I think they will be fine and put some weight back on now."

"You kept your crew out of their cabins I trust? I don't need ruined goods when I hand them off to their new owners."

"Yes, of course, sir," the captain lied. He had made sure his guys only had a short time with the girls every few days and the sailors knew they were under the threat of death if they roughed any of the women up, but the truth was he could not keep his crew happy when they knew there were future whores on board and that they were having to feed and dope up the women every day and yet were expected to receive no *reward*. The women were always turned into heroin addicts as soon as they were abducted; this made them much easier to handle as well as much more complacent. The captain was not a fool, he had done this before, but he was very careful with his charges.

"Good. I will get the first truck to take some girls down here onto the dock in a few minutes."

The delivery trucks sat idling at the entrance to the pier in the cool darkness, exhaust swirling up from the tailpipes giving the whole scene an eerie effect as if the darkness was waiting to take the women's lives and have them vanish into the vapors, gone forever. In a matter of weeks they would have no identity, no names, no background, no home, and no soul. Everything including their dignity would be in the hands of the pimps who would be selling their bodies on the back streets of Europe's finest cities. The smart girls would quickly learn to play the game and cooperate, dress up, wear the makeup, perform for the johns as if they enjoyed it. The dumb ones or the ones with indomitable spirits that couldn't be easily broken into submission would be beaten, starved, brutally raped, and sent to the more despicable clients whose cravings went far beyond basic sex. The perps needed victims to satisfy their wanton lust and were willing to pay mightily for the sadistic opportunity. The General didn't care what happened to them, it was not for him to judge society's foibles; they were just foreign girls from faraway places who seemed to be in unlimited supply and the demand for them never ceased—it never had for hundreds of years and it never would as far as he was concerned.

The trucks he would be utilizing tonight had been modified in the last few days to hold four girls crammed into a secretive small space in the cargo area behind the cab. Up until last week he had been utilizing Ivanowich trucks that had been modified months ago for the same purpose, but those vehicles were never returning to Bosnia again. From the outside, the alterations couldn't be seen, other than a small air vent that was common in most commercial vehicles. To access the hidden area from the inside of the cargo bay, all the legitimate shipment would have to be unloaded and an astute person would have to discern the erratic screw pattern on the rear-facing aluminum panel to see how the mobile prison was accessed. Bottled water and some crackers along with two blankets each were placed in the compartment with the girls, however they usually were too high from the drugs they were injected with right before they were loaded to eat or drink anything for the next 10–12 hours. By the time they sobered up they would be safely handed over to their new masters.

The whole network that had been developed with the Ivanowich trucks and distribution centers that had his people inside the company and running it was now gone, so Afan was improvising—this time. He had no other choice.

The General's cell phone rang, startling him at this hour. He looked at the glowing readout and answered when he recognized the number, "Yes."

"The American is awake; he is still in the hospital. He has a Negro with him all the time, guarding him. What do you want us to do?"

"We must not do anything foolish this time around. Even though he was not who we thought he was, he owes us now for killing your brother and Ahmed, I should say. Any police guarding the hospital?"

"They come and go but they do not have anyone permanently stationed there. Just give me the order and the deed will be done, General."

Afan smiled knowing this man would waste no time seeking revenge for the death of his brother. He walked out of hearing distance of the captain of the boat, giving his blessing to the deed, "Kill him when the time is right Faruk, but be careful. Where is that fucking donkey's ass Tatra?"

"Back in Bratislava, he has security constantly around him. He is quite aware, I think, that we are after him. It may take some time for him to relax, but he will pay eventually, it will just take time."

"Yes, be patient. Call me with any changes and do not make a big scene when you dispose of the American. It must be quiet, we don't need another fuck up like at the countess's place."

The voice on the other end of the call hesitated at the not-so-subtle rebuke; it had not been his fault that the now dead informant at the countess's mansion had given them the incorrect information on who was hunting where. Faruk curtly responded, "I understand sir. I will keep you informed of any progress."

General Afan switched the cell phone off and went back to the task of getting all his valuable shipments off the dock and on their way, thinking, *"All of these problems because of Ivan Tatra. That son of a bitch will be sorry one day. Very sorry."*

CHAPTER 28

Caitlin spent the rest of the afternoon and evening after leaving Matt's hospital room researching the Ivanowich chain of stores on her computer and quickly found that he had indeed owned stores in Bosnia but that they were now all closed, according to their website. The change to the website looked new, but no reasons were listed for the closure. She sat in her room mulling the connection and the consequences; she then decided to call Ivan and see what he was up to and arrange another date or dinner, some way to spend more time with him and extract more information out of him. Whether the shooting at the estate was related to him or not did not really matter to her, she was concerned for Matt; however, she was still supposed to be on her mission, trying to find info on his other suspected dastardly doings.

The CIA and Interpol suspected his company, if not Ivan directly, to be somehow tied to drug smuggling and human trafficking, but had little more than rumor to go on. The human trafficking was the crime that had been the catalyst to her joining forces with the CIA in the first place. Human slavery in the twenty-first century was beyond belief for most people, but she had witnessed it firsthand in Sudan when she had been there with Matt. Young women and boys, even in today's so-called civilized era, could still be bought and sold like chattel to be used as sex slaves or in forced labor by unscrupulous people in many parts of the world with no conscience or concern for another human being's right to freedom or how much degradation they were subjected to. It had become her new mission in life to do all she could to eliminate it.

She dialed Ivan's cell phone and was surprised when he answered on the third ring, "Hello Miss O'Shea, how are you and where are you? I've been worried about you."

"I'm fine Ivan; I was just at the hospital checking up on Matt Simmons. It turns out he finally woke up and will be OK in a couple more days, once he heals a little more. Where are you?"

"I am back in Bratislava. It's good to hear he is going to make it. I know people have been worried about him. When can I see you? Our weekend was so unfortunately interrupted by those Bosnian bastards, and I would like to pick up where we left off in a much quieter location than the countess's estate."

Caitlin wondered suspiciously how Ivan knew they were Bosnians already, since it was only speculation as far as she knew, the police had told no one the shooters identities. She was glad that he wanted to still see her, and this slip of the tongue was perfect—he was playing right into her plan. After loosening up his tongue with a few cocktails one night she might be able to weasel some more evidence out of Slovak.

"That sounds super Ivan. I'm coming to Bratislava on Saturday, will that work? I will call on my way and then we can make final plans."

"OK my little Irish princess, but plan on staying for a few days, all right?"

Caitlin shuddered at the implication, but her desire to get to the bottom of what this bastard was up to helped to override her desire to vomit and tell him to go to hell.

"See you then, sweetie," she said hanging up. Caitlin let all of it sink in for a minute before checking her watch to see what time it was in Washington, D.C., and then dialing the number for Agent Anderson, wondering how much she should actually tell him, especially about Matt's plans.

CHAPTER 29

THE TAXI RIDE TOOK JUST OVER AN HOUR TO GET TO THE hunting estate. The driver nervously watched Zumbula in the rear-view mirror, a tall black man with matching scars across both his cheeks was not an everyday occurrence in Hungary, especially at this time in the morning. He was very happy though when the cab pulled up to the main entrance of the country mansion and Zumbula told him through sign language and the little bit of English that the driver understood, that he should wait and give Zumbula a ride back to the hospital in one hour. The driver eased his seat back after his strange passenger had left the car, leaving the engine idling to keep him warm while he waited.

"It is going to be a well-paid night for once." He smiled to himself, resting his head on the headrest and pulling his felt hat over his eyes looking forward to a little shut-eye while the meter continued to run.

The doorman recognized Zumbula as he approached the front door, bounding up the steps two at a time. The door swung open and the doorman spoke to Zumbula in hushed tones, "The countess would like to speak with you if you have news about Mister Simmons."

Zumbula looked up at the antique clock hanging above the mantle, seeing it was nearly 4:00 in the morning. The doorman noticed him looking at the clock and continued, "She said no matter what time, day or night."

"Wake her in forty-five minutes and I will update her. I am going to get cleaned up and change."

"Yes sir, as you wish. Your clothes are pressed and hanging in your room."

"And Mister Simmons kit?"

"Yes, his as well. Will he be returning to us shortly, if I may ask? Any special preparations required for his return, hospital bed, doctors, anything I can help with?"

"No, not yet, but I will call if we need anything. Thank you for all your help."

"My pleasure sir. We are all very grateful to Mister Simmons for saving the countess's life. Miss O'Shea is asleep in her room, do you want me to wake her?"

"No, thank you."

Zumbula turned down the hallway at a lively step, not wanting to dally at the mansion any more than he had to. He slipped out of the clothes he had been wearing for the past four days in the hospital and debated putting them in the trashcan. The shower felt heavenly and he pampered himself with an extra five minutes of letting the warm water work its magic on the back of his neck. After drying off he changed into jeans and a polo shirt, trying his best to fit in, to look like he belonged in civilization, but laughed when he saw his image in the full-length mirror thinking, "*Look at you, oh great warrior. You look like some kind of American now. Where are your robe and spear and sandals? It is time for a battle. I can feel it in my bones, and I should be dressed appropriately for the occasion.*"

Pulling his small Boyt Harness overnight bag from under the bed he packed one extra set of clothes, a heavy coat and his fancy leather knee-high hunting boots. At the last minute before he zipped it closed he had second thoughts, tossing in a pair of gloves, stocking cap, a woolen scarf, and two boxes of ammo for the 7mm rifle. Zumbula did not like the cold at all, longing for Africa while he walked quickly down the hallway to Matt's room where he packed a matching suitcase with Matt's toiletries and two complete sets of clothes similar to the ones he had packed for himself. Propped against the wall was an aluminum gun case covered in a heavy green canvas and leather cover that he twisted the lock's combination numbers into position and opened. Inside he confirmed that Matt's take down rifle and a 12-gauge shotgun were inside, both disassembled to allow the two weapons to fit in the nondescript case. After stuffing two boxes of 12-gauge shotgun shells into Matt's bag and zipping it closed, he walked back down the hall with the three bags and was met at the bottom of the stairs by the doorman.

"Let me take those, sir. The countess is awake and will see you now."

Zumbula left the suitcases and followed the houseman down a sculpted-ceilinged hallway to the double doors leading into the countess's quarters. She sat propped up in her ornately hand-carved king-sized bed, subtle light cascading from crystal wall sconce lights casting a regal look over the entire scene. Zumbula wasn't sure what the protocol was but after the doorman left the room, closing the door behind him, he slowly approached the bed when she bid him, "It's OK. Come here and tell me how Mister Simmons is faring? I understand he is awake. Is he going to be all right, Zumbula?"

Ignoring the doctor's white bandages wound around her neck and amazed at how beautiful she looked, even at this time of the night, he replied, "He will be fine. He's a tough guy, and he has been through worse. How are you feeling Countess Atwood?"

"I will be just fine thanks to Matt, er Mister Simmons, I mean." She felt a little embarrassed using Matt's first name so informally in front of his friend but continued, "The doctors say I am very lucky to be alive. The bullet just missed the artery in my neck." She turned to point at the side of her neck where the bullet had grazed her.

"What did Mister Simmons say? What is he going to do? When can he leave the hospital? I can have him brought here by ambulance and bring in a doctor and nurse as needed if he wants to, or whenever he is capable of moving out of the hospital"

The desperation in her voice was surprising to Zumbula, but he had suspected even on the first night that they had all been together that she was probably under Matt's spell. Knowing Matt as he did, he wouldn't be shocked if the countess and Matt already had something going on, and she was now confirming his earlier suspicions.

"I am on my way back to the hospital now, and I will let you know or have him call you when he wakes again and makes a plan. Will that be all right, Countess? I must go though; I do not like him being alone."

"Of course, please have him call me as soon as he can. I know the police want a report from him also; I have a friend there who will come to the house for the interview if he wants. How are you traveling and getting around?"

"I took a taxi here. He is waiting outside."

"Tell him to go. I will send a car and driver with you instead. Then when you are ready to do whatever you need to do, you will have my people at your disposal to bring you back here." Before Zumbula could respond she had the house phone to her ear and was giving orders in Hungarian to her staff. The doorman entered the bedroom as if on cue, "I will take care of it, Countess. Please follow me Mister Zumbula."

"Get well and hopefully we will see you soon, Countess. Thank you for the vehicle," Zumbula said, turning for the door.

"Bring him safely back to me, Zumbula," she softly said. He didn't respond, but kept focused as he walked out of the house, wondering what next steps Matt may have up his sleeve, but he was pretty sure they did not include the police or coming back to the countess's estate anytime soon.

CHAPTER 30

FARUK'S CELL PHONE RANG, WAKING HIM FROM THE FITFUL nap he was attempting in the backseat of the car he had stolen in Budapest the day before. Parked in a dark back alley only two blocks from the hospital, he answered in Bosnian on the third ring, "Speak."

"The nigger is not in the room. I just checked and he is nowhere to be seen. The duty nurse says he left a couple hours ago."

"Police?"

"None other than the usual useless hospital security."

Faruk hesitated, formulating a plan with the new information he had just been given, "Good. Now in ten minutes I want you to create a diversion that will get everyone's attention one floor below the American, understand? Something that will get the security guy there and give the nurses something to watch. I will be in the room for five minutes, tops."

"Yes, I understand, sir. There is a storage room on that floor, yes that will work just fine. My watch says ten minutes to the hour right now."

"Mine shows the same so I will be in the hallway outside the American's room in ten minutes," Faruk said as he hung up, climbed out of the car and began a quick walk down the poorly lit back streets toward the hospital. He was thankful at this moment that Europe needed so many cheap laborers and Bosnians were all waiting in line to have the work, legal or illegal work, it did not matter anymore in the new Europe. Faruk's contact in the hospital was a good example of the needs of society today: they needed a janitor who worked cheap, and dozens of illegal Bosnian immigrants were available to do the work and even more Turks and Macedonians or Albanians waited right alongside them. Afan and Faruk had their people everywhere it seemed, usually finding what they needed anywhere in Europe after only a few calls. Every Bosniak had a relative or friend somewhere doing something in most parts of Europe. The contacts all knew they would be receiving a nice cash gift or help for another family member for their loyalty and help.

Entering through the service door just past the emergency entrance, Faruk climbed the fire escape staircase to the third floor, slowly easing the steel door open to peek down the hallway for any sign of other people or nurses doing their nightly rounds. One chubby white-clad nurse waddled away from him to the main nurses' station around the corner. He looked at his watch, and right on time as his watch clicked to the top of the hour, he heard panicked yelling coming up the staircase shaft from the floor below, then the screeching sound of a fire alarm going off. Fire drill procedures would keep everyone in the hospital occupied just long enough. Half the personnel would at first think it was either a routine drill or a prank because fires were unheard of in concrete and steel buildings these days, but they would go to see what the fuss was all about anyhow. All Faruk needed was a few minutes of confusion and he would finish his grisly task and be gone from the hospital before anyone knew he had been there. Around the corner at the end of the hall he could hear one nurse barking orders to the others above the drone of the alarm. The chubby one appeared again, but walked directly to the stairs at her end of the hall and disappeared. Faruk had been told by his contact that at this early time of the morning there would only be three nurses working this floor and the other two nurses would be preoccupied with their opposite end of the floor.

Taking big strides, but not running, he hustled down the hall to room 330 where he had been informed his target waited. He reached into his pocket, pulling out a long razor-sharp folding knife with a serrated blade and flipped it open. He quickly opened the door to the hospital room with no hesitation, ready for anything, but assuming he would only be met by a sleeping man lying with tubes connected to his arms, 5 meters away. He immediately saw he was correct in his assumption. He crossed the private room in a hurry, his shoes making no noise at all on the linoleum floor.

Recalling the General's words to not make too much of a scene, Faruk set the knife on the side table next to the bed and reached for a pillow stacked up on the window sill. Suffocation would be much cleaner than blood from a knife wound marring the scene. The victim would appear to have died from his other injuries, not from murder. Stepping back around to the side of the bed nearest the door where there were no monitors or tubes to hinder his task, he took one last look at the sleeping target. The man lying below him was nothing to him except an enemy, a piece of meat, the man who killed his brother, so he felt no guilt, no remorse, no sense of human compassion whatsoever, only revenge when he pressed the pillow down hard over the American's face.

CHAPTER 31

AGENT ANDERSON'S RESEARCH TEAM WAS ONE OF THE BEST in the business when it came to gleaning details from computers and the World Wide Web, not to mention a vast network of contacts ready to feed him any information they could supply. He himself had spent little time in the field; his role had always been one of administering from behind his desk in Washington and managing operatives in the field, like playing a chess game, moving pieces into position as he deemed necessary while providing them with backup support where and when needed.

"Everyone has a place and a position that they need to be the best at," he had been told by the director when he was first brought into the fold. "Not everyone gets to be James Bond."

In reality, the covert spy business had become one of few field agents nowadays: 90 percent of the work was computer searching, chasing the bad guys and their money through bank transactions, spy satellites, drone strikes when needed, and monitoring email and phone records. So it was with a great deal of satisfaction when his team would find a piece to a puzzle and pass it on to the agents in the field, showing them that they were just as valuable as their storied fellow employees getting all the glory.

"Hey boss, I found this in the newspaper from the *Sarajevo Times*. It seems that there were a couple of guys who got murdered in a road-side attack and then their truck was lit on fire," Scott Wilson spoke out as he stormed into Anderson's office unannounced.

Agent Anderson looked over the rim of his scratched reading glasses wondering where this was leading to. He liked Wilson; he was his kind of guy. A Texan from Midland, Wilson was sharp and self-motivated, not one of the East Coast preppies who typically inhabited government offices around D.C.

"Yeah, so? Who were the guys?"

"No identification was made, seems they were tortured and burned beyond recognition, before the truck was set on fire," Scott replied in his Texas drawl.

"OK, I'm still listening. Spit it out. What has it got to do with anything we are working on?"

"You asked the team to concentrate on the Bosnian connection to Tatra's network of drug and human trafficking, so we started looking into his operations in Bosnia, which came to a sudden end, coincidently two days after this murder took place. Take a look at this photo from the crime scene."

Two bodies tied together back to back in the picture, rigor mortis contorting their shapes into dramatic poses lay on a deserted road, the flesh of the hands, feet, and faces of the victims gone, burned away so only charred bone remained.

Anderson shuddered at the thought of the long drawn-out pain someone would go through from being burned so badly. Analyzing the entire scene laid in front of him on the photo though, he saw immediately what had brought the photograph to his technician's attention. Behind the two bodies, the painted side of the truck had not been completely destroyed and a company logo stood out painted in big letters:

Ivanowich Restaurants

"Tell me a story," Anderson continued.

"All the Bosnian stores closed the next day after this incidence and never reopened. A reporter said he got an anonymous tip and went to check it out and this is the scene he found. Some of the machinery and ovens still remain in all but a couple of the restaurants. All the employees were let go and no one was told why. They just shut the doors and walked away and left a little of the equipment behind. I called the reporter but he wouldn't tell me shit and hung up on me. Kind of weird, those guys usually want to brag about how smart they are and what super sleuth reporters they are."

"Did Tatra have any Bosnian partners? Usually anytime you do business in a shithole like Bosnia you are going to need some local partners to smooth the way."

Wilson beamed from ear to ear while scrolling through his laptop. He was good at what he did and he knew it and couldn't wait to let the cat out of the bag, "I knew you were going to ask that boss, but the only thing I could find was that the titles to all the real estate involved belong to a holding company, but the person who signs for the company is a name you may recognize." Looking up from his laptop he paused for dramatic effect before saying in a country-swaggering tone, "Afan."

"As in General Afan?"

"Yup, the one and only. We did not even know he was holding real estate. It seems a little tame for him, but it's him who owns it, all right."

"So any connection between him and the truck drivers' murders? Seems like an odd business for him to even mess with, the sandwich biz? Not as lucrative as drugs and slaves, that's for sure."

"And extortion and mercenaries for rent and you name it. We can't prove a connection but it sure smells like his modus operandi," Scott expanded on the boss's questions.

Anderson rested his elbows on the desk, pushing his hands together and intertwining his fingers, resting his chin on them to think. *"Would Tatra be stupid enough to get into business with these crooks? How could it help his business? Maybe he had no choice but to make a deal with the devil, or one of his managers unwittingly did. But that's not enough reason to start killing people."*

"While you're thinking, boss, Suzie in banking records hacked into some of the account activity on Ivan's companies and found some oddities. The business was not as successful as some might have thought. He has a lot of borrowed money running his expansion and is borrowing from banks all over Europe. Suzie says it looks like he uses new banks in each new country he starts up in, gets them to fund 100 percent of the start-up costs, but lies about how much he still owes the other banks in the other countries."

"With all this European Union horse pucky, you'd think they would catch on," Anderson mused.

"Not when he deals with local banks, which is what he's doing. He's not using any of the big boys who would soon find out by contacting the other big banks. Dealing with local banks and families that own them, he gains a great deal of goodwill in the local areas where he opens stores, and because he pays his debt to the local guys by borrowing from others who will be untraceable, everybody is happy. Plus, my guess is the local banking families are able to help him with real estate transactions and connections during the start-up phase of getting the stores into new markets. It's complicated, and he must have some very talented and creative CFOs involved and keeping track of it all, that's for sure."

"Good job, Scott. I don't get the connection with the Bosnians completely, but it's there somewhere. I'll let our agents know and see what they can do with it."

As Scott stood to leave the room, he let Anderson in on one other tidbit he had been saving, "When I was checking with our friends at Interpol about Afan's latest doings, they mentioned that they were watching a ship that arrived in Neum today. They say they think Afan has something to do with it, but the cargo appears to only be a load of marble or tile from Turkey. Just thought you might want to know. I'll fill you in on anything else we come across. I've got to go, so long partner."

"Thanks Scott, keep me updated."

Anderson looked at his watch when his phone rang, answering it by saying, "Nice timing Caitlin."

"Matt is awake."

"What kind of shape is he in?"

"Pretty rough, he's going to live, but he's bruised from head to toe. The docs are not sure how bad his internal organs are, so he'll be in the hospital for a couple more days still."

"Good news. OK, let me give you an update on what we have learned."

Anderson went through the details of what he had just been told by his staff, not leaving out any detail or speculation. He finished by telling her, "None of us are that sure what involvement Ivan has with any of the sordid details of what General Afan and his gang are up to, but he must know something. The roadside killings were a message from the Bosnians to him I assume, and my guess is that it was surely him the sniper attack was meant for at the countess's estate. My guess is he has somehow really pissed them off or maybe tried to get out of his arrangement with them. You need to get a closer look at what he's up to so we can put a stop to all this business once and for all. An Interpol agent, Gerard, will make contact with you. He is on our side and is clean; we've worked with him before. He has people working on the same project as us, only from a different angle. Talk to him and see what you can garner, feel free to let him know what we know. This is one of the rare times when we want to work with them."

"Where is he based?"

"He's working between Croatia and Bosnia. He's a sharp guy."

"What about Matt Simmons?" Caitlin asked.

"I'll leave that up to you. I'm sure you can trust him, but I doubt if he'll be any help to you since he's hospital bound and we don't have time to wait for him. Caitlin, don't do anything dangerous or foolhardy. Agent Gerard can handle the dirty work; just help him with info as much as you can, understand? Work on Tatra."

"Sure, I got it. I'll report back in a couple days or as things transpire."

"Roger that and stay out of trouble," he replied, breaking the connection without saying goodbye.

CHAPTER 32

Cold fog of the fall night gave the streets of the Hungarian town a chill that seeped deep into Zumbula's African bones as he climbed out of the front seat of the countess's SUV when it came to a stop in front of the main entrance to the hospital. Taking Matt's overnight bag over one shoulder and leaving his in the truck, he told the driver, "We will be back down here sometime in the next hour or so, depends on when Mister Simmons wakes up."

The driver replied in broken English, "I wait here for you."

"I have to see how he is feeling and if he's ready to move, so we may be a while."

"I wait here for you."

Zumbula smiled as he turned to go through the automatic opening doors, *"He is following the countess's instructions to the letter. Good, that might come in handy later."*

The screeching of the fire alarm sounding off startled Zumbula as he walked through the automatic doors, but no one on the main floor was really panicking about it from what he saw. The administrator at the check-in desk remained at her desk. She picked up the receiver of the phone and dialed a number, while a floor nurse moved a little quicker than normal to an office door halfway down the hall and opened it, but no one was rushing out of the building as if it were truly on fire.

Suddenly panic swept over Zumbula when his intuition sent chills up his spine at the realization that Matt was alone in his room. He ran for the staircase, the elevators in the old hospital being too slow for his purpose. He took the steps two at a time, passing the second floor without hesitation, seeing that no one was working on that floor at the moment. Each floor appeared vacant other than the sleeping patients drugged up for the night resting behind closed doors. By the time he reached the third floor his heart rate was doing double time, his breathing becoming ragged. Sliding around the corner of the third floor hall he ran for Matt's room, feeling better that no one was in the hallway, but it was eerily vacant. Perhaps it was just his imagination, the days of worrying and waiting for Matt to wake up had taken their toll on his psyche.

At the closed door to Matt's room he twisted the handle sharply and stormed into the room. That's when he knew he had not been wrong. His intuition had been correct once more he realized when he startled a stranger hunched over Matt with a pillow in his hands. This stranger turned to face Zumbula menacingly when he heard him rush into the room. The killer was a medium-sized stocky man whose athletic stance told Zumbula he was not afraid and knew what he was doing. The stranger stopped what he was doing and ran for the other side of the bed and that was when Zumbula saw the shining knife laying open on the table.

Being completely unarmed Zumbula ran straight at the bed. Throwing the overnight bag overhand at the table where the knife lay, Zumbula got a break when it hit the table just before the killer could grab the blade, sending it crashing to the floor, scooting under a metal-legged chair in the corner. The killer hesitated in a moment of decision before he decided he would need the knife against the black man who rounded the end of the bed as he got down on his knees to reach for it. Rolling on to his back the blade flashing up at Zumbula, the Bosnian yelled incoherently, "Now you too will die nigga'. Come meet my steel friend here."

Zumbula kicked at the raving man but he was too slow. The blade flashed back at his leg slicing his pants leg but missing flesh. Zumbula needed some sort of a weapon to counter his opponent's lunges so he slung the metal clipboard hanging on the end of the bed at the man like a Frisbee, forcing him to cover his face to avoid a direct hit. Zumbula swept his arm across the windowsill sending a potted plant and a stack of magazines at the killer who was struggling to his feet now and approaching him in a defensive crouch. The killer dodged the brunt of the flying debris while quickly closing the gap between the two of them.

The cold reptilian look in the killer's eyes told Zumbula that this was an experienced foe who would be tough to tame as he backed defensively around to the other side of the bed. The rolling stand that held the intravenous solutions that dripped into Matt's arm bumped onto his back so he slid his left arm behind him pulling the whole stand around in front of him. For a second he wondered if the tubes and needles would come cleanly out of Matt's arm, or if they would rip and tear at his flesh, but who cared, if he didn't stop this guy they would both be dead anyhow. Swinging the pole with all his might at the killer, the liquid filled bags broke on impact with the Bosnian's head covering his face with sticky clear hydration solution.

He staggered back, shaking off the impact, pushing the tangle of the tubes away from his knife hand and wiping the salty liquid from his stinging eyes before coming back for Zumbula again with the knife swaying in a half circle, looking for an opening. Zumbula still had the stand pole in his hands, drawing the killer toward the exit door, the heart and breathing monitors at Matt's bedside ringing and buzzing after the tubes been yanked from his arm and the monitoring electrodes had been pulled off of his chest in the melee. The fire alarm mixed with the screeching monitors created a deafening cacophony of metallic madness in the small room.

Matt had not stirred at all while all the fighting was taking place, making Zumbula wonder whether he had been too late. Perhaps the killer had already succeeded in his mission. It made no difference one way or the other to him now, Zumbula was mad and would seek the ultimate revenge against this fool. The Bosnian lunged at him; he dodged to his left, the thrust just passing his ribs. Zumbula hit him hard with the stand pole across the side of the head, splitting his ear and knocking him off balance. He received two more whacks from the pole to the shoulders before rolling back onto his feet and making a headlong rush at Zumbula, who grabbed for the man's knife arm on impact, holding it away from their bodies while they rolled on the floor toward the door in an embrace of certain death for one of them.

The Bosnian was screaming a blood-curdling yell. He shifted his body weight to take advantage of the momentum of his lunge, lightening the pressure on his arm, feigning giving up before stabbing hard into Zumbula's side. The blade sliced a thin cut 15 centimeters along the bone of his middle rib, but Zumbula didn't feel any pain, just the dull throb of damaged nerve endings. He knew the feeling all too well from his past encounters in the jungles of home. Taking advantage of the cutting the killer continued his momentum, throwing his weight sideways and rolling on top of Zumbula. Yanking his left hand free of Zumbula's grasp, he held him down by the throat with his right hand and raised the knife above his shoulder preparing to stab deep into Zumbula's exposed chest while Zumbula valiantly fought back.

Suddenly out of nowhere from behind a metal hospital chair came crashing down on the back of the Bosnian's skull, splitting it like a ripe melon, the killer collapsing in a bloody comatose heap on top of Zumbula.

There hovering above Zumbula stood Matt in his hospital gown, smiling down at his friend and saying, "You two sure make it awfully hard for a guy to get any beauty rest around here."

"Sorry patron," Zumbula laughed, rolling the assassin off him before standing up and straightening his shirt and coat, wiping a smattering of blood off his dark green waxed Barbour coat. Matt stood unsteadily on his feet acting for manliness sake as if he was OK, but he gladly held Zumbula's offered arm to help him walk back to sit on the edge of the bed. Just then the racket of the fire alarm stopped, bringing an acceptable quiet to the hospital after Matt flipped the switches to off on the noisy life monitors next to his bed.

"We need to get out of here," Matt told his friend.

Only because he knew it was the correct thing to say, knowing Matt would ignore any arguments anyway, Zumbula replied, "You should stay here a couple more days until the doctors say you are better, patron."

"Right," Matt replied dismissively. "Check our friend there on the floor and see if he has any identification on him before the nurse gets here."

While Zumbula went through his pockets, Matt put the knife the assassin had brought with him into his overnight bag piled up on the floor. Matt unplugged the table lamp, carrying it slowly, hunched over in pain to where the Bosnian lay in a heap. Zumbula held up a wallet to Matt then swapped it for the lamp.

"I don't think he's going to wake up for a while, but tie him up just in case."

Ripping the cord from the bottom of the lamp and pulling the knocked out man's limp arms behind his back, Zumbula bent the assassin's knees so he could hog-tie him with the electrical cord.

Matt wrote all the information down from the man's license, mentally inventorying the remainder of the contents for future use before stuffing the worn leather wallet back in the Bosnian's pants saying, "Either this guy is stupid or awful confident he was going to be successful killing me. Professional killers don't usually carry ID on them would be my guess."

The door to the room swung open, startling Matt and Zumbula but they both relaxed when they saw it was only the night watch nurse checking in. Seeing the room a mess, furniture and lamps and IV stands tossed all around with a bleeding man tied up and sprawled across the floor, her hand went to her mouth to stifle a cry of surprise. Matt said calmly to her hoping she understood some English, "Call the police."

The nurse nodded in recognition before going to the bound man to check his pulse and get a closer look at the wound on his head. She then turned to Zumbula who had forgotten in all the excitement that he was wounded also. She made motion for him to remove his coat and shirt, which he did and she stood staring for an awkward moment at the first black man she had ever seen partially naked. Blood glistened against his rock hard muscles while she quickly inspected the cut and then motioned with her hand for them to wait there, mumbling something incoherent in Hungarian and shaking her head while she swung open the room's door to find a uniformed police officer and auburn-haired young woman standing there. The nurse spoke in Hungarian to the police officer while pointing at the man on the floor, before scurrying away.

Caitlin surveyed the scene as she and the officer walked into the room, Matt sitting calmly on his bed, Zumbula standing with no shirt on, a smear of blood oozing from a gash across his side.

"I can't leave you two alone for even a couple hours without you getting into trouble, can I?" she said with a smile. "This is Captain Pushkas from the Hungarian National police. We were coming over to fill you in on some new developments, but it seems you have some things to tell us first." She turned to Zumbula and said, "I heard you came to the countess's estate last night and left without me? What are you two up to and what the hell happened here?"

The captain walked to Matt's bed, extending his hand out to shake, giving Matt a confident firm grip, "Mister Simmons, pleasure to meet you. I have heard a lot of things about you. Very sorry you had to get mixed up in all this. Tell me what happened here?"

"You need to ask my friend, Zumbula. I was sleeping through most of the action."

Zumbula proceeded to give them all an abbreviated version of the incident, ending it when he told them Matt hit the guy over the head with the hospital chair.

Reaching into his coat pocket, the captain flipped open his cell phone and made two quick calls, speaking in Hungarian the whole time. When he was finished he told them, "There will be local police here in a few minutes to secure this room and another hospital room for our attempted killer here until he recovers enough to be moved to our jail. Perhaps he will be able to tell us more about why he did this, who he works for, things like that."

"I doubt it, but you can try," Matt replied. "Don't bother with guards in this room either, because I am checking out as soon as we get Zumbula's side repaired."

"You should remain here sir; I can guarantee your safety from now on. You are in no condition to be moved."

Caitlin walked to Matt's side, holding his hands in hers, saying gently to him, "He's right Matt. There is no rush to leave now, we have plenty of time."

"Get a doctor in here as soon as possible, and then we are leaving. Has one of you got a vehicle?"

Zumbula nodded yes.

"Caitlin, pull this last needle out of my arm would you? There are some band-aids in the top drawer. I assume this bag has my clothes in it," he asked, looking at Zumbula.

"Oui, patron."

"I will need an official statement from the two of you. Where are you going?" Pushkas asked.

"How about we come by your office tomorrow after lunch and sign whatever you have typed up based on what Zumbula said, will that work?"

"Yes, I believe so. There may be additional questions after we interrogate the attacker."

"Good we will see you then. Now if I could have some privacy, as soon as my nurse Caitlin is done. I need to go into the bathroom and change before the rest of the officers get here."

The captain got the hint and left the room saying over his shoulder, "As you wish. I will wait outside the door."

When the door closed, Caitlin said to Matt, "We need to have a talk. I have some surprises for you."

"I can't wait. Let me get dressed first," Matt said, with a wry smirk spreading across his face. Mentally he felt fine, but he was still physically weak, the last twenty minutes had taken a toll on him. He would have to take it easy he told himself, if he had the time to . . .

CHAPTER 33

ALL THE EXCITEMENT WITH THE ATTEMPT ON MATT'S LIFE had the hospital buzzing, a cadre of police and investigators milled around the halls making it difficult for Matt, Caitlin, and Zumbula to slip quietly out the back door of the infirmary after a chubby doctor in his early forties had taken Zumbula to a small examination room to clean and stitch closed the ugly slash on his side. The doctor gave him a tetanus shot for good measure while Zumbula stood unflinchingly with his hands held over his head, refusing any painkiller or Novocain during the process of being sewn up. The doctor was amazed that anyone could stand there calmly, not flinch or grimace as the needle penetrated the skin with all its nerve endings screaming out on the surface.

Caitlin and Matt sat alone side by side on his rumpled hospital bed, waiting on the doctor to finish up his work on Zumbula, Matt listening intently to the tale Caitlin was weaving for him about her involvement with the CIA again and how she had ended up here in Hungary coincidently at the same time Matt had. She filled him in briefly on whom the suspects and players were and why her people thought he and the countess had been shot at mistakenly, who the Bosnian players were, and how they assumed Ivan Tatra may have been involved.

When she paused, he asked gently, "Why would you get back into this dangerous game? You don't need the money? You could be working for any Foundation or any cause you choose. This is not a game these people are playing as you can well see here today, Caitlin. This is rough shit, and people are getting killed and it is far from over."

Caitlin had thought about this question many times before, knowing the madness of it all, realizing the potential danger but feeling in the end it was all worth it and told him, "Because I care, Matt. Just like you, and by the way who are you to tell me about staying out of trouble? You are here right now in the hospital and off we go—just like Sudan all over again. But the truth is I'm doing this because I have decided that I am not going to stand by and let terrible things happen to innocent women and children who have no one to look out for them. These bastards we are dealing with, the Bosnians and possibly Ivan Tatra, need to be dealt with firmly and the local police, no matter where they are, put these crimes against women at the bottom of their list of priorities, if they even put them on the list at all. Prostitution is the oldest profession in the world they joke, but it is mainly enslavement in most cases nowadays, women taken from their families as young girls, facing horrific humiliation, abandonment, in some cases being sold by their families for a few dollars in the poor rural areas where girls are second-class citizens at best. Matt, I was lucky, I was born into a family, even though my mother died when I was young, where I was given opportunities and the ability and the resources to do something very special in this life, and I have decided that I am not going to waste that chance. I'm going to do something about it."

Matt listened to her impassioned words, her Irish accent creating a mystical, almost theatrical tone to her speech, a tone that stirred Matt's passion while tugging at his heartstrings at the same time. He had seen firsthand what slavery and abuse could do to a woman when his wife Bianca had been kidnapped in the Central African Republic a few years earlier. He had witnessed the way Rashid had turned her into a harem girl, a possession that he could do whatever he wanted with, like owning livestock, forcing it to do whatever he chose, however he chose, whenever he chose. Matt had seen what the abuse and kidnapping and degradation could do to a person, how it had turned the love of his life into a monster capable of killing her only baby boy and taking her own life in the process. Matt felt the rage—not ever having avenged what Rashid had done—begin to build up in him, the rage of knowing that the devil Rashid still walked as a free man somewhere while he Matt Simmons spent night after night, day after day with a hole in his heart where a family used to stand.

His voice cracked just a little when he replied to her, "Don't forget I know a little something about this subject as well. What can I do Caitlin, how can I help you?"

Caitlin looked at the floor for a second to break the gaze of Matt's blue eyes when they began misting up. She had told Agent Anderson that Matt would help them if they needed him when she had been on the phone with Anderson earlier and now it was confirmed. Now she was free to fill Matt in on everything that had transpired, "You remember Agent Dennis Anderson, the guy you worked for in the Sudan affair when you saved Bianca?"

"Sure, how is he?"

"He is fine, and says I am to tell you that you are officially, but not really officially, back on the CIA's team for this case and that you would know what that means and that you agree to the code and contract you signed last time. Do you need another copy of it to sign?"

Matt chuckled, "No I understand and of course I agree to the terms. The point I remember most is that if we get caught, they will deny their involvement, but if we succeed they will take all the credit and we can't say anything about it to anyone. I'm hip to the routine. Do we or the boys from Washington have any backup here in Europe?"

"A guy named Captain Gerard is on our team, according to Anderson. Apparently he has worked for us closely in the past. Seems he and Anderson go way back to the Balkan wars and he has been an ally ever since. He is our expert on all things Balkan and all the complexities that go with it. I'm not sure just how involved he can be in his official role, but he gives us a fallback go-to-guy, at least here in Europe."

Matt let it all sink in: the Bosnians, Ivan Tatra, the countess, and how what was supposed to be a business hunting trip had now turned into another dangerous mission—one in which he was already wounded before he even knew what was going on!

"It sounds to me like the first thing we need to do is go see your boyfriend up in Bratislava. Is he expecting you for a return date?"

Caitlin frowned at the inference to her and Ivan once again and stood up from the bed, hurt at the comment and walked toward the door, "I am doing my duty, my job Matt, that's all. Please don't joke about that. But yes, I was planning on going today. You can come if you think you are up to it."

Matt felt like an ass that his little jibe had not gone over as well as he planned and replied meekly, "Hey kiddo, I was just joking. Don't take it that seriously."

Caitlin turned back toward him when she reached the door replying, "If you are coming, get your shit together and I will meet you at the main entrance downstairs. I'm going to arrange for a ride home for the countess's driver with the one that brought me over here and we will use her Rover that brought Zumbula over."

With that she let the spring on the door slam it closed behind her, leaving Matt alone in his room to change into his street clothes and wait for Zumbula.

"You really know how to make 'em happy Matt, old boy. Way to go."

CHAPTER 34

Caitlin drove the Rover in silence for the first two hours heading north to Bratislava. Once the traffic congestion of Budapest was left behind it was a gorgeous drive through the rolling hills in the crisp, clear air of an autumn day. The oaks leaves had changed to their annual fall color, offset by the dark green pines, the rain from the weekend having washed the smog away leaving crystal-clear landscapes to wind through in the comfort of the powerful Range Rover HSE. Matt reclined his seat after a half hour hoping that time would heal Caitlin's disappointment in his comments while he rested and napped, letting Mother Nature do her duty healing him up. He was seriously hurting physically. He had not brought the pain pills with him because he was concerned about how groggy they made him. He was sure he was going to need all his wits about him in the next few days but was regretting his hasty decision to leave them behind when every bump in the road made him wince in pain.

Matt woke when he felt the SUV slowing to a stop to refuel on the outskirts of Bratislava. Caitlin and Zumbula both got out to stretch while an attendant began filling the car's tank. Matt opened his door but struggled with his legs, they didn't want to cooperate with his brain's commands. Using his hands to lift them and swing them out to the concrete was a monumental struggle. Pain shot up his side when his broken ribs reminded him to take it slowly, that he was far from healthy yet. The walking and stretching for 10 minutes helped considerably, along with a diet Pepsi and a muffin from the convenience store attached to the gas station.

Matt offered to drive for a while but Catlin refused, saying she was fine. Matt checked with Zumbula to see what weapons and ammunition they had with them. After hearing the count of the shotgun and rifle, Caitlin told him, "I also have two pistols, both nine millimeter Berettas. One is in the glove compartment for you."

Caitlin's cell phone made a short buzzing sound letting her know she had a message so she picked it up and hit voice mail.

"Hello Caitlin, not sure where you are, but I am confirming our date for tonight. Please come straight to the house, I believe you know how to get here. I will be waiting and we can make plans once you arrive. Call me or my assistant Marina and let us know your ETA, baby. Ciao."

Caitlin cringed at the thought of having to make like she was romantically interested in this jackass, however it served a greater purpose and she would make whatever sacrifices were necessary and hoped Matt would at least understand her predicament. She looked at her wristwatch, and then redialed the number. When Ivan's answering machine came on she left him a brief message, "Hi Ivan, I am an hour out so I should see you at your house around 5:30 tonight. I am driving a dark-green Range Rover, Hungarian license plate number 54HTWS. Let your security know so they will let me through the gate and I will see you then. Bye."

Having listened in while Caitlin left the message, Matt got down to business after she pushed the end button asking her, "How much security has he got at the house?"

"Some at the entrance gate. It is a five-acre compound surrounded by a wrought iron and stone wall with Alsatian Shepherd guard dogs running free inside protecting the property. I'm guessing he has stepped it up since the shooting at the countess's estate. but we will find out pretty quickly."

"Any cameras inside or out?"

"On the outside and on the wall yes, but I have never seen any inside. Typically this is a really safe place to live so he's been pretty relaxed when it comes to home security."

"Good," Matt replied.

They drove on in silence, Zumbula gazing out the window, watching the autumn colors fade as the sun dipped toward the cold horizon, looking forward to the next part of the inevitable action that seemed to follow the patron everywhere he went. His blood flowed powerfully in his veins, he was alive once more and the adrenaline of adventure coursed through his arteries.

THE GATE LEADING into the 300-year-old Slovakian estate swung open on cue when the Range Rover came into view, two guards dressed in civilian garb giving the Rover a cursory look as it passed but not stopping it for an inspection after being given the vehicle's description and plate number and being instructed to let it pass by the boss. Beginning its life as a Slavic prince's wedding present to his young and ravishingly beautiful Polish bride, the oldest daughter of Poland's royal family, the stone mansion with its corner turrets resembled the larger castles of Europe without the upkeep and complete ostentatiousness that goes along with owning a true castle. The majestic home had survived because of its beauty, its architecture, and its location nestled along the banks of the Danube. Each of the world wars had seen it occupied by the German army when they arrived, but the soldiers had spared it of any ransacking or pilferage, such was its elegant personality.

Matt let out a low whistle when they motored through the open gates and began the drive up the manicured crushed rock driveway hemmed in by landscaping that was second to none, toward the waiting mighty oak entrance doors.

"Damn, now this is a house. Just when I thought I was doing well, I see this. I'm going to have to go back to work if I want to have any chance of competing with ol' Ivan."

"He told me it was a dream come true when he purchased it. He says he grew up in a small town near here and was in love with it since he was young and poor," Caitlin responded.

"A guy needs to sell a lot of Ivanowich sandwiches to get this kind of real estate. Something doesn't add up here if you ask me."

When they arrived at the front door, a butler dressed in the appropriate attire came out to the vehicle and opened the doors, greeting them in broken English, "Welcome, welcome. Please come in. Mister Tatra is waiting for you in the study, Miss O'Shea. He did not tell me you were bringing friends. I will make alternative arrangements. You are all staying the night?"

"I don't think we are," Matt replied.

"Fine, I will send someone out later for your luggage if you change your mind. Please follow me," he said, turning to lead them through the massive double doors, their iron knockers fashioned into gothic lions' heads, hanging heavy on the thick, ancient oak. Matt let the others get a head start, then retrieved his pistol from the glove compartment, discreetly tucking it in his belt at the small of his back hidden under his coat. He had the Bosnian assassin's knife in his pants pocket for backup just in case. It was difficult for Matt to keep up with the others due to the pain of walking upright, but he struggled on, hiding the injury as best he could.

Ivan greeted Caitlin warmly when she walked through the doors first into the walnut paneled study, antique books filling the shelves warmed by a crackling fire, with a bottle of French Bordeaux resting on the ornately carved desk next to two wine glasses.

"Ma cherie, there you are," he said, walking toward her with his arms dramatically open anticipating a hug until he saw Zumbula walk in through the doors a moment after her.

"Well, what do we have here, a surprise guest?" Grimacing when he looked back at Caitlin, assuming his romantic plans had just been cancelled he continued, "Baby, you should have told me you were bringing a friend. I would have made arrangements. I believe we have met before, haven't we?" Ivan said holding out his hand to the black man standing before him. "Ah yes, at the countess's, that's it. You were with Mister Simmons if I recall correctly?"

Before Zumbula could respond or shake his hand, Matt slowly walked into the study, a little hunched over in pain, but still firm in his handshake with Ivan who had lost all of his false bravado suddenly, wondering what the hell was going on, but trying to play it cool until he figured it out.

"Speaking of the devil, there you are, nice to see you once again, Matt."

"You too, Ivan. Nice place you have here."

"Thank you, it's kind of big, but it's home. How are you feeling? What may I ask brings you gentlemen here? I wasn't expecting you, and Caitlin didn't tell me she was bringing any guests along."

Matt looked around the room admiring the workmanship replying, "We thought we would tag along and see the countryside. Never been out this way before and wanted to see your house, see how the other half live."

Ivan wondered at the oddity of the situation. He did not like surprises but pretended to not be rattled.

"Of course, come in, please take a seat. Can I get you a drink? We were going to eat in one hour. I will have my man put on a couple more plates." Ivan pushed a button on his desk and a few moments later the butler entered the room.

"Would you like wine or a cocktail, champagne?"

"Wine is fine for me," Caitlin replied.

"Diet Coke for my friend, and I will have a beer, please," Matt replied.

Ivan repeated the order in Slovakian to the butler even though he understood the orders in English.

When the butler left the room to retrieve the order from the bar, Ivan turned back to Matt, "I believe I heard you were in a car accident and were in the hospital, true?"

"Yes, I just got out today."

"And you came straight here? Are you OK now?"

"Yes, I'm all better, just a few bruises."

Ivan could tell by the way Matt eased himself into the leather armchair that he was not OK, appearing to be in substantial pain the way he moved so slowly, like a stiff old man.

Caitlin sat in another leather armchair across from Matt while Zumbula remained standing, arms folded across his chest next to the door, relaxed but intent. Ivan tried to appear casual, however Matt noticed by the way he paced the room nervously attending to tiny details that he was rattled.

"Well, it's good you are OK. It was a shame what happened at the countess's estate, all that shooting. Who would have thought some crazy Bosnians would do something like that. Any clues from the police as to who, what, or why?"

Matt let Ivan's words sink in. Ivan had mentioned the Bosnians, yet Matt like Caitlin was sure no one outside of this room and the CIA in Washington knew that Bosnians were involved in any way. The words solidified Matt's opinion of Ivan's involvement in the whole fiasco, and it was time to get some answers.

"No, not much has come out yet. Who told you the shooters were Bosnians? That's news to me," Matt replied.

"My assistant mentioned it, I believe. He must have heard it from the police."

"I understand you had some shops in Bosnia, but they closed suddenly a few months ago. What happened there? Anything you want to tell us about that might have something to do with the attempted murders?"

"Bosnia is a hard place to do business. They are a crazy people, those Bosniak, very hard to deal with so we just shut the restaurants down rather than continue losing money," Ivan answered, waving his hand dismissively and trying to change the subject. "Ah well, I am glad it is all over and done with and that everyone will be OK. Tell me again, what is it you do in the States, Matt?"

"A variety of things, real estate, shipping, things like that. So tell me, did you have any of the Bosnians as partners in the restaurants? Did a couple of your employees get killed in Bosnia?"

"What is this, all these questions? You act like you are the police or something," Ivan said, openly irritated by the direct questioning.

Caitlin stepped into the fray with a soothing voice, "Matt was shot at and the countess was wounded. Anything you can tell us might help the police find out who the culprits are, Ivan. We aren't blaming you for anything, we are simply asking questions."

Ivan stared at Caitlin, then back at Matt, then approached Caitlin, wagging his finger at her, "What, you are involved in this as well?" Ivan's voice rose to a higher pitch, he had had enough, "I think this little tea party is over. You all need to leave, and I mean right now. I don't need to answer any of your ridiculous questions! Who do you think you are talking to?"

Matt sprang up from the chair, all his injuries no longer hurting and grabbed Ivan's arm from behind, catching him off guard and twisting it up hard between his shoulder blades and roughly forced him face first onto the suede overstuffed sofa's cushions. Ivan let out a surprised cry of pain when he was knocked off his feet. Zumbula took two steps to the study's door and closed it, twisting the lock before casually walking over to where Matt had Ivan pinned down on the sofa, watching the proceedings with a smirk on his face, ready to help. He knew Matt's short temper better than anyone, so when Ivan had gotten up on his high horse, it was only going to be a matter of moments until Ivan would learn about it firsthand. Caitlin, a little surprised by the swiftness of Matt's attack, stood one meter away and drew her pistol from her purse and slipped the safety off.

Matt pressed Ivan's face into the cushions, making it hard for him to breath and impossible for him to call out for help, speaking menacingly into his ear, "Look shithead, I'll tell you when we are done and I can guarantee we won't be done until I get some answers. Now we can do this the easy way or the hard way, it's totally up to you and I have all night. In the last few days I have been shot at, almost killed in a car wreck, had someone try and smother me in the hospital, so I am in no mood for any bullshit, capiche?"

Matt let Ivan's head come up so he could breath and answer his question, which only brought a struggle and response of, "Fuck you, you can't do this. You don't know who you are screwing with. Do you know who I . . ." Matt crammed Ivan's face back into the suede cushion before he could complete his sentence. He pushed him down even harder, one hand right at the base of his neck.

Ivan yelled a muffled threat, "I'm going to call the police!"

Jamming his arm further up his back to the point where he thought he might be about to separate his shoulder, Matt told him, "My African friend over there has a couple nasty things he learned in the jungle, and he really enjoys doing them to European white assholes. I'm going to turn you over to him in just a second, but I'll give you one more chance. What is the name of your partner in Bosnia, huh?"

Ivan let out a muffled scream at the pain from his wrenched shoulder, Matt eased up a little on the pressure before pulling his face up so he could answer and take a breath, "Let me go! You will pay for this! Shitttttttt!"

Matt pushed his face down harder than before, making sure he could not breathe at all and brought his knee hard up into Ivan's testicles, feeling him scream a muffled cry buried in the pillow. Zumbula waited his turn impatiently, hoping to give the Slovak a whack or two, maybe break a couple of fingers, just to get even for the past week's problems.

"No problem, asshole, the hard way sounds fun to me. What do you think Zumbula?"

Ivan struggled for his life. He had never been roughed up like this before—he had always been able to talk or buy his way out of any problem and now he was truly afraid. Matt lifted his head up briefly once more and Ivan mumbled trying to catch his breath, "You do not want to know, trust me; they are bad men, very bad."

He let out another scream when Matt yanked his arm up even harder hissing, "You let me decide that shithead."

Even though he knew he had Ivan ready to talk, he figured a little more pain would lubricate the Slovakian's vocal chords and have him begging for mercy and talking all night. A loud knock on the door interrupted the action and Matt nodded to Zumbula who walked over to it, unlocked it, swinging it open and letting the butler enter. Zumbula stepped behind him closing it quickly behind him to prevent the butler from rushing away once he saw what was happening to his boss. The butler, shocked upon seeing the alarming scene before him, dropped the silver tray containing the drinks, glass and ice scattering across the floor upon impact. Caitlin led the shook-up butler over to a high-backed chair where he sat sweating profusely, staring at Caitlin's pistol and his boss wrestled to the couch in obvious pain from these strangers in his house.

Matt couldn't care less if the butler watched the proceedings. He knew the last thing Ivan would do is go to the police with any information or tell them about Matt's visit to see him. Matt finally let Ivan's head come up for air and the Slovak sputtered, "OK, OK, I'll tell you what you want. Shit! Stop it, that hurts, damn it! Aghhhh."

Matt let him sit upright on the couch, releasing his arm; Caitlin sat two meters away in an armchair, her pistol trained on Ivan's chest, ensuring that Ivan not have a sudden change of heart.

"Tell me the story shit for brains, I want to hear it all," Matt growled.

"You have been warned, and I don't care how they kill you now and they surely will, believe me," Ivan spat out, rubbing his shoulder. "You are a dead man now, so I don't care what you know."

"Thanks for the warning, but I don't have all night. Start talking," Matt replied.

"It all started when I was approached by a couple of Bosnians who wanted to open some of my stores in Bosnia. I don't normally do franchises, I have always owned all the stores myself, but their timing was good." Ivan hesitated, thinking about what he was going to say next before continuing, "What the hell, the truth is I was deep in financial problems at the time. I had grown too fast. I was out of cash and the banks and my existing investors were on my ass for their payments. I had always paid my investors good returns, and the banks had always been waiting in line to loan me more money. Strategically, Bosnia made sense because I had just opened a new distribution warehouse in Croatia, in Zagreb, and the more products I moved through that facility the better. Anyway, they approached me with a plan to split the profits 50–50, and they would put up the front money, so I said yes and we got started. The stores made good money right from the beginning, which is rare. Real good money, and my money showed up on time from them and they kept up their end of the deal. The first sign that something was amiss came when one of my managers in Croatia noticed and reported to me how many of our drivers and warehousemen operating out of Zagreb were Bosnian, and he didn't trust them. I dismissed it at first because Bosnians will work for cheap, so it would make sense to hire them, but they and the Croats don't always get along as you know. He also commented in the email that the volume of business moving through the Bosnian stores put them in our top 10 locations, which was great news but it didn't make sense due to the small size of the stores. In other words, it is hard to move that many sandwiches through a store of that size."

Ivan looked around the room, looked at Caitlin with her pistol, glanced at Matt, and saw the frightened look in his butler's face, before continuing, "I decided to take a secret trip there to see how they were doing it, figuring if nothing else I might learn some new sales techniques, but when I watched the operations I could tell they were not moving as much as they said they were. I thought maybe they were taking our product and selling it on the side, so I had the next delivery truck tailed by one of my security men. He reported some oddities to us but that was the last time we heard from him." Ivan hesitated, letting the statement sink in with his audience. "Inquiries to the police turned up nothing; the guy just disappeared, vanished. I tried to ignore the obvious, I needed the cash flow and I was recovering from the hole I had buried myself in, but I had a private investigation firm snoop around a bit and that is when I learned who I was actually dealing with. You two sleuths ever hear of a man named General Afan?"

"Nope, fill me in," Matt answered.

Caitlin did not say anything; she just listened to what he had to say.

"Turns out he was a popular general during the war, probably should have been hung for war crimes and now he runs what could be called the Bosnian Mafia. He is into all kinds of shit, and if you want to do business in most of that country you need to work with him or his thugs one way or the other."

"Nice business partner," Caitlin chimed in.

"Looking back now I should have done better research in the beginning on who was actually backing the deal, but I was desperate and I would have made a deal with devil at that point." Ivan turned to face Matt, saying, "I need a drink, how about you?"

"Sure, sounds good. Zumbula keep an eye on the butler when he goes to get them, eh?" Matt ordered. Ivan gave the butler the orders and he left the room with Zumbula close behind.

Ivan waited until the door closed behind them then continued, "I don't want my houseman hearing the rest of this and when he returns, I am going to send him out of the room again and I will show you a video that will get your attention."

"All right, go on."

"I figured it was time, I should get out of the deal as quickly as I could, I knew they were up to some sort of no good. I don't to this day know exactly what it is they are doing, but none of it makes sense. Who buys wholesale sandwich product and sends it on a ship somewhere else? That is one of the things we found out that they were up to. Unless the boats are set up with specialty refrigeration most of the product is going to spoil in a few days. There isn't that much money in reselling wholesale food, trust me, otherwise I'd be doing it. I finally had enough money to be able to get out of the deal and the last thing I needed was my company name being tied to some criminal activity by the Bosnians. Can you imagine the field day the press would have if the word got out that I was connected to whatever shit the Bosnians are up to? It would bankrupt me. So I told my guys to go get all the equipment and computers out of the Bosnian stores in a midnight raid so to speak, thinking that would teach them a lesson about screwing with me and sever my ties permanently at the same time."

Ivan fell silent when the butler and Zumbula returned with the drinks. Everyone silently took a couple hasty sips, until Matt asked Zumbula, "Ivan and I need to discuss something in private. Would you mind taking the butler into another room and keeping an eye on him?"

The butler understood, rising to follow Zumbula out of the room. Matt gulped some water down quickly that the butler had brought in, the pain was really getting to him now from all the exertion of wrestling with Ivan, but he didn't want to let on how much it hurt. Caitlin watched him out of the corner of her eye and could tell he was hurting but did not say anything in front of Ivan.

Ivan stood and walked over to the television perched on the highly polished walnut cabinet, turned on the screen, and hit a button on the CD player.

"You know all I know now, but I have one more thing to show you. I am telling you upfront what you are going to see will make you sick and is beyond belief, but you will truly know who and what you are dealing with after you see this. The morning after I sent the trucks into Bosnia to retrieve my store gear and computers, we were told that one of the trucks with two employees in it did not come home. This video was sent to me that morning through our own computer email system that they had hacked into. Are you sure you want to see this? It's unbelievably disgusting."

"Turn it on," Caitlin replied, wishing she hadn't a few minutes later.

CHAPTER 35

"COUNTESS, IT'S MATT SIMMONS. HOW ARE YOU?"

"Hello there, stranger. How are you? I heard you left the hospital a little early? More trouble? Everything all right?"

"Yes, everything is fine with me. How is your neck?"

"Oh, I'll be fine, I might have to make a trip to Paris and buy some new scarves. It looks like I will be wearing them on a daily basis for a while," Countess Atwood joked.

Matt chuckled along with her, glad to hear she was taking the shooting in stride, "Wow yeah, think of all those ensembles that now need matching. I don't think it's going to be a quick trip in Paris."

"Maybe you can join me? I have a beautiful flat near the Eiffel Tower, and I will need someone to carry my bags."

"I could probably be talked into that. Let me know when you are going. Hopefully it won't be for a few weeks, since I've got some unfinished business to take care of. Speaking of that, I'm sorry about wrecking your Rover—what a waste of a beautiful machine."

"Thank God you lived through that wreck. I saw the car, and it is completely totaled. The Brits build them right, lucky for you. I can always get another Rover but you would be a little tougher to replace, I am afraid."

"Thanks also for loaning me the new one; I promise I will take better care of this one. Would it be all right with you if I held on to it for a few more days, and then I will bring it back to you all nice and shiny, scout's honor?"

"Of course use it or anything else I have as long as you need it. Where are you now? Are you heading this way?"

Matt hesitated for a second, not sure how much he should disclose before telling her, "I'm on my way to Sarajevo. I have a little business there I need to tend to, but I should have your car back in a few days."

"Matt, don't do this. I have heard some of the background of what happened to you and I, and those people are not people you want to get involved with. I have spoken with the police commissioner here, and the authorities are looking into it. Leave it to them please; you don't need to get any more involved than you already are. I'm going to be OK and so are you. That's enough isn't it?"

"Oh, I'm not going to get involved in anything, don't worry," Matt lied. "I'll let you know when I'm coming back. I have to run now; I'm glad you are OK and thank you for all your help. Take it easy and stay in bed like a good girl. Be sure you do what the doctors tell you."

"Be safe and hurry back, Matt. I need you to doctor me a little. There are a few things about what happened between us that I would like to discuss further when you get here. Don't worry, I'm not going to try to tie you down, but we need to talk, OK?"

"Sure. I'd enjoy that, see you in a few days. Bye bye and thanks again."

The countess hung up the phone and hated herself for opening up to Matt like she had; she was acting like a teenager with her first crush. Not very ladylike that was for sure, but she did want to talk to Matt further, and it did not really matter if he was going to be around in the future. She just wanted to bounce some ideas around, get his opinion on which way to go, since he had been through a lot more than she had when it came to relationships. Sure, she hoped he would stick around. After all, she had fallen head over heels for him, and their lovemaking in the hunting stand had been the best she had ever experienced. She dreamed about it nightly and longed for more.

What the experience with Matt had made her realize was that it was time for her to drop the charade of being happily married to a man she rarely saw, who was an absentee father, who ran around on her as he wanted to, and who did not even have the common courtesy to hide it anymore. No, she had decided while recuperating, with plenty of time to think, that it was time she moved on and found that vibrant, fulfilling life that she knew waited out there for her, the one she deserved. If Matt wasn't the man for her long term, she would find someone else, but no longer would she go through life alone, with no passion and no love.

SITTING ON THE edge of his bed in one of the hotel's terry cloth bathrobes, Matt switched the phone off just as he heard Caitlin walk through the front door into the two-bedroom hotel suite's living room that they were all sharing in Old Town Sarajevo. Zumbula was wrapped in a bath towel, camping out on the sofa after stripping off his dirty clothes and using Matt's shower. He then gathered up all of their used clothes placing them into the overnight laundry service and having room service come and get them. He told them he wanted the fastest service possible and no starch, they needed them quickly and didn't have extras to replace them. He was guaranteed the clothes would be back before 7 in the morning.

Caitlin's arms were full with one bag of bandages, disinfectant, and tape, the other with a mix of snacks, deli meats, and cheese and a six-pack of beer that made a loud thud sound when she set it down on the coffee table.

As Matt walked stiffly into the living room, Caitlin said, "I got what I could. Not many stores are open at this time on Saturday night here in Sarajevo, I'm afraid. How is the pain, Matt? I got you the only over-the-counter painkillers I could find."

"Thank you, Caitlin, those and a couple of beers should do the trick—I hope."

"Before you fall asleep, Matt, you should know I spoke with Agent Anderson, and he says we can expect a contact call from Interpol. He says they have a wealth of information about who was behind the shootings and that we should share whatever information we have or that we gather in the next few days with them. He said and I quote, 'Tell Matt that Interpol is in charge and he needs to work with them,' unquote. He also mentioned when I told him what Tatra said that he thinks Tatra is into the criminal part a lot more than he is admitting. They are going to keep an eye on him, he's not off the hook yet."

"Sure, I would agree with that," was exactly the reply Caitlin knew Matt would give her. He walked over to the grocery bag, unloading its contents onto the counter before popping the top on a can of local beer she had bought and taking a long pull off it. He tossed a can of soda pop to Zumbula, popped a half dozen of the painkillers into his mouth and took another swig of beer before asking Caitlin, "I can't offer you any Irish whiskey, lassie, but I could spare a beer if you would like?"

"Wow, what an exciting date this is! Two half-naked wounded, stitched-up men in my hotel room, with me playing nurse and getting to drink semi-warm beer! This is special, isn't it? This is exactly why I dedicated my life to the spy business, for these kinds of thrills."

They all laughed and made small talk for the next half hour, letting the day's adrenaline work its way out of their systems until Matt finally stiffly rose out of his chair announcing, "I'm finished; I will see you all in the morning. Zumbula, you need anything?"

"I am fine, patron; I stole a pillow and a blanket from your room already, and I'm going to sleep here. Sleep well patron."

"You too. Caitlin, good night, and thanks for the meds and the beer and being our nurse. Sleep tight and don't let the bed bugs bite," he joked, stretching and leaning over, his ribs screaming in pain at the movement, to kiss her on the forehead.

"You too. I'm calling it a night as well," she replied, watching him hobble toward his bedroom while she walked to hers.

Matt let the bathrobe fall to the carpeted floor, painfully slipping between the expensive cotton sheets. He knew he had overdone himself today and that he needed to take a few days off to let his body heal and thought, "*Maybe tomorrow will be a slow day and I can relax.*"

He flipped off the light switch, staring into the darkness and waiting for the pain pills and alcohol to kick in until he heard a light knock on the door that adjoined his room to Caitlin's. The door eased open, a table lamp from her room backlighting her perfect figure clad only in a bra and a miniscule pair of sheer panties, her luxurious hair falling freely over her shoulders. She hesitated in the doorway for a brief moment to make sure Matt got the full affect of the backlighting from her room before whispering, “I thought you might need a nurse to give you a massage, for medicinal purposes only, of course.”

“Oh, but of course,” Matt softly replied, an ear-to-ear grin cutting across his face in the darkness when she gently eased the door closed behind her.

CHAPTER 36

DEMIR HAD BEEN BORN INTO ONE OF THOSE MIXED-RELIGION families in the Baltics that could have been the saving grace for the Bosnians and Serbs over the past 200 years. In so much of the mountainous areas, the various religious factions overlapped and lived peacefully, most of the time. Orthodox Christians, Catholics, and Muslims in many villages lived in harmony out of necessity. Intermarriage, while not common, was tolerated, depending on the man-to-woman ratio in the multiple-religion regions.

Such was the case for Demir's father who was an Orthodox Christian Serb and fell in love with a Bosniak Muslim woman. The tiny villages they grew up in sat less than two kilometers apart in the disputed border hills. The majority of the inhabitants of the hills kept their own faith, attending services but celebrating the variety of holidays and traditions of the region's religions together. The number of hardcore radical, religious fanatics was minimal in the hill country, the hate-filled fist-pounding, condemning preaching from the Orthodox priests and mullahs espoused only in the churches and mosques of the central parts of each country.

The neighbors in the hills, hoping and praying that the bloodshed that had taken so many of their sons, daughters, and family members in the past would never happen again, lived peacefully. Entire generations had been wiped out in a couple of the early wars, and cooler heads—those who were bent on surviving on their poor subsistence based farms and not so much worried about which God was right—had no desire to rekindle the fervor one more time. If a man wanted to marry outside his religion, so be it.

The generations of children born to these mixed families, the ones not forced into one dogma or another, were free to go about their lives in the hills without the hatred that was ingrained into the children living in other parts of the country. That is, until the wars and the fighting started up once again in the early 1980s.

Suddenly the peaceful coexistence was shattered when the various factions' armies showed up in the villages, killing everyone who was not of their faith. Brothers from mixed families having to choose sides, families ripped apart as the haphazard troops descended on unsuspecting townships or farms. *Genocide* it was called by the powerful European and Western countries that stood by and let the civil war and bloodshed rage on.

The Serbians had the upper hand with well-trained troops and armament and were eager to put their unlimited supply of weapons to use in ridding the countryside of Bosniak or forcing them to flee to Bosnia and taking their land in an effort to expand the Serbian borders. Taking no prisoners made it easier for the army to scour the mountains of any resistance.

Bosniaks retaliated in their own vicious way, taking their hatred out on any Serb they could get their hands on, whether the local Serbs had been at peace with their Bosnian neighbors or not. This was war at its ugliest and such was the case when Demir's tiny village was set upon an hour before dawn by ragtag Bosnian troops.

The sheepdogs barking gave the village a warning that something was not right. The inhabitants were aware that trouble was brewing in the surrounding hillside but had been told the troops were not moving in their direction. After all, they reasoned, who would want their tiny, nonstrategically based hamlet? Unlike other villages that had a chance to flee and seek refuge across the safer borders if trouble was brewing, these people had no chance of escape.

When the ruckus from the dogs began, Demir's mother put her two younger children in the hidden cellar dug into the floor below the wooden stove then covered it back up with the floor boards and an old carpet. At 12 years old Demir was considered too young to fight even though he was handy with the old beat-up rifle that his father used to shoot wolves that harassed their domestic sheep and goats during the frigid winters. His mother forced him into the other cubbyhole underneath a small hatch in the wooden floor where he would also be safe, just in case.

It was still dark and cold when the shooting started close to their house; he could hear his father and mother arguing with each other, his father telling her to take the horse to the next village and get help, his mother saying she was not leaving her family and would stay and fight. His father was too busy to argue anymore when their home was suddenly ruthlessly sprayed by .50-caliber machine gunfire from 500 meters away on the ridge overlooking their farm. The concentrated fire cut the wooden home to shreds, the cracking and snapping of wood as the bullets ripped through was soon replaced by the smell of wood smoke, a fire had begun from the heat of the tracer rounds searing through the dry planks, just like the Bosniak planned.

Demir's father yelled for his wife to stay down, never mind the flames as he ran to what was left of the front room window to take a few shots back at the troops firing on him, but they were all out of range for his 6.5 mm open-sight hunting rifle. He held high and shot a couple rounds in the general direction of the incoming fire, hoping to at least slow down the rapid fire, but the act was his last moment of bravery. A hot round from the .50-caliber machine gun on the hill almost cut him in half. Blood and gore splashed across his terrified wife standing two meters away from him in the shadows.

The Bosnians sneaking up on the farmhouse saw him go down and rushed the house now that they were facing no more resistance, finding Demir's mother weeping over what was left of her husband's body when they burst through the front door. Rape being the tactic for punishing any enemy women they caught, the soldiers wasted no time hauling the helpless crying woman begging for mercy outside, taking turns like rabid animals as she screamed out that she was a Muslim.

"You're a pig who sleeps with Christ's men, now you will be treated like the whore you are," one of them yelled while the others laughed.

Facing certain death if he ran to his mother's aid, Demir laid helplessly hidden, tears running down his cheeks, praying for help for his mother. As if the scene in front of him was not wretched enough for him to experience, Demir's worst nightmare quickly came true when he heard his little sister cry out for her mother from her hiding place. The soldiers quickly found the two kids hiding beneath the floor, but were in a hurry to move on and catch up with the bulk of their army so, out of expediency, not mercy, they shot them both in front of their mother, before leaving her sprawled across the yard to bleed to death.

Five minutes after quiet had returned to the farm and the soldiers were out of sight, the house he was hiding beneath now engulfed in flames, Demir escaped in a run out through the back door, running to his mother's unconscious side. He tried everything he could to save her, but soon realized she was not going to make it, she was bleeding profusely. He held her head in his lap and sobbed for the last time in his life, as she exhaled her last tortured breath, and he vowed vengeance while he carried the guilt that he should have done more, for the rest of his life.

Fleeing through the woods and river bottoms for several days until he stumbled into a UN refugee camp, he was given food and water and kept safe until the fighting subsided a couple of years later. Driven to succeed by guilt and revenge and to make something better of himself, Demir attended school, got good marks, and was eventually recruited to attend the police academy back in Serbia. Speaking both languages perfectly, he was able to fit in as a Serb, even though the Bosnian tongue was what he had grown up speaking most of the time.

An agent from Interpol reached out to him one spring day, just before graduation, offering him a position with them and explaining how his skills could be useful to the international police agency, especially in the Balkan region. He performed extremely well at more extensive training in subterfuge, computer-related tracking skills, and special techniques for undercover work, which led to Interpol putting him to work immediately. With the ability to blend in as either a Bosnian or a Serb, or if need be get by as a Croatian, he was soon working undercover on a series of successful missions in the Baltic states, driven by a silent guilt that ate away at him daily.

When the opportunity presented itself to work for Agent Gerard on a case to gather information on the former Bosniak General Afan, he applied for it and pulled whatever strings he could behind the scenes to get the job. He did not want to seem too anxious to get the work, but he wanted it more than anything he had ever wanted in his life. Immersing himself in the mission once he received his commission to work on the project, he spent the better part of two years undercover leading up to tonight, working at small menial jobs for the General's variety of legitimate businesses, patiently gathering what information he could glean, working his way slowly into the General's sidekicks' inner circle until he was eventually offered a position driving one of the delivery trucks that he soon discovered moved off the port from Neum to a variety of undisclosed destinations.

Tonight was the second time he had made this run from the port, and this time he realized the cargo was much more valuable as he watched the General actively supervising the loading of each truck when it pulled onto the dock next to the cargo ship. He and the other drivers were kept more than 100 meters away during the secretive loading process. After one of the lieutenants drove the trucks to where Demir and the other drivers stood shivering in the night air, they were given explicit directions on where to make the delivery. So Demir drove off as instructed into the misty darkness to make his appointed rendezvous.

Revenge is the most powerful motivator of all, especially if a person can control his or her emotions and go about it in a systematic way. In Demir's case, he had lost all emotion years ago when his mother had died in his 12-year-old arms, so he was calm as he shifted through the gears onto the main road heading north. He was relaxed and confident, and tonight he was going to deal out some serious payback to the beast who had been in charge of the raid on his family farm so many years ago.

CHAPTER 37

CAITLIN'S PHONE RINGING ON THE NIGHTSTAND IN HER ROOM woke both of them from a dead sleep at 7:30 in the morning. Caitlin scrambled naked from Matt's bed and rushed to catch the caller but was not quick enough. She stood shivering in the room and waiting for the person to leave a message, so she went to her bathroom to retrieve her cream-colored silk robe. Catching a glimpse of her reflection in the full-length mirror, she smiled at the image. Her shoulder-length auburn hair was tousled in a wavy mess, her makeup smudged at the corners of her puffy morning eyes, and she had the most wonderful feeling of having made the best love she ever had in her entire life. Although she had needed to be very gentle with Matt—on a couple of occasions throughout their passionate lovemaking he had cried out in pain when a certain position affected his injuries—she found his touch and skills incredible. She was truly amazed at his stamina, urging him on, pushing him further until the two of them finally collapsed into each other's arms, spent but relishing the warmth of the luscious afterglow of making love. For an hour they cuddled, quietly talking about everything and anything until the day's activities caught up to them and they both fell into a deep sleep nestled in each other's arms.

The phone beeped that she had a message, pulling Caitlin back to reality. She did not recognize the number, and a strange man's voice with an unrecognizable accent spoke to her when she played the message back: "Miss O'Shea, Agent Gerard here. I was given your number by our mutual friend in DC and would like to meet with you and your two friends this morning if it is possible. Please call me back at this number as soon as you can."

Caitlin walked back into Matt's room where he sat propped up on one elbow smiling at her.

"Sorry I was not up to my best last night. I hope you will forgive me and give me a chance to redeem myself one day when I am healed up?"

Climbing onto the bed she gave him a peck on the forehead replying, "If you are lucky, maybe. I hope I didn't hurt you?"

"I'll live," He said rubbing his side gently, realizing he should have taken it a little easier last night. "Who was that on the phone?"

"Our Interpol contact, he wants to meet this morning."

"Sure, we might as well get this over with. Maybe he will have some useful info for us. After a shower and some breakfast we could meet up, if that works for you?"

"I'll call back and tell him," Caitlin answered kissing him quickly on the nose before hurrying back to her room to get ready.

Matt waited until Caitlin left his room before hobbling to his shower, letting the warm spray run over his bruised and beat-up body, the warmth relaxing the stiff joints somewhat. Dressing into the change of clothes Zumbula had packed for him he walked into the living room where Zumbula sat fully dressed with a complete breakfast spread out on the table for them, delivered just moments before to their room by the luxury hotel's room service.

"Patron, I took the liberty of ordering breakfast. I thought perhaps you needed to eat to help regain your strength this morning," Zumbula quipped with a smirk painted across his face. "I thought perhaps I was going to have to come in and rescue you a couple of times last night when you yelled out in pain. Are you OK this morning?"

"Never felt better my friend, never felt better. Does Caitlin know we have breakfast here?"

"Yes, she will be out in a minute." Zumbula walked over to the window and continued, "Patron, there are two cars on the street in front of the hotel with what looks to me like undercover police or some other agency in them and there is at least one more man in the lobby of the hotel who is not a customer. They ignored me too much when I went out to get some fresh air this morning."

Matt took his cup of coffee over to the window and, hiding behind the curtains, looked down onto the main street in front of the hotel to confirm Zumbula's theory.

"Ah yes, the black Mercedes and the silver Peugeot?"

"Oui."

"Not very subtle. You sure they were government types, or maybe they are the bad guys we are looking for?"

"Government in the Peugeot and in the lobby, but the Mercedes could be either. I'm not sure."

Caitlin entered the room, dressed smartly for the day, asking, "What are you two up to?"

"Got your cell phone handy?" Matt quizzed her.

"Sure."

"Call the agent back and when he answers, tell him he can come up to our room in five minutes."

"But I told him we were meeting him at the café in the town square in a half hour. I didn't tell him where we are staying."

"I'm pretty sure he knows already, call him and we will soon find out."

Caitlin hit the redial button for the last call while Matt watched the Peugeot at one end of the street and Zumbula watched the Mercedes at the other end. The number went through and the agent's cell phone began to ring.

Matt said, "Bingo," when he saw the passenger in the front seat of the Peugeot answer his cell phone. Matt nodded to Caitlin to go with what he told her.

"Agent Gerard, you might as well join us for coffee in our room rather than waiting for another half hour to meet."

There was a pause on the other end of the line until he replied, "Very well, as you wish," and then hung up.

The passenger door opened on the silver Peugeot and the man sitting there climbed out and jaywalked across the street and entered the hotel lobby. The Peugeot pulled away from the curb and drove slowly down the street.

Matt walked from his position at the window to a chair at the table and said, "Zumbula, how about passing me the toast, will you?"

CHAPTER 38

Agent Gerard smiled at the three people waiting for him as he entered the luxurious hotel suite that the American had rented under his own name. He was a little embarrassed about being spotted waiting outside the hotel; he had underestimated the American and the Irish woman, something he would not do again. When he had spoken with Anderson at the CIA in Washington earlier, he had filled him in on a little history of the three people standing in the room, about their escapade in Sudan. Gerard had found them in Sarajevo easily and would himself have been more subtle about his hotel room and certainly would not have checked into it without using false names. Perhaps, he thought to himself on the way up in the elevator, perhaps the Yankee was doing it intentionally; trying to draw the crooks to him, let them know he was here in their backyard. Come and get me. A ballsy tactic for sure, but also a quick way to get taken down if you were not stealthy and well prepared for what these Bosniak specialized in.

"Hello, thank you for the meeting. I am Agent Gerard," he said, shaking Matt and Caitlin's hand. Zumbula stood quietly in the corner of the room watching the window, not making any effort to greet the newcomer.

"Sit down please. Would you like some breakfast or coffee?" Caitlin asked.

"Coffee with milk would be fine, thanks."

Matt poured him a generous cup, and then slid it across the table to where Gerard took a seat and began to speak, "Let me get right to the point, if I may?"

Matt nodded for him to continue.

"I know you are after certain Bosnians who were involved in a shooting in Hungary last week and . . ."

Matt interrupted him, "Who also tried to kill me in the hospital."

"Yes, I heard about that also. I'm glad they were not successful. But what I was saying is we understand your personal and your CIA's ambition to bring the culprits to justice, but I have to ask you to leave it to us at Interpol to rectify the problem. We are right in the middle of a deep undercover operation that is nearing its conclusion and any interference could cost the lives of some of my best men who have been working on this project for years."

Matt broke in, "Tell us a story about our mutual friend Afan. Seems like a bad apple that thinks he is indestructible. Everyone tells us he is up to no good. Why not just move in and arrest him, get it over with?"

"A couple of reasons why, Mister Simmons. First he is very well connected here in Bosnia, a real-life war hero local people believe was responsible for keeping them from becoming slaves to the Serbs. He has the police in his back pocket; the Army reveres him; he has a lot of dirty money to pay off those people he needs; and he is as ruthless of a human being as ever walked the face of the earth. He has been smart enough to not leave the country, because he knows if he did and he was caught, he would be arrested on war crimes charges instantly. No one has ever said they would testify against him, and he's pretty smart about not getting his hands dirty in the crimes and corruption he is involved in, he lets his subordinates take care of the details."

"Sounds like Mafioso," Caitlin chimed in.

"You've got it, the Bosnian version of it anyhow and they have been at it as long as the Italians have been, trust me. Prostitution, human trafficking, drugs, the hard stuff as well as pot. He still holds in hidden warehouses a huge supply of military equipment, ammunition, and weapons left over from the war, most of it stolen from the United Nations when they were in here trying to make peace. We are in the process of confirming right now that he has a shipment of drugs and probably women or girls that has just arrived in the country, and we are tracking it and hoping to make a bust soon, so you can see why I need your cooperation."

Matt let all the news sink in. This was a big boy the authorities were dealing with, not some punk criminal they could just waltz in and arrest. Matt was going to need help and it certainly was not going to come from the local authority that was for sure. Matt contemplated out loud, "I saw the guys who shot at the countess and me. If I see them again while we are here, I could ID them for you and you could snatch them up? I'll testify against them. None of his guys here know who we are; we can play tourists, check things out, and report back to you. We need some more weapons though and I was hoping the CIA sent you word about that since we are a little undergunned if any action starts up."

Gerard cleared his throat, had a sip of coffee, and then spoke, "Actually I was thinking it would be safer for all of us if I took you all to the airport and got you out of harm's way while you can. You should be in a hospital from what I hear."

"That's not going to work for us. My colleague here, as you may know, is very involved in international human-trafficking cases—let's say she's on a mission and breaking this one up would be right up her alley. She brings a certain set of abilities you and I do not possess that can be very effective in fighting crime," Matt said nodding toward Caitlin.

Gerard looked her over. He had been told by Agent Anderson that she was very pretty and no man could resist her and as she stared back at him he knew exactly what Anderson meant. He could also see a toughness behind her piercing green eyes and realized she could indeed be very useful in certain scenarios, but he had to keep this situation under control. He had too much at stake on this mission to risk unwanted interference. He replied, "I am supposed to have something going down in the next couple days, and I want no interference from you three, OK? So promise me you will wait until I give you the OK before you go snooping around, or else I will need to call my friend back in DC and have your asses hauled out of here right now, all right? Are we on the same page?"

Caitlin chimed in, "Just tell us what to do, let us help where we can . . ."

Caitlin was interrupted by Gerard's cell phone ringing. He looked at the number, then up at Matt and Caitlin saying, "I need to take this call in private. May I use another room?"

"Use the bedroom on the left, please."

Gerard brought the phone to his ear and began speaking in Serbian while he closed the door behind him, listening intently to the hushed but semi-panicked voice on the other end, "I didn't know I was being followed. I made several evasive moves, doubled back on my route and never saw anyone tailing me, but now there are two vehicles, one on my tail and one alongside me on the passenger side. They have made motions for me to pull over but I'm not going to. I'm staying on the busy roads hoping they won't do something stupid or start shooting at me in the middle of a busy road. Do you still want me to go to the warehouse rendezvous point, or what? I need some backup right now. They know I'm not lost. They're pissed off, and some kind of shit is about to start."

"Give me your exact location now."

Demir told him the cross street he just passed heading west, Gerard recalling the exact spot from a restaurant he frequented located on the opposite corner.

"Head for the warehouse rendezvous, it should take you 20 minutes maybe 25. There are some of our men there. I'm on my way. How many guys in the cars?"

"Two in the back car and four in the front one. They are on their cell phones. I'm sure there will be more pretty quickly, probably the city cops too."

"I'm bringing backup, don't worry," Gerard said, more out of habit than belief, pushing the end button before walking back into the hotel room. He started to dial his driver's cell number to tell him to meet him at the front door when he remembered that he had sent him back to the office for an hour to catch up on the endless paperwork.

Gerard spoke to Zumbula who was still standing, watching out the window, for the first time, "Is that silver Peugeot still out there?"

"No, it left right after you got out of it. The black Mercedes is gone also."

"A black Mercedes is not my men."

A sinking feeling struck Gerard, leaving him no option but to include the American and Irishwoman and whatever nationality the black guy was in his new plan, "Let's go. We need to take your car, now I don't need all of you, but I have a man in trouble."

"Sorry, but we are a team," Caitlin quickly replied.

The three of them threw on their coats. Matt and Zumbula stuck pistols in the back of their waistbands and Caitlin grabbed her purse containing her Beretta and everyone's extra clips tucked neatly inside. They all hurried down the hallway and down the stairs past the lobby to where the Rover waited for them in the parking lot.

CHAPTER 39

"He will not pull over. I am telling you, he is avoiding us and he is not driving to where he was told to go," Ahmed yelled into his cell phone. "Ask the General what he wants us to do. We are on the main road leading to the warehouse section of town. This isn't a good place to run him off the road or make a scene. We can't shoot out his tires here, there are people everywhere."

Mirsad listened carefully to the facts of the situation because he knew he did not want to face the horrific consequences if he made any mistakes when he relayed the news to the General. Trying to stay composed he replied, "Stay close to him. One car in front and one in back until I get back to you. Let me see what the General has to say—don't make a scene until you hear from me and don't let him out of your sight, whatever you do."

He pushed the off button, then hit auto dial for General Afan's cell number; it was answered on the second ring.

"Yes."

"Sir, Mirsad here, we have a situation." He went on to fill the General in on the situation, and then waited a few seconds in silence for his boss's measured response.

"Tell them to stay with the truck; don't let it out of their sight. I am on the way. Actually never mind, I will call our men following the truck myself. What is his cell number?" Afan hung up after jotting down the number, letting the scene play out in his mind. The truck was heading into the industrial section of Sarajevo, which was good, because it meant fewer bystanders to worry about than in the bustling heart of the city. He knew the area well, having several buildings in that area under his control, warehouses that were filled with a variety of armaments and watched over by discreet guards. He had lots of resources to draw from in this part of town, so this was good. Why the driver of the truck would attempt to hijack any of his illicit cargo was beyond him. Everyone knew it was a guaranteed death sentence to double-cross General Afan.

"What a fool! I will have to make a good example of him to discourage any other idiots who think they can do the same." A smile crossed his face when a variety of his favorite torture methods he had used in the past snaked through his demented mind.

DEMIR TOOK THE exit off the main thoroughfare turning right onto the wide road designed and built for large commercial trucks when the city was rebuilt after the war had ravaged large pockets of the city. He lost the car that had crowded in front of him earlier but the car following him stayed close to his tail when he made the sudden turn. In the big delivery truck he had no chance of outrunning the pursuers. All he had going for him was size, as long as he kept moving. Demir looked down at the fuel gauge, a pang of doubt tearing at his guts when he saw he had less than a quarter tank left. Help was on the way he knew, but they better hurry up he thought as he turned down a one-lane side street, tall brick walls supporting older warehouses towering toward the heavens, crowding in on each side of the truck as it rambled on.

These old warehouses on the surrounding blocks had somehow been spared from rockets and mortar fire; they were some of the few survivors of many wars. Demir knew the town well and this shortcut would get him to the rendezvous location quicker, and the guys tailing him would not be able to overtake him because there was no way two vehicles could go side by side through these old city one way streets. He felt safer, more confident when he looked into the side mirror and saw the driver of the car behind him yelling animatedly into his cell phone.

Movement in front of the truck startled Demir, reactively hitting the brakes, the smile disappearing from his face when he had to stomp the brake pedal to the floor, all the tires screeching and smoking when he tried to avoid hitting the black Mercedes sedan that had pulled out from the left on a side street and stopped dead center in the middle of the road he was on. The passenger and driver of the sedan leaped out of the driver's door, rolling away from danger seconds before the sliding delivery truck slammed into the German built car, crushing the passenger side in. The truck's momentum pushed it three meters to where the two vehicles stopped, intertwined in a smoking, crushed metallic embrace.

Demir's arms ached, he was sure he had broken his left forearm from holding on so tightly to the steering wheel of the truck upon impact with the car. Panic set in and a glance in the mirrors showed the men in the car behind him scrambling out the doors, running toward him with guns drawn. He pushed the redial button on his cell phone with his right hand leaving the phone sitting on the seat, his arm hurt too badly to hold it up to his ear.

Agent Gerard answered on the first ring, "Where are you now?"

"Sixteenth Avenue and Forty-Fourth Street, heading west on Sixteenth. Roadblock on Forty-Fourth, and the follow car has me stopped and pinned in from behind. Six men total, all armed, not looking good."

Gerard knew the place Demir described, a bad place indeed to be stuck in with its narrow one-lane streets, weaving through the old section of the warehouse district.

"We will be there in five minutes or less. Do what you can to hold them off."

Gerard felt his heart race when he heard through the cell phone the sound of men yelling at Demir, pounding on the door to the truck, followed by the rapid staccato beat of an automatic weapon's bullets ripping through metal. He could hear more yelling, louder now, glass breaking, Demir yelling back at the Bosnians, the clear sounds of a man getting beaten, before the phone went dead.

"Turn left here!" Gerard yelled to Matt who was driving the Range Rover like a crazed maniac through the streets of Sarajevo.

"At the light, turn left again." Matt ran the red light, swerving to miss an oncoming Fiat sedan that was innocently motoring in the opposite direction. The Fiat honked loudly at them as it turned out of the way at the last second. The Rover's speedometer pushed 120 kilometers per hour as Matt straightened out waiting for his next instruction.

"Right at the next alley," Gerard said, one hand on the dashboard, the other holding onto the door's armrest when Matt put the vehicle into a four-wheel drift sliding around the turn. Matt had misjudged just how skinny the alley was, careening off the stone wall, sparks flying off the driver's door, crushing the door mounted rearview mirror.

Gerard dialed another number, speaking quickly to the person on the other end of the line when they answered, "Beneton, I need you to come from the east side on Sixteenth, OK? The truck is surrounded at Forty-Fourth Street, and our man is in trouble. At least six bogeys, all armed, assume automatic weapons. You know what our man looks like, shoot to kill anyone else, we are coming from the west behind them in a dark-green Range Rover. Myself, one woman, one African man, and one grey-haired man, we are all armed with pistols only. Hurry up; we will be there before you. There should be backup in another ten to fifteen minutes."

"Got it chief," Beneton replied before passing on the information to his partner hurtling at top speed toward their assigned destination.

Gerard turned to Caitlin and Zumbula sitting in the backseat saying, "Anderson told me you guys know what you are doing, but this could get really nasty in a couple minutes and now is your chance to bail out if you want to. I don't want to be held responsible for you getting hurt or anything else."

Caitlin replied immediately as she drew her pistol from her purse, "We can help, don't worry about us."

Zumbula just nodded his chin in affirmation toward Gerard, his hand resting casually on the 9mm on his lap, his other hand firmly gripping the armrest.

"The next road should be Sixteenth and that's where the truck and cars are. Turn right."

Matt did, his tires screaming when he yanked the steering wheel over to enter the tight street. The Rover tipped up on two wheels giving all the occupants a moment of panic until it leveled off when Matt straightened it away, pushing the gas pedal to the floor. Straight in front of them a cluster of people, a parked car and a delivery truck stood waiting in their path 100 meters ahead.

CHAPTER 40

Enraged, the Bosnian pounded his fist on the driver's side door of the delivery truck, brandishing his Mac-10 mini machine gun, yelling for the traitorous driver to open up. Demir ignored him as best he could while laying toward the passenger side on the bench vinyl seat, hoping to avoid any flying glass when his window was smashed in. Demir kicked himself for not having armed himself for this mission, but knew better than to arouse any suspicions by being caught packing a concealed weapon of any sort by the Bosniak. A thump behind his head on the passenger side window made him sit upright when he saw another Bosnian working the locked door handle to no avail. The Bosniak backed up, moving away from the window so he would not get caught in any ricochets and squeezed off a burst of bullets that shattered the window, sending diamond-like shards throughout the cab. Demir felt the tingling sting across his face and neck as he was peppered with the tiny glass shrapnel. Having no other choice, he put his hands over his head in surrender when the bearded man came through the now open passenger door. Ordering Demir out of the truck and stepping off the gas tank step to let Demir pass, the Bosnian swung his weapon hard upon the back of Demir's head when he passed him, crushing his skull. Demir collapsed to the ground in a crumpled heap, spittle running out of the corner of his mouth until the Bosnian squeezed two rounds into his face.

The driver of the Mercedes yelled at the men from the follow car, "Get the girls and the shipment out of the truck now, right now. Load everything up in your car and get it all out of here! Let's go, hurry up people!"

The towering brick walls encased the narrow road throwing an eerie light on the commotion that gave the effect that it was already late evening while the men rolled up the rear cargo door of the truck and began handing the variety of bundled packages of dope in an assembly-line fashion out of the truck and into the trunk of the Citroën. The driver of the Mercedes quickly worked the screws holding the secret panel in place until it fell away exposing the four women huddled in a drug-induced shivering panic inside. Grabbing the closest one by the arm he roughly yanked her to her feet hoping the others would follow, but they didn't, they just sat holding on to each other, cuddling in hopeless optimism that their drugged nightmare would soon end.

"Come on bitch, into the car with you," he spat, dragging her to the end of the truck bed. "Here take this one down to the backseat," he yelled at one of the other men. The young woman smelled of urine, feces, and days-old body odor, her filth concealing the beauty she possessed, the beauty that had destined to her enslavement at the hands of bandits in Uzbekistan. The Bosnian on the ground lifted her frail body down to the pavement, and then shoved her roughly into the backseat where she groveled on the floor trying her best to hide.

All of the Bosnians stopped what they were doing when they heard the squeal of tires at the intersection of the road behind them and saw the fast-approaching grill of a Range Rover, the engine roaring as if it was going to commit suicide and smash full speed right into them. Seeing that this car was not one of their own, several of the men who had weapons close at hand began shooting at the Rover hurtling directly toward where they worked unloading the contraband.

CHAPTER 41

Fifty meters from where the car and delivery truck sat parked on the thin street, Caitlin leaned forward in the backseat, saw the speedometer resting at 110 kilometers an hour and asked Matt as casually as she could muster, "You got a plan, laddie?"

Bullets pinged off the hood and front grill; a random burst cracking the front windscreen, just before another blew a hole through the center of it. Gerard returned fire, leaning dangerously out the passenger-side window, the walls of the buildings rushing past him less than half a meter away.

Matt yelled over the noise of the air rushing in through the windows, "Keep your heads down and brace yourself, we are going to give them a little wakeup call with the Rover then come out shooting. Which guy is your agent, Gerard?"

"I don't see him; they may already have killed him. I heard a lot of shooting over the phone line before it went dead. His name is Demir and he has short black hair, average height, average weight. Kind of looks like the rest of them."

"Matt," Caitlin yelled, pointing at the back of the truck through the broken windshield, "there are some women there in the back of the truck."

This complicated Matt's reckless plan; however at this point he was too committed for a plan B to emerge, all he could hope for was that the big truck could absorb lots of impact and their injuries would be only superficial. Another burst from a machine gun blew away the rest of the windshield, causing Matt to duck and swerve slightly, scraping his SUV's passenger side down the building, a shower of red sparks and screaming metal trailing behind. Gerard had luckily just pulled himself in to reload right before the Rover had scraped along the wall. He shot with calculated precision at the fleeing men through the broken-out windshield able to aim better now using both hands to steady his .45-caliber semiautomatic. He dropped one man to the left of the truck as he tried to run, and then hit another dead center in the chest standing in the driver's doorway of the Citroën, blood spraying red across the brick wall behind him.

Matt straightened out the SUV, yelling, "Hold on!"

Then, with all his strength, he shoved both feet onto the brake pedal, all four tires locking up, burning rubber, and smoke billowing from under the vehicle while the occupants of his car all braced themselves for a certain hard impact with the tail end of the parked Citroën. Bosnians scrambled like rats from a fire past the truck to escape the impact.

The Range Rover's factory equipment is so superior to almost any other vehicle on the market, the braking system being no exception; the big, oversized discs obeyed the command to lock into place immediately. The SUV's speed dissipated just as Matt had planned it would, but the overall effect of the attack was enormous, smoke billowing in stench-filled clouds, tires screaming, and all the while Gerard took precise shots at the fleeing hoodlums who panicked at the sight, not returning any fire at the Rover as the surviving Bosnians continued to scramble for safety.

Agent Gerard dropped his pistol onto the seat at the last minute placing both his hands on the dashboard to brace for the impact and Caitlin let out a muffled scream when the Rover smashed into the back end of the Citroën at a skidding 30 kilometers an hour. The sound of crunching metal and plastic and glass was deafening when the Citroën careened into the delivery truck, wedging its hood firmly under the hydraulic tailgate. Zumbula was the first one out of the Range Rover, leaping up onto the crippled Citroën's hood, then jumping smoothly into the cargo area of the truck where the three remaining girls lay huddled together, shivering in each other's arms, wondering what new nightmare awaited them from this striking-looking black man reaching down to lift them to their feet. Figuring they likely did not speak any English, Zumbula lifted and turned the first girl so she could see Caitlin standing on the Citroën's hood now, arms open wide inviting the frail teenager to come to her. Even in her chemical-induced stupor, the girl understood that the woman she gazed at was there to help her, so she stumbled toward her, with the other two following close behind with Zumbula's rapid assistance. Matt and Gerard kept up a steady consistent shot sequence from behind the shelter of the truck at the four remaining Bosnians who hunkered in a variety of hiding places out of harm's way along the walled street in front of the truck.

Matt yelled up to Caitlin when she was climbing down from the hood, "Caitlin, throw me a couple more ammo clips. Get everyone into the Rover."

Caitlin tossed him two fresh ones from her coat pocket while she loaded the three girls into the back cargo area of the Rover and was about to close the hatch door when Zumbula showed up with another woman with a bloody nose, her hand dangling at an odd angle with a broken wrist, that he had discovered on the back floor of the Citroën.

"This makes four, this should be all of them," he said forcing the crying girl into the crowded Rover.

"Let's go," he yelled out to Matt and Gerard. Gerard responded by turning and crawling along the wall toward the Rover, but Matt simply ducked down for a second, waiting a few moments for the Bosnians to show themselves now that the shooting had died down. One of them crouching in a doorway made the first mistake by leaning out and firing his Mac-10 machine pistol randomly toward the truck in an effort to lay down some covering fire so his partners could make a move toward Matt. Matt watched, looking under the Mercedes he saw a man's legs, exposed up to the shins, but hesitated hoping another combatant would show himself as well. Number two mistake by the Bosniak, another shorter man appeared behind the first man, both of them now in line with each other while they shuffled cautiously toward the side of the crushed Mercedes. Matt let them get another 10 meters closer, then two-tapped the 9mm, the first shot catching the back guy just below his knee and the other shot destroying the lead man's left shin bone. The scream of the knee-capped man had the desired effect of keeping the other two Bosnians at bay for a few precious minutes while Matt ran in a crouch to the idling Rover and jumped in behind the wheel. Gerard, sitting in the front passenger seat held onto his left arm with a blood soaked bandana telling Matt when he looked over at him, "Lucky shot, I'll be OK. Go, go! Let's move."

Matt tried to throw the Rover in reverse and swiveled in his seat to watch where he was going, ordering Zumbula, "Keep the girls down so I can see."

In no mood to have a discussion Zumbula raised his hand as if he was going to slap one of them, which had the desired effect of making them all duck down out of Matt's line of sight. The Range Rover responded grudgingly to the reverse command of the shifter, some severe damage to the engine compartment apparent when the fan belt began screeching and the grinding of the transmission's gears created panic for everyone on board. Jamming the shifter back and forth a couple of quick times, Matt swore at the wounded British SUV until it finally lurched backwards into a rapid serpentine-like reverse down the street. The rear bumper from the Citroen was wedged in the Rover's front end, sending a shower of sparks behind it as it scraped the street during their hasty retreat. The suspension had been severely bent on impact with the Citroën making steering the Rover a deadly guessing game. Matt careened off both sides of the buildings lining the street, fighting the wheel, pushing the vehicle beyond its crippled limits, but valiantly able to make it to the first cross street.

THE BOSNIANS, FEELING more confident with some space between themselves and the Rover, made a dash to the Mercedes where they shot the remaining rounds in their machine pistols at the zigzagging Rover while it spun recklessly out of sight around the corner onto the next street.

"Shit," yelled the Bosnian, pulling his cell phone out of his coat pocket to call the General.

"Sir, some fools in a green Range Rover have ambushed us and taken the women and four of our men have been shot. Two white men, a black man, and a woman are in the Rover. They are trying to escape on Forty-Third Street, heading north. Our vehicles are disabled, theirs is barely running."

"What about the other cargo?" the General hissed into the cell phone.

"It is all here, but someone should come right away to get it, before the police show up. There has been a lot of shooting."

"Don't worry about them, if they show up before I do, tell them you work for me and you want their captain there immediately. Do not leave the shipment for any reason, am I clear? You have already fucked up bad, but there may be hope for you if the cargo stays safe, got it?"

The Bosnian fully understood the General's orders, they were very clear. His voice trembled when he replied, "Yes, General. I understand, sir."

General Afan was steaming with rage, whoever this bastard was who had tried to hijack his shipment was going to pay the price and it would not be quickly. He would take his time, maybe days to punish the bastard.

"*Four more men down, how can it be? This wasn't just one man involved in hijacking my stuff! It must be a rival group, maybe the fucking Serbs!*"

He leaned over the front seat commanding his driver, "Faster, faster! Get us to Forty-Third and Sixteenth now. We will come after them from that direction." He dialed his cell phone once more, getting the other carload of his men on the line.

"Where are you?"

"Sir, we are at Thirty-Second and B Street. We heard the news of the hijacking, and we are on our way."

"OK. Put two men on the shipment when you get there and guard it until the others show up, then you and one other man go to Forty-Third, come up Fifteenth, and find the car the hijackers are in. It's a dark Range Rover, smashed up they tell me. Get my women back and try and capture the hijackers alive. Only kill if you have no other choice, wound them if you have to, but I prefer them alive. It sounds like there are only four of them, one is a woman."

"Got it, sir."

CHAPTER 42

Gerard spoke quickly to Agent Beneton while Matt tried in vain to restart the Rover after whipping around the corner out of sight of the Bosnians.

"Yes, we are on Forty-Third between Fifteenth and Sixteenth. We need all available bodies now. I have four rescued women, one woman agent, and two civilian men with me. We are low on ammo, and our vehicle is disabled. Do not, I repeat, do not trust the police to be on our side. Attackers are General Afan's men, heavily armed. Let the U.S. Embassy know of possible arrival soon, also British Embassy as backup. All Interpol agents are directed to advance on this area immediately. Have the men at the rendezvous warehouse abandon it and come and help us now. Set up a perimeter of roadblocks if possible to stop Afan's backup men, or at least hold them off for a while. No one is to enter the area."

Matt heard the commands, noting that Gerard was speaking English to his mixed-nationality staff and that was typical protocol for Interpol, but that he noticed he had failed to tell his men that he was wounded. Matt tried the SUV once more but gave up for good when it did not respond.

"I'm afraid the Rover gave up on us. Let's go, get the girls, we need to find a place to hide out until the cavalry gets here to save us."

The doors flew open. Caitlin ran to the back of the SUV quickly opening the hatch door.

"Come with me, hold my hand," she said and even though none of the girls understood English they all followed her lead after tumbling out of the back.

Matt and Gerard reconnoitered the buildings on the street in front of them, looking for one that may be open on a Sunday, which was not likely in an industrial area. Smashing in a front door was not an option since that would leave obvious sign where they had broken in and lead the pursuers directly to them.

Zumbula sprinted down a small alley leading off the deserted street and began systematically checking the access doors that led out to the alley. These were the kind of doors that were installed for building code compliance, for safety in case of fire, but were typically utilized as access for employees to come and go outside and have a smoke or steal goods out the back door. The third door he tried did not open but was loose on the hinge, loose enough that Zumbula backed off, took three steps back, then charged at it putting his shoulder hard into the steel door just above the lock, the door springing open on impact.

"Patron, this way," he yelled down the alley to Matt. Caitlin led the girls down the alley and through the door while Matt and Gerard covered their escape, making sure no one followed them. Caitlin flipped on the light switch next to the door revealing a high ceilinged storage facility, with palletized boxes of what appeared to be some sort of manufactured goods, stacked five meters high in neat rows, illegible Cyrillic black print stenciled across the sides of the cartons. Matt and Gerard ran the length of the alley ducking through the open door, quickly closing the door behind him, flipping the lock into its correct position and securing the door.

"Call your men and tell them where we are. We should be fine here for a bit, but sooner or later the Bosnians are going to go door-to-door until they find us."

Gerard looked to his cell phone to make the call but realized he had no signal through the thick stone warehouse walls.

"I have no signal, no bars. Perhaps if I go up to the offices I can get a call out."

Matt felt the chill of being cornered run up his spine, trapped in this building. He didn't like it one bit. They were in no position to wage a standoff considering the lack of ammo and the burden of the young women to take care of. He liked to be out in the open where he had options, not stuck in one spot, but with this entourage he was now supporting they were in no position to continue running. All they could do was hope and pray that Gerard's men arrived before Afan's did.

"OK, see if that will work, but stay low and don't let anyone see you from outside on the street. Wait, before you go, let me look at your arm. Did the bleeding stop?"

Gerard turned to go, saying, "It's fine, the bleeding has subsided." Then he headed for the exit door that led to the offices 50 meters away in the far corner of the warehouse. Caitlin got the women settled in, sitting on top of some low wooden crates in the middle of the building, hidden behind several pallets that had been pulled down from the high shelves, ready to ship out.

"Matt, I am going for some water; these girls are dehydrated and very weak."

He stared back at Caitlin, their eyes locking for a fraction of a second, each of them smiling for just a brief moment, but long enough to give the other person a reassuring, confident look that everything would be OK.

Matt walked over to her, putting his arm around her shoulder and giving her a hug, replying, "Don't turn on any more lights than you have to and stay out of sight from the street, baby. Maybe there is a bathroom near the offices—you can get some there."

Caitlin reached up with her hand as if she was going to caress his chin but tweaked his nose instead, telling him, "I'm a big girl, I'll be careful."

Matt watched approvingly as she walked away, wondering how in the hell he had ever gotten himself into this mess, but happy for some crazy reason that she was there with him.

CHAPTER 43

Afan's car slid around the corner, the driver pushing it for all he could get out of it. In front of them he finally saw, parked in the middle of the road, an abandoned, battered Range Rover, steam rising from the radiator, the windows blown out.

"Faster! Get to that car there, that is the one. They must have run away unless someone picked them up," Afan yelled.

Screeching to a halt when they arrived at the rear of the car, all four men bailed out of their car, guns drawn searching for any clue of which way the hijackers might have gone. They fanned out with military precision, checking the side streets, looking for anything out of the ordinary. Afan's cell phone rang in his pocket, making him wonder who the hell was interrupting him now.

"Yes, what is it?" he growled.

"Sir, I just received a call from the security monitoring service we use on all our buildings, and they say the alarm at our storage building on Forty-Second Street has gone off. That building is near where you are, and I'm not sure if it means anything but I thought you should know."

"I am a block away from there, but I do not hear any alarm going off."

"It is a silent alarm sir, so it doesn't attract any attention from the authorities. That was your idea, if you recall."

A wicked smile crossed the General's ruddy face, "Well done. We are going there now. Tell the others. It must be them, it cannot be a coincidence, and it is too close to where we found their car. Give me the key pad code for getting into that building."

He covered the phone and yelled, "Men, get back in the car, we are going to the storage warehouse around the corner. Hurry up, let's go!"

Driving at a moderate speed so as to not to draw too much unwanted attention, the Bosnians drove past the glass-covered entrance to the offices of the warehouse without slowing down while a local delivery truck passed going in the opposite direction. Nothing appeared out of order, it was closed, and the lights were out just as they should be on a Sunday.

"Turn around at the corner and ease back on the same side of the street as the office, then park where we can't be seen from the offices," the General commanded.

The driver did as instructed, and they rolled to a stop next to a lamppost where they could not be seen getting out of their vehicle. The men hustled out of the car; all four of them stealthily approached the offices, slipping along the side wall of the building, hugging the concrete, weapons ready. No other vehicles or people could be seen coming from any direction in this commercial area. The General let the driver lead the way, not wanting to take the first bullet, just in case this was another ambush. After peeking around the edge of the glass from a crouched position, the driver gave the group a thumbs-up sign that everything was OK to precede, and they ran up the stairs to the aluminum-and-glass front door.

General Afan tapped in the code to stop the alarm and unlock the door, which responded with a solid electronic click of the bolt sliding out of locking mode. Two men rushed in, weapons at the ready, covering the driver and Afan who followed right behind them and closed the door. Movement from behind a desk near the corner of the office made the driver swing the muzzle of his Uzi submachine gun toward it. Quicker than the driver could respond, two meters from the right of the movement, Agent Gerard brought his pistol over another desk, holding it in his one good hand, the other one bleeding heavily, dangling at his side, double tapping two shots at the startled driver who reflexively ducked at the secondary movement. Bullet number one hit him high in the shoulder blade; number two missed him completely, slamming into the wall. Gerard ducked for cover after the shots and saw that he was outnumbered four to one and cornered like a rat.

The Bosnians hit the floor in unison, the driver grabbing at his painful wound but remaining silent, resetting the Uzi slung across his shoulder to a less painful spot. Afan looked at the other two men giving them sign language to spread out and draw fire from a wider area. They quietly crawled into their places 10 meters apart and when they were set, the General rose slightly above the desk he hid behind and shot a burst from his Mac-10 in the direction of their assailant.

Gerard knew this was his chance, he had watched from floor level waiting for movement so he could shoot another of the four attackers and when the General shot, he rose from his position enough to shoot a quick volley at his attacker. Before he could get a shot off though, he was caught in the cross fire of the two Bosnians he had not seen move to his flanks, taking the full charge of the rounds into his upper torso and head, dead before his head slammed onto the tile floor, dark blood pooling instantly around his lifeless form. The General ran to where he lay to make sure he was dead and recognized the finished man instantly.

"Ah, Agent Gerard, we meet again, one last time I am afraid." The Bosnians gathered quickly around the dead body to get a look at the man that was no stranger to any of them; they knew who he was, who he worked for, and why he was after them. His cell phone lay on the floor next to him, the light of the dialing face lit up indicating it was being used until the General leaned down, hit the end button then dropped it on the tile floor, crushing his heel into it.

Afan didn't like the fact that Interpol was involved in this, an uneasiness telling his guts that they should all leave right away, but he knew they had no choice but to take out the rest of the agents who were in his warehouse now, the one that held millions of dollars' worth of military-grade weapons. No one could know about this stash. This whole day didn't make any sense at all now. He had thought he was dealing with some rookie hijackers, or some small-time competitor. Now he had a real problem on his hands, one that was going to take drastic measures to make it right once more. Interpol was no one to mess with and he had done his best to stay off their radar as much as he could, but obviously now that Gerard was here, Afan knew he was a target.

"No one leaves here alive," he mused, turning to go to the door that led into the warehouse.

"Check the rest of the office and the bathrooms before we go out to the warehouse. They are all in there I would imagine. We have them cornered, but be careful, who knows what they have for weapons."

He instructed the man on his left, "Call the other car and tell them to cover the back of the building. Do not let anyone escape."

The men fanned out to search the restrooms and break room, moving catlike through the halls, anticipating resistance around every corner. The driver stuffed paper towels in his shoulder wound when he saw that the break room was clear, effectively stopping the trickle of blood running down the back of his shirt while the other two men continued down the hallway. The lead one stepped back from the door to the women's bathroom when he noticed that light was showing under the crack below the door. He pointed with his Uzi so his partner would see it also. They signaled for the General who joined them and then cautiously opened the door, while jumping back out of the line of fire in case someone waited for them inside the washroom.

Nothing happened when the door swung open so the men entered the room in a rush, spreading out as much as they could, one of them going to his belly so he could see under the stalls. No legs appeared there, but the two half-filled plastic containers surrounded by spilled water on the floor made the General sense that someone had just been in here and was probably still be in one of the stalls hiding.

Afan spoke in rough English assuming the rest of the people in his building must also be Interpol agents, "You are outnumbered and at the count of three my men are going to shoot through the stalls and you will die. Surrender yourself and live or stay where you are and die. One, two . . ."

"Wait," a fragile female voice from behind the third stall door said.

"Hands up, where we can see them, come out slowly," Afan barked.

Caitlin walked meekly through the doorway, hands above her head, her face humbly looking toward the floor hoping an act of innocence might garner some sympathy from the killers.

One of the men walked quickly to her when they saw she was unarmed, grabbed her arms and folded them behind her back. She let out a squeal of pain before the man slapped her across the back of the head, knocking her to the floor. Grabbing her by the elbows he propped her upright to look at the General who rattled off a series of questions while holding Caitlin's face, his calloused hands squeezing her cheeks so hard she thought the skin would tear away from the bone any second.

"Where are the others? How many are there? Who are you; we know you are with Interpol. Talk to me bitch!"

Caitlin's mind raced, she wanted to stall for time. She knew Matt had heard the shooting just like she had when she was retrieving water for the girls. He would be securing the area, getting the girls to safety, maybe running out the back door to save them all.

"No he would never leave me here; he will come and get me. He is making a plan, unless he thinks that in all the shooting they killed me too. Even still he won't leave me here, I'm sure of it."

Another smack across the top of her head from behind made her wince and try to pull away, but the General had her in a firm grip and only squeezed tighter making her cry out.

"They have already left the building, all of them. Please don't hurt me. I didn't do anything I swear, they left me here alone."

"How many are there, how many?"

"Eight, ouch, eight. I'm telling you!"

"Lying bitch, there cannot be eight, you only have one vehicle, eight plus you two would not fit in it." Afan was screaming now and his men backed off, they saw the rage building up, a rage they knew better than to be close to when it exploded. The General backhanded Caitlin across the face, causing a trickle of blood to ooze out of the corner of her mouth, and she felt sure a tooth had been broken.

"Let me have your pistol," he said to the driver. "I am done with this witch; she is of no use to us." The driver stepped forward, handing over his loaded 9mm. Afan stuck the muzzle up to Caitlin's forehead; she stared back at him, directly in the eyes, daring him to pull the trigger.

Her defiance in the face of certain death made Afan pause for a brief moment and the driver cautiously said, "Sir, maybe we can use her to negotiate with the hijackers, with the Interpol guys. She may be of some use alive."

Afan eased the barrel off her forehead and pushed her roughly to the floor, kicking her hard on the ass, knocking her flat on her belly on the tile floor. Caitlin stayed there, not moving, taking in the moment, her mind racing and attempting to make a plan of her own, even if she was outnumbered.

The men spoke in Bosnian, so she did not understand when the General said, "I think that they are all still in the warehouse, cornered like the vermin they are. They will not leave her behind; these imbeciles have ethics and a code of fucking honor. They do not know what happened in all the shooting but they will not run out on a woman and leave her with us. Let's go see what they do when they see we have her as our hostage. We must kill them all, whoever is in this building, you understand? We can have no witnesses, no one to tell what they saw inside this warehouse. We do not need trouble from the idiots at Interpol. I can smooth everything over with the locals, but not them. Let's go men."

General Afan reached down and grabbed Caitlin's wrists, overlapped them behind her back, and wrapped his arm around her neck, forcing her toward the door, "Let's go see who your friends are, baby."

CHAPTER 44

Automatic gunfire rattling from the offices at the end of the warehouse surprised Matt and his instincts made him rush toward it before he calmed himself and took stock of the situation first and remained behind the pallets. Rushing through the only entry door to the office was certain death; he could tell from the sound that there was more than one gun shooting and only a couple of the shots came from a semiautomatic pistol, which was all that Gerard had with him. Caitlin had left hers behind when she went for water, so she was unarmed in the face of all the danger. Gerard and Caitlin were most likely both dead by now, he reasoned. Matt looked up to God and whispered a little prayer that Caitlin was still safe while he contemplated what his next move was going to be.

He looked over at Zumbula who had the women congregated behind a couple of pallets. They sat in a huddle, all hugging each other, a look of terror etched in their faces, all staring up at him like frightened kittens after the sound of the gunfire. Zumbula gave the women a sign with his hand to stay put, and then hurried over to Matt's position where they both had a clear view of the office's steel door.

"The agent will be dead," Zumbula said, stating the obvious.

"Yes, but hopefully not Caitlin. Maybe she is hiding."

"Maybe, patron, maybe."

"Grab Caitlin's pistol and the clips out of her purse, I think we are trapped. There may be more of them covering the back door by now."

Zumbula ran over and dumped all the contents of Caitlin's purse onto the floor and threw two clips to Matt, checked Caitlin's pistol making sure it had a round in the chamber and flicked the safety off. As he moved behind a stack of pallets the office door swung open and

Caitlin appeared, a stout heavyset man holding her as a shield in front of him, a pistol crammed into her right temple. Matt and Zumbula stayed hidden behind the pallets.

"Hello my friends," Afan yelled into the warehouse. "It seems we have a situation. You have something I want, and I have something you want." Matt peeked through a space between the boxes, but did not respond or give away his location.

"We know you are still here. I have men at the back door covering it, so you have nowhere to go," Afan lied. He looked around the dimly lit building; only one bank of lights was turned on near the back entrance door.

He turned to the driver speaking in Bosnian and ordered, "Turn on all the lights."

The powerful lights came on and lit up the entire building's interior a second later.

"Now here is what you will do. You will bring me my girls and I will trade them for this one I have. A fair trade, I believe, you get one and I get four. You have one minute to do so or you will get to see her die and then I will just kill you all afterwards. I am a reasonable man, but an impatient one, I am afraid. So show yourself, bring them to me now."

Matt had no clear shot at the man holding Caitlin. He had her held up in a perfect shield other than his head showing next to hers bobbing back and forth as he spoke, but making it an impossible shot from this distance with a pistol. He looked over at Zumbula who glanced back from his crouched position and with a nod of acknowledgment he began to silently crawl forward, concealed behind the rows of shelved pallets and cardboard cartons. Matt watched Zumbula, not sure what he was up to but his movement was spreading them out and giving them more of an angle of attack and at the same time not making them an easy target if shooting started. Matt sat tight, weighing his limited options. He too had to get closer, so he slipped on his belly past five more pallets closing the gap by at least seven or eight meters as the Bosnian jabbered at them. He could not see Zumbula from his new position; however, assuming the wily tracker was still pushing forward, he tried to continue to do the same, stealthily sneaking forward on his belly.

"You are pushing my patience, thirty seconds more and this lovely redhead explodes before your eyes," Afan yelled again. Making a move to get their emotions fired up, Afan stuck his tongue out and ran it sloppily up the length of Caitlin's neck and into her ear yelling, "Oh, she tastes so good, yummy. Maybe I am changing my mind and me and my men will just keep her, you can have the whores instead we will have our way with this one. I don't care one way or the other, but you can save yourself if you want to." Caitlin stood rock solid, not moving a muscle, hoping that the longer the Bosnian talked, the better the chance was that Matt would devise a plan, now that he knew what was happening.

Zumbula arrived crouching at a dead end. He had run out of cover and was still 20 meters away from the door. He stared through a gap in the boxes, willing Caitlin to look at where he was, melding his mind to hers, focusing all his energy towards her in an attempt to get her attention. She was staring at where the girls were hidden, thinking that Matt and Zumbula would still be there. The man holding her turned to bark something at someone behind him and seeing him turn Zumbula took a chance, waving his hand above the pallet to draw her attention. Matt saw Zumbula's movement and instinctively brought his pistol up to get a firm rest on top of the pallet of boxes he was hidden behind.

Caitlin caught the movement of Zumbula's black hand out of the corner of her eye. She turned her head slightly to see what he was doing, realizing that he was making sign language with his hand for her to duck down. When Afan turned to yell at his men behind them his grip around her neck had relaxed somewhat, giving her the break she needed. She had been acting meek and compliant up until now so when she made her move the General was not expecting it.

Caitlin let her shoulders go limp, just the way she had learned at the CIA camp in Maryland where they taught her a variety of fighting techniques for a woman to use against a larger adversary. Rather than resisting or fighting back, she simply relaxed her posture, let her body go limp and slipped straight down, slithering out of Afan's arms before he had a chance to react. Trying to hold onto her limp frame was like wrestling with Jell-O and proved futile, and the next thing he knew she was lying prone on the concrete stoop and he was fully exposed to anyone in the warehouse. Matt's first bullet hit the Bosniak dead center in the middle of his chest; knocking him back a step before the second round thumped him just below his ribs. He dropped his weapon and grabbed for his chest, the wind and life having been knocked out of him simultaneously, but Matt put another insurance shot into him just in case.

Zumbula had been hoping Matt would be ready when Caitlin hit the concrete so when the shooting started he rushed directly at the doorway in an attempt to rescue Caitlin who he watched roll onto her back after grabbing the pistol that Afan had dropped. She fired three quick rounds through the doorway into the office, rolled onto her knees, got hold of the hand railing on the wall and leapt in a single graceful bound over the three stairs onto the warehouse floor.

Sirens could be heard screaming closer and closer toward the warehouse. General Afan's driver was hiding around the corner wall of the offices interior, wondering what the hell he was going to do next. The General was definitely dead, the driver knew, because he had been splattered with blood, bone, and lung chunks when Afan was shot. Lying in the hallway behind Afan's body were the two other men who had come into the office with him, both mortally wounded, one of them moaning loudly while his blood ran freely into a growing puddle of gore on the office's tile floor.

Not wanting to face any kind of authorities, especially without the now-dead General's backing, the driver made a headlong dash out the front door and sprinted down the street to their parked car. He could see speeding police vehicles in his rearview mirror approaching the scene three blocks behind him, so rather than draw attention to himself by speeding away from the scene, he simply put the big Mercedes into drive and eased down the street using his turn signal before he made the first right turn he came to. Once he was around the corner and out of sight he put the pedal to the floor, the big V8 roared its approval and sped away.

ZUMBULA WAS AT Caitlin's side when she landed on the warehouse floor, the two of them running to Matt.

"Matt, Agent Gerard is dead. I saw him on the floor of the office," Caitlin quickly said.

"Let's get out of here then, back the way we came in. I'm not sure who those sirens belong to but if it's the local cops they may not be too friendly and we will have a lot of explaining to do," Matt replied as they all ran to gather up the frightened girls. Zumbula got a hold of one of the girls around the waist and another by the arm, pulling her to the exit door. Caitlin took the other two by the hand, leading them behind him. Matt had the door open when they arrived; he had looked both ways up and down the alley and seeing that no one was in it so he led them all away from the main street that the office fronted. The girls were very weak, the drugs were wearing off, they had not eaten in days and they were not able to keep up with Matt who hobbled his way in front of them, in obvious pain at the exertion. Caitlin and Zumbula struggled to keep them moving knowing every second counted in their effort to escape the scene of so much bloodshed. Twenty meters from the end of the alley, feeling like they were going to make it, two unmarked cars slid to a stop blocking the alley and two men dressed in business suits jumped out of each car, pistols drawn and pointed menacingly at Matt and Zumbula.

"Freeze, Interpol, halt where you are," one of the men yelled.

Relief swept over Matt hearing that these guys were Interpol; he raised his hands over his head but continued running toward them yelling back, "We are with Agent Gerard; move your cars around the corner out of sight of the local police cars that are coming. Quickly, do it now!"

Hearing their boss's name used and seeing that the man had several women with him, which matched the description Gerard had given them on his cell call to them, they tipped the muzzles of their weapons down. Gerard had thankfully told them where to come to and help him, right before he was killed. They had listened to the whole killing of their boss on his cell phone that stayed on through the entire event. The drivers of the Interpol cars hustled the vehicles 15 meters farther up the road out of the line of sight of anyone entering the alley from the opposite direction. The two remaining agents ran forward to help carry the stumbling girls around the corner and into the waiting vehicles.

"Everyone lay down in the backseats," the agent in charge ordered. "We are getting out of here, now." Zumbula was in the lead vehicle with all four girls. Caitlin and Matt climbed in the rear one.

As they sped away around the next corner, Matt spoke to the head agent, "I'm sorry to tell you that Agent Gerard is dead. He was a very brave man."

"Thank you for confirming this, yes I know. I was speaking with him on the telephone when the Bosniak shot him. I heard the whole thing." There was a slight hitch in the agent's voice; emotions were running high and Gerard's death had certainly rattled him. He continued after an awkward pause, "Two more of our vehicles are approaching the office now and they will retrieve his body. They will keep the local police busy while we get you people to safety. You have caused quite a commotion here in Sarajevo today. It has been quite a day for all of us, Mister Simmons."

Matt lay on the backseat holding Caitlin in his arms, nuzzling her ear with his nose and quietly replied, giving her a playful hug, "Yes it has . . ."

CHAPTER 45

ANDERSON SAT AT HIS GOVERNMENT-ISSUE GREEN METAL desk, overlooking the traffic jam working its sluggish way out of Washington, D.C., reviewing the Bosnian case files, putting them in order, happy to be closing an operation successfully for once. It seemed to him that nowadays, he always had more cases coming to his attention than he could handle and not enough agents to deal with them all, and rarely did they ever seem to come to a positive conclusion. The Bosnian case had been one he never even wanted to be involved in, but sometimes when asked by another agency like Interpol for assistance, you did what you could to help out, if for no other reason than they would owe you favors that could be called in later.

When Interpol found out the identity of the man Anderson's agents had killed, they were ecstatic. Years of investigations by Interpol and the UN had found that General Afan was involved in a multitude of criminal activities; however, he had been impossible to convict of anything, because no one dared testify against him and he was considered by most Bosniak to be a hero, no matter what sordid business he was involved in. He and a small group of cohorts controlled vast parts of the government, all the way up to the president, and as long as he stayed inside Bosnia's borders he had continued life as a free man.

After Afan's death, the crooked local Bosnian authorities were quickly rounded up, brought into meetings with Interpol, the European Union, and United Nations representatives and told in no uncertain terms that they were to cooperate with Interpol to break up what remained of Afan's activities before someone else stepped up to take it over or expect to pay the price for their lack of help. The massive largess from Europe and the UN that the country survived on would dry up instantly if they did not cooperate, it was clearly explained.

Arrests of minor players in Afan's schemes were made, equipment confiscated, the war supplies sitting in some of the warehouses were returned to the UN and the drug and human trafficking came to an end, if only temporarily.

ANDERSON LEANED BACK in his chair putting his hands behind his head. He knew it would not take long for another group to get the businesses back up and running, because supply and demand for the vices they fueled never ended and someone was always willing to fill the need—it was just a matter of time.

The girls Caitlin had rescued and all the others who were on the tramp steamer were liberated from Afan's clutches and offered a free trip back home but they all refused the offer. Home had been where most of their trouble had started, because girls were considered of no value in many of the Muslim and third world countries they came from. Opting to stay in Europe at foster-style homes, the girls would get help from volunteers until they could get back onto their feet, learn a skill, and become productive members of society.

Caitlin O'Shea ran the whole new venture of helping the girls get settled with the passion and drive of a zealot, setting up new homes, raising money for the cause and awareness to combat the slavery of prostitution and to curtail human trafficking worldwide. Countess Atwood had become a fellow champion of the cause, funding many of the start-up hostels and homes herself. Anderson was sorry to see Caitlin go; she quit the CIA right after the warehouse shootout to spend all her time at the new activity. The two of them made a verbal agreement that she would stay in contact with him and feed any information she garnered from the girls or her sources directly to him, and he promised to help her cause where and when he could. He had come to realize that the same people who were involved in this racket were generally involved in lots of other unsavory activities, including terrorism. Occasionally, a small tidbit of information led to a much bigger can of worms.

THE THICK MANILA file labeled "Matt Simmons" was still open, laying to the right of the pile on his desk. Anderson had just spoken with him via telephone last week, somewhat surprised to hear that he was already back in Portland, ensconced in his mansion with his friend Zumbula and the African's wife and young son. Matt sounded a little sad and reflective when he told Agent Anderson that Caitlin had decided to stay in Europe and work full time at her cause. Simmons told him they were trying to make plans for a rendezvous, but Caitlin was a busy girl. When Anderson asked about the countess, Matt said they stayed in touch, she was all healed up from her wound, but he would probably not see her again since they were living in two different worlds. Everything else was going fine, Matt told him although Anderson swore he heard a tone of resignation in Simmons voice that he had never heard before. Maybe Matt missed Caitlin, or maybe it was the Countess he was pining for?

Matt asked Anderson about Tatra and what had happened to him. Anderson filled him in on the ongoing investigation into all his activities; it seemed there was more going on than met the eye with Tatra. Matt knew for sure that that was the case. Even when he was interrogating him at his castle in Slovakia, Matt could tell he was not giving him the whole story and he agreed with Anderson's assessment of the situation.

Matt told Agent Anderson at the end of the call, "You got that right, he was lying about something. If you need a hand getting that bastard, let me know." Anderson detected a certain dislike in Matt's voice, something personal and something more than the current case was flowing below the surface, a little jealousy perhaps.

Agent Dennis Anderson looked at his watch. It was already 6:00 p.m. and he had to attend another one of the countless dinner parties as required by his superiors. Taking one last look at the remainder of the "Matt Simmons" file, a smile crossed his face. While he read the last pages of the dossier, he thought, "*You will be calling me soon, Mister Simmons, I know your type. No wife, no steady girlfriend, living in the house where your wife killed herself and your child. Nope you won't last long living the boring mundane life that most people consider normal. All that money you have, you could stay home and get fat and be happy, but you won't. You are a killer now, a man of action, seeking revenge with a chip on your shoulder that you dare everyone you meet to try to knock off. You will be bored and calling me, it won't be long and I'm sure I'll have another job for you when you do.*"

Anderson closed the file but kept it separate from the Bosnian case, setting it in an active rack on the credenza behind his desk. He always had a use for guys like Simmons, always . . .

The End

ACKNOWLEDGMENTS

I WOULD LIKE TO THANK MY FAMILY FOR THEIR CONTINUED support of my wandering ways and for still being there, waiting with open arms whenever we are able to all get together and celebrate everything that means family. The term *family*, in the traditional sense, has certainly evolved for us in the past 20 years, however the basic principles that keep a group of people together and united have not changed, at least not in strong families like ours. Sacrificing your time for family, looking out for what's best for your family, making sure that all the family is taken care of in every regard, and above all giving your unqualified love to those people you call your family will keep families strong for a long time to come.

I would like to thank all my Yugoslavian friends for being Yugoslavians. I went to school with, played soccer with, and had a best friend growing up that were from the countries that used to be part of the country that was named Yugoslavia in my days of growing up. In those days we never heard of Croatians, Serbs and Bosnians, they were just Yugos.

I would like to thank Josip Tomljanovic and the real Ivan Tatralov for their ideas and inspiration while I was writing this novel and for touring me around their respective countries of Croatia and Slovakia.

A big thanks goes to the former Miss Hungary Adrienn Lipp, who showed me the sights around Hungary and helped with an assortment of details on Hungary and educated me on the rich culture of Hungary.

A special note of recognition must go to the real Pamela Atwood who along with her husband Stan made a serious contribution to a political action committee when called upon and Pamela was rewarded with being a character in this book. The Countess in this book is of course a fictional character in all of her descriptions and actions and implications and the real Pamela Atwood is much prettier, a greater huntress and is much smarter than her fictional namesake. The real Miss Atwood would never fool around with a guy like Matt Simmons . . .

As always the love of my life who inspires me on a daily basis, the lovely Miss Shelley Mason, encouraged me, tolerated my hermit-like writing sessions when I had deadlines to meet and stuck with me when I didn't have the time to give her all the undivided attention she so richly deserves. I apologize now for being me and hope she realizes there is a bright light at the end of the tunnel.